SAVING THE SELKIE'S HEART

ELLA ROSE

ALSO BY ELLA ROSE

THE SELKIE SEAS SERIES

<u>Novels</u>
Losing the Selkie's Skin, a Selkie Seas prequel novella
(https://books2read.com/losingtheselkiesskin)

Stealing the Selkie's Heart, Book 1
(https://books2read.com/stealingtheselkiesheart)

Saving the Selkie's Heart, Book 2

<u>Short Stories</u>
"Watched" in *Worlds Apart*, A M/F selkie flash fiction story
(forthcoming)

"The King's Anchor" in *Beyond Atlantis*,
(http://books2read.com/DSPBA)
A M/M selkie short story

For R and L.
I pray for the day you find your HEAs.

CONTENTS

1. Chapter 1 — 1
2. Chapter 2 — 15
3. Chapter 3 — 30
4. Chapter 4 — 47
5. Chapter 5 — 52
6. Chapter 6 — 68
7. Chapter 7 — 87
8. Chapter 8 — 103
9. Chapter 9 — 112
10. Chapter 10 — 126
11. Chapter 11 — 139
12. Chapter 12 — 152
13. Chapter 13 — 167
14. Chapter 14 — 180
15. Chapter 15 — 192
16. Chapter 16 — 202
17. Chapter 17 — 219
18. Chapter 18 — 225

19. Chapter 19   237

20. Chapter 20   244

21. Chapter 21   250

22. Chapter 22   259

23. Chapter 23   273

24. Epilogue   278

Afterword   284

Acknowledgments   286

About the Author   287

CHAPTER I

1861, Isle of Selbane, in the Hebrides off the west coast of Scotland

"Happy birthday, Lyall!"

Lyall closed her eyes and held her breath, remembering the whisper of air as she blew out the candles on her birthday cake. The hiss of fabric as she pulled apart the ribbon of her present, her parents' expressions mirroring each other with anxiety and hope written clear across their faces—her mother's eyes had held the trace of tears as Lyall pulled aside the plain burlap cloth covering the present bundle, her father's eyes hard as stones in his face as he gazed on with a frown wrinkle between his eyebrows. The feeling of the pelt beneath her fingers, soft as the finest silk, as the coarse burlap fell away and her sealskin, the birthright she'd only just learned was hers a few weeks prior, fell into her lap.

The sealskin was snow-white—which her mother explained was lanugo, the soft baby fur designed to keep young pups warm in their seal form—and small, small enough to cover her thighs like a child's blanket.

"Don't worry. You'll grow into it," her father had promised.

Now she held the sealskin up to her chest and inhaled, taking in the cedar box scent of the container the sealskin had rested in for the last twenty-two years. The water lapped at her waist, chilling her skin as she stood in the ocean water of the cave.

She glanced over her shoulder, careful not to disturb her long blonde hair that covered her bare breasts, and peered uncertainly at her parents. They stood together on the shore next to one of the large boulders that lined the cave beach like sentinels, her father leaning heavily on his cane, one arm around her diminutive mother's shoulders. They were the only ones in the cave, which had been exactly to Lyall's liking for her first attempt at changing into a selkie, like her parents.

Her mother gave her an encouraging smile, which Lyall tried to mimic. But the shivering from the cold water made her teeth chatter as she turned back to face the outlet of the cave, where the water flowed into the larger expanse of the sea.

She was naked, as her parents had insisted she must be, as she held the baby sealskin up to her chest. It provided instant warmth, as if someone had recently worn it and it radiated the body heat from someone else.

She closed her eyes again and took a deep breath.

"Fasten the hooks first," her mother had explained at the house earlier that morning. "They'll be small and difficult the first time. But you'll get the hang of it soon." She'd smiled at Lyall with a look filled with pride.

Lyall had squashed the fear that rose in her at her mother's words. In truth, she was petrified of her first change, which her father warned might be painful the first time. She was a sucker for pain, barely handling even splinters without tears. So the thought of full-body anguish was terrifying to her, though she kept that part quiet. She couldn't bring herself to squash the naked hope in her parents' expressions whenever they spoke about her birthday or her first change.

The thought wore on her as her birthday approached, filling her with both dread and anticipation in equal measure. What if she didn't do it right? Was it possible to only half-change and be stuck as a half-seal, half-human? What if she turned all the way, only to find herself unable to handle the pain of the change without throwing up or embarrassing herself?

Or worse, what if it didn't happen at all?

Her parents had mentioned, a few weeks ago and only once, that some children born to selkie parents in their human forms could never change into their selkie forms, even with the sealskin.

Lyall shivered at the memory of that thought. The pressure to perform, to make the change the first time, sat on her like a weighted blanket, a sopping, dreaded mass on her shoulders that bowed her over as she stood in the water of the crystal-lined cave.

She glanced around, noting the quartz that covered the ceiling of the cave, catching the dying rays of the sun's light and making them sparkle like diamonds. This had been the cave where her best friend Una had captured the selkie man Ronan, the action that led to her parents' admission that they, too, were selkies, and potentially her, as well. It was a sacred place, Una had told her, set just off the inlet that led to the ocean. It was a place of secrets, of beginnings, and it had been the first place that popped into Lyall's mind when her parents asked her where she wanted to change for her first time.

Had her birthday party been only that morning? It seemed like so long ago already, as if days had passed in between her opening of her present and walking down to the cave and shucking out of her clothes behind one of the large boulders inside. Then she'd wrapped herself in a blanket and waded into the water, clutching the sealskin as if it were a lifeline.

And, she supposed, it was. To another world. Another life. Infinite possibilities.

Hope welled in her, chasing away the fear. Anything was possible today. It was her birthday, after all.

She smiled to herself and positioned the sealskin over her shoulders like a cape, as her parents had instructed on the walk to the cave. She tried to fasten the tiny bone hooks that lined the edge of the small sealskin, but she could only manage a few. They scratched at her collarbones as she shivered in the water and waited for the change to happen.

"Picture yourself as a seal," her mother called from behind her.

Her father made a hissing sound of displeasure. "Leannán, that's not helpful," he groused. "She doesn't know what that feels like!"

Lyall felt her confidence slip. He was right. How was she supposed to picture something she'd never experienced?

"Well, what do you think she should do, Prion?" her mother huffed. "I've never had to teach this before. I just did it."

"Lyall, honey, just think about your sealskin covering your entire body. Picture yourself covered in fur, and let the change happen as it will." Her father's voice rang with the air of authority. The air, Lyall had learned only weeks ago, of a commanding general and leader of their selkie clan warriors, the Anchors. It had shocked her to learn that her gruff, loving father was actually a prince of the Liath Clann selkies and the Strategic Commander over all the Liath Clann Anchors. It was a title given to him by his father, King Righ, once it was apparent that his selkie skin, damaged maliciously by a rival siren, would never allow him to transform into his seal form anymore.

Lyall could feel the pressure creeping back over her shoulders, the weight of her father's lost ability pressing onto her skin. What must it cost him to watch his daughter transform in the way he hadn't been able to for decades? This moment was important to her. She had to change.

She curled forward, willing her body to transform. Her hands clenched into fists at her sides, knuckles turning white with the strain of her desire.

Change! she demanded of her body. *Turn into a seal! Let this work!*

Her body trembled as she braced for the change, the pain that her father said would claim her. Her stomach flipped into knots from the anticipation, the hope and the dread that warred with each other as she hoped and prayed for the change to happen.

Seconds ticked by, turning into long, lonely minutes.

Finally, gasping as she let out the breath she'd been holding, she called over her shoulder, "Am I doing something wrong? Shouldn't it have happened by now?"

Silence met her question.

A few more seconds ticked by, and she risked a glance over her shoulder. Her parents still stood where she'd last seen them, but their faces were carefully neutral, holding none of the happy anticipation that had been on their faces all day.

As she watched, they glanced at each other, sharing a long look. Then her father nodded once, and her mother stepped forward, beckoning with one arm.

"Come here, Lyall," her mother said in a grave voice.

As Lyall turned and waded back to shore, she saw her father turn and hobble out of the cave. She stopped, shocked at the depth of the hurt that seared through her. Was he so disappointed in her effort that he couldn't even bear to look at her?

She waded to her mother, watching her father's slow progress, noting the stooped slump to his shoulders. Her questioning look found her mother's gaze, and her mother pulled her into a firm hug.

"It's ok," her mother whispered into her hair.

"What's ok?" Lyall asked in confusion, trying to pull back to look her mother in the face. But her mother held her fast. "Should I try again? Did I do something wrong?"

"No, baby, you did nothing wrong. It's just that—"

"It's just that what?" Lyall asked, panic rising in her at the realization that her father had left because they were going home again. Her attempt to change was over. She had failed.

"It's just that we knew this might happen." Now her mother leaned back to clasp Lyall's face in her chilly hands. She peered into her daughter's eyes as she spoke in a soothing voice, as if Lyall were a frightened animal. "It was a long shot that it would work, and—"

"That's it?" Lyall said, her disappointment making her voice break on the last word. "I should try again!" She gestured to the water, half-turning as if to go back in, the sealskin hooks scratching like small fingernails at her throat. "I can do it if I try again, I know I can! I'll just—"

"No."

"—try harder this time!" The panic rising in her made her feel full of frantic energy, as if she had to move, had to speak faster, had to *do* something, anything to fix what had failed. Where *she* had failed.

"Lyall, no." Her mother's voice was sharp, sharper than she'd ever spoken to Lyall before, and the tone stopped her like a slap to the face. She stared incredulously at her mother, noting the pity that slid along her face. "We're done. It didn't work. It's okay."

"But..." she began, but her mother put a finger to her lips, stopping her words. *But it's not okay.* The words burned against the backs of her lips, burned hotter than the shame that flooded her body.

She had failed. Her sealskin was just a pelt. Her father had left. She had failed.

Her mother gathered the wet blanket and covered Lyall with it, placing the blanket over the top of the useless sealskin.

The wet wool instantly warmed her, even as she started shivering, not from the cold but from the depth of her failure. This had been her chance to prove she was special. That she was worthy of something bigger than herself. She'd always felt out of place, had never felt like she belonged among her group of friends. And now she knew why: not because she was something special, but because she so spectacularly *wasn't*.

Her shoulders bowed under the weight of the heavy, wet material. Her mother placed an arm over her shoulders and steered her towards the cave entrance, pausing to stuff Lyall's discarded dress in a satchel brought along for that purpose.

The women walked in silence as they stepped out of the cave and into the dying rays of the sunset's light. Up ahead, Lyall saw her father making his slow progress through the tufts of sea grass as the sandy beach yielded to the sturdier dirt of the island. She glanced at her mother and saw the lines on either side of her frowning mouth, set like rows carved into granite. Though they never would say it, Lyall knew her inability to change disappointed them. That this had been a turning moment for them all, a great potential that had come crashing down on their hope like the waves of the deep sea.

A breeze gusted, lifting Lyall's hair and caressing her face like her mother's hands had moments ago. She felt coolness on her cheeks and realized that she was crying silent tears that coursed down her cheeks leaving salty trails dried by the wind. It whistled past her ears, and the sound was like a sigh that whispered *failure failure failure* in time to the beating of her broken heart

SHE BEGGED OFF HER mother's solicitous attempts for company back at the house. Her father, upon arriving, made his way to his bedroom and shut the door, cutting off any attempts at reconciliation. The sound of the door clicking shut had carved through Lyall with a finality she didn't know what to do with.

So she said she needed to visit her best friend, Una. But once out the door, she didn't head south towards the house Una shared with her selkie husband, Ronan, but instead veered west towards the home of Lucas Hew, her boyfriend.

The walk was short, but by the time she made it to his house, her eyes were puffy from crying and snot was leaking down her upper lip. She knocked on the door, not knowing what she was going to say or how she was going to explain showing up unannounced on his doorstep, but only knowing that she longed for the comfort of his arms around her. She needed to be held by someone and told she was still special, even if she couldn't explain why she needed to hear it.

The door opened to reveal a smiling Lucas, caught mid-laugh at something happening inside. But when he saw who it was, his face sobered.

"L-L-Lyall! I didn't expect to s-see..." he broke off as he took in her disheveled appearance. "What's wrong?"

"I... I just..." But she was sobbing so hard she couldn't get the words out. So she flung herself into his arms, pressing her tear-soaked face to his shoulder.

But instead of putting his arms around her, he grabbed her shoulders and gently pushed her away. "Lyall, now isn't a good t-time."

"What?" Lyall asked, confused, as she wiped away a tear from one cheek. "Why?" She couldn't understand why she wasn't already in his house, seated in front of the fireplace while he offered her tea and demanded to know who had hurt her.

"Who is it, Lucas?" called a laughing female voice from behind Lucas.

I know that voice, Lyall thought.

She looked questioningly at Lucas, who had a strange blush working its way up his face.

"N-now, L-L-Lyall, I did-didn't know you w-were coming tonight," he said in a stern voice.

His stutter is worse when he's nervous, Lyall thought.

She tried to step around him to enter the house, but he sidestepped into her way, blocking her. She gazed up at him in shocked wonder. "Why are you behaving this way, Lucas?" she demanded, sniffling. Her dismay had faded and angry irritation was taking its place. "Who's in there with you?"

Lucas stared at her with an expression she couldn't immediately place. After a long moment, she realized, with a shock, that it was pity. Pity was written clear across his face and there wasn't an ounce of sympathy mixed in.

Lyall drew back with a hand on her chest.

"Lucas?" the other voice demanded from inside. And Lyall realized she did recognize it.

"What is Donalda Roid doing here?" she asked. She felt as if she were spinning, as if the ground beneath her feet were shifting like sand. It suddenly became very hard to breathe.

"Now, Lyall, this isn't w-what you th-think," Lucas began.

Then, from behind him, two pale hands slid over the tops of his shoulders and down to his chest. Donalda's curly brown ringlets cascaded like ribbons over one of his shoulders as she pressed herself to his back and peered around him.

"Oh, Lyall!" Donalda exclaimed in surprise. "We weren't expecting you tonight." She grinned at Lyall and her smile brought to mind for Lyall rows of shark's teeth. She gazed at Lyall while she remained draped over Lucas's back.

Lyall felt drained of emotion. She tried to summon anger, betrayal, rage, but all she felt was a detached sort of shock that filled her like ice.

Lucas looked pained, as if the whole ordeal was embarrassing for him. "Lyall," he began, then stopped as she took a step backwards.

"Were you ever going to tell me?" Lyall whispered, pressing her fists to her stomach. She felt queasy and as if frozen pieces of herself might burst apart if she didn't hold herself together.

Lucas glanced over his shoulder at Donalda, then back to Lyall. "I was going t- going to tell you—"

"When?" Lyall's voice was a whisper.

"About a month now," Donalda offered with a toothy grin.

Now Lyall recognized a feeling inside her, a burning warmth that seemed to thaw her from the inside out. She fanned the flame of it, encouraging it so that she could process the scene before her. "And what about Tamhas?" Her voice shook, but she was proud to hear that it didn't falter in the wind. "What does he think of this? And so soon after you've been betrothed?"

Now Donalda's face turned mulish and her mouth puckered up. "What he doesn't know won't hurt me," she groused. "Besides, I can't stand to be around someone who reeks of fish all the time." She pressed her hands into Lucas's chest, hugging him tight. "Not when there's other fish in the sea, right Lucas?" She purred the words into Lucas's ear, and Lyall could see his discomfort change into something softer, something intimate, as if she wasn't standing there at all.

Like a snake striking, Lyall's hand flashed through the air and connected with Lucas's cheek with a ringing clap. Then it reversed mid-air, flying back the way it came so that the back of her hand slapped the other cheek.

Lucas reeled from the impacts, one hand going to press against the side of his face as he gaped slack-jawed at her.

"That was for sneaking around behind my back!" Lyall raged, recognizing the ember inside of her as a fire of betrayal. She let go of her control on it, letting the feelings wash over her like waves of regret and anger. "And that was for making me fall in love with you!"

Tears began coursing down her cheeks, leaving scorched trails on her heated face. She turned on her heel and marched away, heading towards the safety of her own home. Behind her, she heard Lucas calling her name and the muffled sound of Donalda trying to coax him back inside the house.

But inside her mind, she raged. Raged against the betrayal and the smug smirk on Donalda's face as she draped over the man Lyall loved. Raged against her own stupidity, which seemed to be the brightest emotion of all. She poured out her tears in wave upon wave down her cheeks, which felt as hot as a forge.

How could he do this to her? When she'd given him so much of her own heart. Was this all that love offered? Betrayal and pain?

Typical, a voice inside her head whispered. *How typical of you. To throw away your one shot at happiness, just like you threw away your shot at being a selkie.* The voice was insidious in her mind, and it whispered to her the entire way home. Whispered how pathetic she was, and how everyone saw it but her. Told her that nobody would ever love her the way she wanted and that wanting it made her a bigger fool than before.

By the time she made it home, her eyes felt swollen and hot from the crying. She eased her way into the house, noting from the darkness that her parents must've gone to bed already. She slunk to her bedroom and threw herself face-down on the bed.

"Stupid girl," she whispered to herself. "Foolish, stupid creature. How could you ever have thought you were special?"

The darkness had no answer, but, in her mind, she gave up, relinquishing her hold on the angry flame that had burned inside her all the way home. She closed her eyes and clenched a pillow to her chest and curled into a ball, letting the final wave of self-loathing wash over her. She succumbed to the pain, feeling as if there were small needles pricking every inch of her from the inside out, like small spiked creatures trying to scratch their way out of her skin.

And she did nothing to stop it. Instead, she clenched the pillow tighter and let the darkness claim her.

CHAPTER 2

CEANNAS TRANSFORMED AS HE stepped from the surf onto the pebbled beach in front of Lord Prion's house. He had been summoned, along with a handful of other Anchors, to meet Lord Prion early that morning.

Ceannas suppressed a surge of irritation as he slung his sopping sealskin over his shoulder like a discarded coat. He ran his free hand through his dripping auburn hair, flicking away the water as the cool air bit into his skin. It was the day before the Migration to see the Great Elder, an event that only happened once every fifty years. There was much to be done, much preparation to be made before the entirety of Liath Clann made the trek, and he didn't appreciate the interruption to his day.

Not that he would ever admit such to Lord Prion. The older selkie's temper and expectations were legendary, and he held little room for failure. For Ceannas to refuse his summons would be a grave insult, possibly even punishable by being forbidden to make the Migration with the rest of the clan.

Ceannas shuddered at the thought—to be unable to protect his clan, when that was the entire nature of his existence as an Anchor, was unthinkable. He had taken the Anchor's Vow when he was still a pup, had sworn to protect his clan and its royal family for as long as his life was worth living. Though the vow allowed for sexual partners to be taken along the way, there were to be no mates, no family to distract him from his promise to his clan. It was a vow he took very seriously, a vow he considered higher than no other.

Next to him, five other men and two women emerged naked from the water, holding their sealskins. A selkie's sealskin was vital to his or her existence, and they took great care to protect them at all costs. To lose the sealskin was to risk being lost to their human form for the rest of their preternaturally long lives.

He knew the clan well remembered the story of Lord Prion, who had neglected his sealskin decades ago and had let it be permanently damaged by a rival siren. Or of their own Anchor, Ronan, who had let his sealskin be taken by a human, binding him to her until she gave it back to him. The stories were legendary because they had happened within the recent memory of the clan, and everyone was on particular guard with their skins since.

He let the rest of the Anchors step from the water, scanning the horizon for threats almost unconsciously as he waited. His senses were on high alert, as they always were when he changed forms, and he led the Anchors up the sandy rise, among the clumps of sea grasses and small bushes, to Lord Prion's door.

Ceannas knocked three times in the pattern of Anchor greeting, and the door opened. A grave-faced Leannán, Lord Prion's wife, met them, her long hair tied back into a plait. Though her face was usually full of smiles and welcome, today there was nothing but reservation in her expression as she stepped aside and silently gestured for them to enter.

They all stood awkwardly just inside the threshold as she closed the door behind her. It surprised Ceannas to see three figures seated on the couch in the living room: Lord Prion, who sat with his hands resting on his cane in front of him; Ronan, his best friend and former Anchor; and Una, Ronan's human mate.

The memory that Ronan had found his True Mate, the other half of his heart in this human, swept through him, sending a brief longing in its wake. To find something more than just a mate, to find the other part of your soul that was fated by destiny to be yours and no other's... it was a mythical concept, but one that had turned out very real for his friend.

Ronan gave him a grave nod in greeting, which he returned. He tried to communicate a question with his eyes—*why are we here?*—but Ronan had already looked away towards Lord Prion.

The naked Anchors knelt to one knee and placed their fists over their hearts. "My Lord Prion," they said in unison. He nodded to them, gesturing for them to rise, his sharp blue eyes piercing in their intensity.

But his strength was belied by a wracking cough that tore through his body as he began to speak. The cough was wet-sounding and came from deep within the chest. Ceannas's own sternum hurt just hearing it.

"Is this everyone, Uncle Hugh... I mean, Prince Prion?" Una asked Lord Prion. Ceannas remembered that she'd only learned of her "uncle's" selkie affiliation a few weeks ago. It must be difficult for her to process, being a human and finding out her surrogate family was not only a mythical creature but also royalty among them. She eyed her uncle with open concern.

Lord Prion glanced at her absently, as if he'd been jerked from deep thought at her words, then nodded. He tried to stand, bracing himself heavily on his cane. His knees wobbled, then another cough wracked his body, sending him crashing back onto the cushions with his hand held to his mouth.

The cough lasted several seconds, causing dread to rise in Ceannas's chest. This was no winter cold, he guessed. Not from the deepness of the sound and the small rattling at the end of his gasping breaths. He realized that Lord Prion looked different, as well: thinner than he remembered from a month ago, with a gauntness to his cheeks that spoke of a rapid weight loss. Even his clothes, once well-filled-out, now hung on his frame like a scarecrow's clothing.

Lord Prion, looking for the first time all of his one hundred and twenty years, sat with glazed eyes as he wiped his hand discreetly on a handkerchief supplied by his daughter, who appeared suddenly from one side of the room.

Ceannas's attention sharpened. He'd barely noticed the blonde girl sitting to one side of the room, away from everyone else, in an armchair. It was unlike him not to note everyone in a room, and he cursed himself for his poor situational awareness. Some defender he was, he groused at himself. Not even noticing a harmless girl.

Though, he had to admit, the term "girl" barely applied to her anymore. He'd seen Lord Prion's daughter, Lyall, from time to time in his duty as Anchor. He noted the golden shimmer to her hair as it tumbled over one shoulder, the creamy look of her skin, her rounded curves under her homespun gown.

Then he chided himself. Harmless she may be, but she distracted him like few others, regardless of the fact that he'd only seen her a few times. Each instance had captivated his attention like he was a raven looking at a shard of sparkly glass, and he hated it. Nothing should distract him, least of all some human girl who had the misfortune of not being a full selkie. Besides, being the prince's daughter ensured she'd be forever off-limits. He pitied the selkie who dared handle her heart, given who her father was.

Lord Prion let loose a rattling sigh, slicing through Ceannas's ruminations. "I'm sure you all are wondering why I called you here," he began, his once-strong voice now harsh and gravelly from the hacking of the cough.

Ceannas noted a smear of blood on his handkerchief as Lord Prion tried to stow it out of sight under his thigh. The sight alarmed him, but he remained silent. He wondered if Ronan, on Lord Prion's other side, noticed the blood, too.

"I'll keep it simple, if only because I lack the breath to be verbose," Lord Prion rasped. "I'm sick. Very sick."

Lyall made a squeak of surprise and Ceannas spared a glance in her direction. She sat very straight in her chair, her expression one of shock and dismay. *He hadn't told her,* he realized. *The bastard didn't even tell his own daughter he was sick.* He felt pity for her, for learning his father was so ill in front of a room full of strangers like him.

Leannán made a small noise, and Lord Prion glanced at her, then at Lyall. "No, you're right, my dear." He sighed. "I suspect it is fatal. The selkie healers cannot figure out the source of the cough, but they suspect it is some sort of wasting sickness. As I cannot reveal our kind to the humans, I cannot visit a human doctor to learn about human maladies.

"But from the research done by our healers, the condition is irreversible." He gave a brief, apologetic glance to his daughter, then added. "I'm sorry. I'm sure this comes as a shock for you all."

Ceannas wasn't sure what was more surprising: the admission of sickness or the apology. He'd never heard of Lord Prion apologizing to anybody for anything, even when he was in the wrong. The action led credibility to Lord Prion's words, and he felt a heaviness settle in his chest.

This wasn't Lord Prion speaking, delivering information with his typical aloof and presumptuous attitude. This was Prion the selkie, admitting a very personal piece of information to his loved ones. It wasn't a side of Prion Ceannas had ever seen before, and he didn't appreciate the empathy he felt now.

Prion was known as a sharp leader, a risk-taker who spared few individuals' feelings in his orders. He'd always seemed, to Ceannas, to be a king delivering his orders from on high, never consulting with the selkies he commanded before sending them out on their orders. Though Prion had some excuse given his lack of a sealskin, which prevented him from leading alongside the Anchors below him, Ceannas felt it was a dereliction of duties not to take the Anchors' desires into account. He thought Prion to be superior in attitude in a way that rubbed Ceannas wrong. He never liked the sense that he was beneath anybody, even his superiors. It was too close a feeling to what he'd felt his entire life under his father's thumb.

But, regardless of his general dislike of the prince, Ceannas had to admit that he was one of the best Strategic Anchor Commanders he'd ever met or heard of. The man was a prince among generals, and he was sorry to hear that his command was coming to an end. He wondered how long Lord Prion had left. Would he still be there when they returned from the Migration? Was there time to hand off his duties to another, to keep the impact on the clan as small as possible?

Dimly he realized he should respond somehow, probably with something discreet or with sympathy. But his Anchor's mind couldn't stop ticking over the ramifications of Lord Prion's death and what it would mean for the clan.

Lost in his thoughts, Ceannas barely noticed Ronan put a comforting arm over his wife's shoulders as she sat in shock.

"You... you can't be dying," Lyall ground out. Leannán stepped over to her daughter and began to rub small circles on her back, but Lyall pushed her hand away and stood. "No, I refuse to accept this! Find another healer from some other clan. Go see the human doctor and pretend to pass as human." She flung out a hand to indicate Ronan. "He did it! And nobody said anything!" She looked frantically around the room, her eyes landing on Ceanna's. "There's got to be something you can do!"

"There is no magic that can save me now," Lord Prion said. "Our healers are the most experienced I've ever seen, and they cannot do anything more."

"I refuse to believe this!" Lyall's cheeks flushed with emotion as she started pacing in front of the couch. Ceannas saw Lord Prion and his wife exchange a grave look. "There must be something you can do. Anything!"

"Maybe the Great Elder can do something," Ronan broke in. Everyone turned to look at him. "They say he is a creature of great magic. If we could only get Lord Prion to him—"

"The distance is too great," Lord Prion said. "If I could change, I could avoid this entirely, but—"

"We could charter a ship—" Leannán began.

But Lyall turned and pinned her father with a piercing stare. "What do you mean *if you could change?* Are you saying changing into your seal form would fix this?"

Lord Prion gave a pained glance at his wife, but he nodded. "My healers have advised that my illness is a human one. If I could change, there is a chance the magic of the change would cure the illness, as it is incompatible to seals."

"Then we find you a sealskin!" Lyall exclaimed. Her eyes grew wide as an idea hit her. "I have one! You can use mine! Since I can't—"

"It doesn't work that way," Lord Prion said gently. "It has to be a sealskin bound only to me. Yours is already bound to you, though you have never changed with it. I would have to kill another selkie and take their skin to make it work."

"I volunteer myself," Ceannas and Ronan said at the same time.

They looked at each other in surprise, then Ceannas stepped forward. "My Lord Prion, let me volunteer my life for yours. I would gladly give up my life for this clan. You are too important for us to—"

But Lord Prion waved him away with an angry hand. "Don't be ridiculous. I would never ask that of anyone! Least of all *you*, Ceannas."

Ceannas ignored the stab of hurt that sliced through him. Was he not enough? Was his life somehow not worthy? His Anchor's vow, the commitment to the royal family that he staked his life on, had required him to step up, despite his personal feelings for the man. But to be told his vow wasn't enough? It hurt both his ego and his integrity.

"You all are too important to the clan," Lord Prion continued. "Especially on the eve of the Migration. We need all our Anchors to keep the clan safe. My life has been long, and I've come to terms with this decision." He sat back in his seat, regaining some air of regalness as he placed both hands on the head of his cane.

"Well, I don't!" Lyall exclaimed. "I refuse to come to terms with it! If we could somehow repair your sealskin, are you saying you could change and be well again?"

Lord Prion exchanged a glance with Leannán, and it was pained uncertainty. Ceannas knew they didn't want to get her hopes up. Hadn't they tried for decades to solve that particular problem? According to the stories, Lord Prion and Leannán had once even sought a *buidseach*, a shaman among selkie-kind. They'd found her, but she reported she lacked the power to heal it. Had said that kind of magic was too powerful and that she didn't know of anybody who could do it.

"It's unlikely that will happen," Leannán said. "There is no way to repair that skin. Trust us, we've tried."

Tears welled in Lyall's eyes. "But there has to be some way." Her voice was barely a whisper. Ceannas saw the other Anchors look away in discomfort, but he watched Lyall. He noted the single tear track down one cheek, saw the heaving breast as she tried to keep control of herself. He pitied her for her situation.

Though he'd been glad when he'd left his father's dwelling to be his own man several years ago, he knew others didn't share his distaste for their fathers. His had been brutal, abusive, and had little tolerance for a pup's weaknesses. But he'd trained Ceannas to be vicious, though Ceannas only showed that side in battle, and had taught him he could depend on nobody but himself. It was a vital lesson for an Anchor, though he wished he could have learned it under different circumstances.

Leannán took Lyall in her arms and the girl began sobbing, as if the physical contact broke what little self-control she had left. With an apologetic look, she ushered Lyall out of the room.

Lord Prion heaved a heavy sigh and turned to regard the rest of the Anchors. "I am entrusting you with the lives of all our clan members on this Migration. And, Ceannas, as Lead Anchor, this will primarily fall on you to leave my brother free to oversee the entire Migration. Be ever-vigilant. I have heard rumor..." He glanced towards the back room where his wife and daughter had disappeared. "...of some sedition among our group."

Ceannas frowned. "Sedition? Of what sort?"

"The war with the sirens. It lasted ten long years, which was about nine years longer than it should have." Lord Prion growled the last part of this sentence. "When we received the peace offering earlier this year, we assumed it was a genuine gesture of peace. And our treaties with them have gone well."

His piercing blue gaze narrowed as he looked around at them. "But I have heard of some who disagree with this peaceful break. They feel the sirens haven't gotten their fair share of pain and would reignite the war anew. There's been rumors that a small band of them have been meeting in secret for months. My intelligence suggests they will make a move soon to show their hand. I believe it will happen at some point during the Migration." He pointed a finger around the circle at all of them.

"Therefore you must be hyper-vigilant! We can have no such warmongering among us. To refuel that hatred between the two groups would be disastrous for us all. And I fear violence may occur when the seditious movement comes to light. We must protect all of our members, even those who would disagree with the king and queen's orders."

"You aren't suggesting we protect those who are plotting against the king and queen?" one of the female Anchors, Hilda, asked. She was tall, with long blonde hair to her waist, and she looked ready to fight at a moment's notice. She was an asset in battle, Ceannas noted, and a worthy Anchor. Her current job was as personal protection for Queen Mairi, and she took her job seriously.

"Only as far as we need to in order to keep them safe. Even from themselves." Lord Prion's face was stern as he regarded Hilda. "I mean it: violence only begets more violence. If... *when*... they make their move, we will be on our guard and will protect both those who are innocent and those who would seek to overthrow the king and queen's peace treaties. Don't worry," he added, as Hilda smoldered. "They will come to justice should they openly defy the king and queen.

"But this Migration should go without a hitch. If they don't make their move, all the better. We will deal with this when you return."

If you're still around when we return, Ceannas thought bitterly. He hated to think about what might happen to the seditious members of the clan once Lord Prion was out of the way. It might embolden them to act. Or they might spin his death to serve their own purposes. Either way, he could see no good end to this once Lord Prion was gone.

"We will do our duty," Ceannas said, clasping a fist to his heart. The other Anchors, including Ronan, followed suit. "Do not worry about the clan while we are gone. We will handle any threats accordingly." He glanced at Hilda, who smiled grimly at him. They were on the same wavelength.

Another cough wracked Lord Prion's body. As Una bent to tend to him, sliding the bloody handkerchief from beneath his leg, Ceannas gestured to the other Anchors that it was time to go.

They bowed to Lord Prion, who waved them off in dismissal with one hand while he coughed, then let themselves out the door.

Once outside, Ceannas turned to the others, who formed a loose circle around him. "We will be on our guard more than normal," he told them in a firm voice, the voice he used to direct armies. "Any breath of these traitors comes to my ears immediately, understood?" The others nodded. He interlinked his fingers and cracked his knuckles. "And I will deal with them. Got that?"

Hilda grinned and it was a savage thing. The other Anchors nodded again, then turned to make their way back into the ocean. Some donned their sealskins before they even reached the water and changed so that they could waddle into the waves.

Yet Ceannas hung back, letting the others go before him. He glanced back at Lord Prion's house. The news troubled him, both of Lord Prion's illness and the subtle movement of traitors in their midst. Had he spoken to anyone who had hinted at restarting the war? He tried to remember all of his recent conversations. Had anyone mentioned in passing that things were better during the war? Or had anyone dismissed the peace treaties as anything other than a vital necessity? He couldn't remember, and that was a problem.

"You're slipping, old friend," said a familiar voice behind him. He grinned and turned to see Ronan standing a few feet behind him.

"When did you learn to be so quiet?" Ceannas teased. "You haven't had to practice those skills in some time. Especially now that you've exchanged the Anchor's life for the married one. Why were you at that meeting, anyway? I thought you'd absolved all your Anchor duties."

"I like to dip my toe into the clan's business from time-to-time, stay abreast of the clan's movings. But I came tonight because Prion requested both Una and I attend. As family, though, not as clan members." He nodded ruefully. "But married life *does* suit me," he acknowledged. "I rather enjoy not having to be on my guard all the time anymore."

"But don't you miss it?" Ceannas asked with a sly wink.

Ronan smiled, then it faded. "Not when there's treason on the horizon. Sedition? In Liath Clann?" He shook his head. "And here I thought the war was behind us."

"Well, it's still behind *you*," Ceannas teased. "I'm the one who has to deal with it now. You get to sit on your comfortable couch at home and get fat while *we* do all the work to keep the clan safe."

Ronan grinned and patted his lean stomach. "I do like getting fat." Then he sobered. He stepped forward to clasp Ceannas's shoulder. "Be safe, old friend. If Lord Prion thought the rumors serious enough to warrant a warning to the Anchors, there must be more truth to them than he's letting on. Be on your guard."

Ronan's words made Ceannas's stomach flip uneasily, but he grinned to cover it. "Always. Unlike *some* former Anchors, *I* never stop being on my guard."

"Like you were just now." Ronan smirked.

Ceannas flashed him a haughty look. "I knew you were there the whole time."

"Sure you did," Ronan laughed. "Well met, Ceannas."

"Well met, Ronan." Ceannas turned and pulled his sealskin over his strong shoulders as he dove into the water. He curled forward, letting the change take him over, then followed in the direction the other Anchors had taken, back to the caves where their clan currently sheltered on the other side of the island.

But the entire way, one thing consumed his thoughts: not Lord Prion's words, but by the high flush on Lyall's cheeks as she raged against her father's announcement. She was a fine creature when riled, he thought. And he would do well to remember her words about having a spare sealskin to give her father. It was something he would have to bring up to the Great Elder when they arrived off the coast of Asia in a few weeks' time.

"You can use mine! Since I can't—"

What had she been about to say? What was it she couldn't do? The thought plagued him, more than it should have, as he swam. Then, too soon, he was back at the clan's cave system and he put the thought out of his mind.

Lord Prion's daughter was the least of his worries on the eve of the Migration. He would do well to remember that, too.

CHAPTER 3

LYALL COULDN'T SLEEP THAT night. Echoes of her father's grating cough sounded throughout the house and each one made her heart stop. She knew they happened in his sleep, and her mother said he slept through them, but Lyall wondered how that could be. How could he so casually be dying while his mind slumbered?

She'd been shocked at the news of how bad it had been. She'd known it his illness to be persistent but fatal? That was new information. She wondered how long her father had known it was that serious. Sure, he'd been thinner lately, joking about being "fighting fit" for the first time in decades. And the cough had been around for a few weeks. But deadly? No, that had never crossed her mind.

There had to be something she could do to help. Some way of being useful.

She wondered if the money she'd saved at Madam Ruagh's dress shop would cover the cost of the town doctor. She didn't have much, but surely she could convince Dr. Hew to help.

But getting her father to go to the doctor would be difficult, especially since he believed it to be a waste of time. For the first time, she wondered how good the selkie healers were. How much did they know of human issues? And could they do magic?

But her father had said they'd done all they could.

Tears welled in her eyes and trickled down her cheeks. Something had to happen, even if she didn't know what. Then she remembered something: hadn't Ronan suggested someone who might know better than the healers? The Great Elder? This creature had to have more magic than the rest of them, for such a title.

If she could get her father to the Great Elder, perhaps he could save him.

Or, a voice at the back of her mind whispered, *perhaps you could bring the Great Elder to him.*

It was a gamble, to be sure. But perhaps she could convince the Great Elder to come back to Selbane with them instead. Then the weight of that decision settled over her. Selkies migrated every fifty years to go see this Elder. That had to mean the Elder was very important.

Or very old, her mind whispered.

She sat up, horrified at the thought. What if the Great Elder was too old to make the trip, the way her father was too sick? She *had* to find some way to bring the two together.

She got out of bed and opened the cedarwood box at the foot of her bed. From it she pulled her sealskin, its white mass glowing in the darkness of the room. Maybe she could get the Great Elder to unbind her sealskin from her so that it could be her father's. She couldn't change anyhow, and it was only a sore reminder of her failure.

She hadn't even wanted it to come back to her room after her failed efforts at changing that evening. Hadn't wanted to touch the thing. But her mother reminded her that such things still had purpose and utility.

"Your sealskin is the greatest thing you'll ever own," her mother had told her before they entered the house after her father. "Someday you'll come to understand that."

Was this the purpose her sealskin was made for? To help her father shift again and survive?

An idea hit her like a stone to the head, striking so hard that her sealskin dropped from her suddenly numb fingertips.

Her father's sealskin. That was where the damage was done. If that was repaired, he could shift again. He wouldn't need her sealskin to do it, when he already had his own bound to him through its own special magic!

But how to get it to the Great Elder? She spun from the room and raced on silent feet through the familiar dark halls and into the living room. Above the mantel place was a familiar box, one she knew held both her mother's and father's sealskins. They were symbols, her mother once told her. Reminders of what they'd given up, symbols of their commitment to each other. Her mother could still change but didn't, out of love and respect for her father.

What would she give up to save him?

"I've got to change," she whispered to herself. She couldn't trust one of the Anchors to deliver the skin, not on such short notice. But if *she* could make the trek and guard the sealskin herself...

It was a shot she had to take.

She stepped to the mantel and opened the box, removing the thick masses of sealskins. Her mother's was on top, neatly folded into a tight rectangle. Her father's was below, folded together as best as it could. She set her mother's aside and lifted her father's sealskin.

It was a mess, a tangled patchwork of rips where the grey blubber shone through like gaping lips, all criss-crossed over each other like vines. She thought of her own pristine sealskin, the clean white lunago that seemed so beautiful. This mass of fur and blubber was not beautiful.

But it could be again, if she succeeded.

As the idea formed in her head, ideas jumbling over one another like marbles in a bag, she raced back to her room. She fetched the small satchel her mother had stuffed her dress into earlier in the cave, then paused. What to carry? The bag had to be light and small enough for her to carry in her seal form. Which meant only one change of clothes and the sealskins would fit.

Well, she could wear her one set of clothes down to the water. She stuffed her sealskin and her father's into the bag, then raced back to the kitchen.

Should she leave a note? Let her parents know where she had gone? They wouldn't be alarmed that she was gone before they woke up—she often got an earlier start on the day than they did and headed to work before they were about. But once she didn't return home?

She shook her head, making her blonde curls bounce against her shoulders. No, a note might tip them off too soon. She had to be well underway before they got wind of her disappearance, far enough that their reach couldn't touch her before she finished her mission.

So she went to the door, unlocked it, then turned and looked over her shoulder. This was no vacation she was undertaking. It would be the longest time she'd ever left the house, since she knew the trip took weeks just to arrive. And then there was the return home.

"Please still be here when I return," she whispered, brushing at the tears that welled in her eyes.

Then she opened the door and stepped out into the night.

SHE MADE IT TO the cave about an hour before dawn. The entire trip to the cave had her jumping at every noise, constantly looking over her shoulder to see if she was being followed. There were so many things that could go wrong. What if her parents woke and checked on her in the night? What if she'd missed the clan, and they'd left already? What if she couldn't make the change after all?

No, she thought, as she entered the cave and quickly shucked out of her dress. She couldn't think like that, couldn't let those kinds of thoughts enter her head. They would only weigh her down.

Naked, she laid her dress onto the pebbled beach and pulled the satchel with her father's sealskin cross-bodied over her chest so that the strap settled between her bare breasts. Then she pulled her sealskin from the bag, marveling at the weight of it, even dry. The fur was silky underneath her hands, and the dark gray blubber underneath was dried and stiff.

How did this work again?

She shook the skin, then draped it over her front like an apron and waited for the magic to happen.

Nothing.

She held out her arm and draped it over. It covered her from shoulder to wrist, and the flippers hung limply down either side.

Nothing.

Knowing it would be useless, she tried the same motion on the other arm, but again, nothing happened.

She growled in frustration. She'd never seen the selkie Anchors change when they visited, though she'd tried peeking from the house windows. But the bluff hid the shoreline from view, and she'd seen nothing.

Maybe she was wearing it wrong?

In a flash of inspiration, she remembered how her mother had arranged the skin over her shoulders. She swung it around the back of her like a cloak and draped it over her shoulders so that the side flippers lay across her collarbones.

The waves whispered as they slid over her skin as she forced her chilled fingers to fasten the tiny bone hooks, what felt like dozens of them, to get the skin to close around her like a coat. Then she held it in place and reached up to pull the flattened head over her own blonde curls.

She waited, feeling the water lap at her ankles with icy teeth.

Failure, failure, it seemed to whisper to her. The old fear from last night crept over her and she shoved it back with a mental push. This wasn't the time to worry about impressing her parents. There was more at stake here.

She closed her eyes and pictured her father as he'd stared at her from the shore that afternoon. Let herself remember the hope and fierce determination sparkling in his eyes. He'd been proud of her then, she knew. Proud of her for doing what he no longer could.

You can do this, she thought to herself. *Remember that feeling.*

A tingling sensation crept over the back of her neck, like ants crawling over her skin. She twisted her head, trying to get rid of the feeling, but it intensified. It spread across her shoulders, everywhere the pelt touched, then continued down her arms and spine.

This is it! she thought with a feral grin.

She closed her eyes, surrendering to the change.

But as the tingling encompassed her body, it changed, becoming more intense, sharper. It felt like bees were stinging her and she cried out as the sharp sensations pierced her skin.

She curled forward, falling to her knees as the stinging intensified. Then she realized something strange was happening to her arms. They felt shorter, stronger as she lurched onto her hands so that they bore the weight of her upper body. Behind her, her legs stretched out, and she began to cry. Her legs burned as they fused together, turning into one strong tail with two flippers on the end.

She was being consumed by fire and her mind raced to figure out how to end it. Pain was everywhere, turning her brain into a single alarm of terror. She had one thought—*what's happening to me?*—before the change crashed over her and everything went black.

IT WAS STILL DARK when she became aware of herself again, with the night air around her seeming unchanged from her last conscious memory. Her mind felt sluggish as she tried to figure out where she was. The pebbles of the beach underneath her were like small, hot balls, and she longed to cool her skin in the water that lapped at her head.

She tried to raise herself up, intending to crawl into the water to relieve the pressure, but her body wouldn't respond. Her entire being felt like it belonged to someone else as she tried to move her legs to push herself forward. But she only rolled herself on one side, tipping over like a barrel. There was a sensation of choking from something wound around her neck, and she remembered her satchel lying cross-bodied over her torso before she entered the water.

She let out a startled cry as she rolled and was startled to hear a strange hoarseness to her voice. The sound she'd let out sounded like a bark rather than a human's cry. She tried to lift her legs again, and she rolled over on her back, half submerging herself in the sea. She squinched her eyes shut against the brine of it and wriggled harder.

Immediately, she felt lighter, more in control of herself. She wriggled her body again, trying to use her hips to lurch herself further into the water, and it worked. She slipped under as a wave crashed over her, carrying her forward into the dark coolness of the water.

It was like another world. She wriggled her body again and felt the pressure of the water change as she swam forward. Angling upward, where she knew the surface to be, she tried to stand, knowing she was in shallow water still. But her legs couldn't find the sandy bottom and her arms didn't feel right as she moved them.

She fought to kick her legs to breech the surface again, but her body didn't work the way it was supposed to. In a panic, she thrashed, kicking and moving her arms as hard as she could, certain a rip current had caught her that would pull her down forever. The band of leather around her neck felt like it was pulling against her, as if trying to keep her under water.

In desperation, she opened her eyes, intending to kick her way to the surface with her dying breaths, if need be. But she froze as she saw the sight of the sea floor below her.

Several feet down, she saw a clump of brain coral surrounded by an assortment of fish so brightly colored it was as if they had sunlight filtering down on them. She looked around, her panic momentarily forgotten, as she saw the strange world of life hidden just below the surface.

It was like nothing she'd ever seen before and she hung motionless in the water, letting the current push and pull her in whatever direction it wished as she took in the tableau in front of her.

How could she see under the water? And how was she able to hold her breath longer than she'd ever been able to before? She glanced around her and saw the darkness of the rest of the ocean stretching out before her. What else lay under the water? What exotic things could she find if she went a little further?

Motion caught her peripheral vision, and she turned, sensing something moving close to her body. She craned her neck, bending her body nearly in half, impossibly limber, and saw the rest of her body. It was covered in glossy dark fur. Where her legs had been, now was a long body that tapered to two flippers clenched together as a tail.

She had done it! She had changed!

Then she remembered: she had to get to the surface. She flicked her tail in a single, strong stroke, and she shot upward until her head broke the surface of the water.

She let out an explosive breath and hung there, unconsciously moving her arm flippers from side to side to keep herself afloat as her tail moved in gentle side-to-side motions.

Ducking her head below the water again, she kept her eyes open. She saw, as if looking through clear glass, the life teeming under the surface of the water. Then she raised her head out again. Her sight changed, becoming more blurry.

Interesting. Obviously her seal eyes were more accustomed to water vision than above-air vision. Gathering her breath, she dove beneath the surface again.

Now that she realized her body was a single, long muscle, moving through the water was easier. She tested her abilities, turning left, then right, aware of the movement of her flippers on either side as she torpedoed through the water with ease.

Turning wasn't so hard, she found, and neither was hanging suspended in one place in the water—she held her position easily once she stopped trying to move forward. It was as if her body was made for motion, like it wanted to be moving as much as possible. The slightest effort propelled her forward at a surprising speed.

She noticed the noises around her, the slight gurgling of the water as it rushed past her ears, the whoosh of the waves as they crashed above her head. And further out, just beyond what she could make out, small squeaks and barks.

That sounded like the noise she'd made on the beach. Maybe that meant she was close to others of her kind!

She swam to the surface, took a deep breath, and dove beneath the water, delighting in the effortless way she moved through the water. As she swam, she tried not to focus on the things she saw: the fish darting in and out of the coral reef below her, the large stones that sat like humped sentinels here and there, the thick chunks of driftwood that lay like discarded limbs.

Focus! she reminded herself. *You're trying to find others like you.*

The barks got louder as she followed them, twisting and turning through the water for the sheer joy of the movement. Then she saw them, slim shapes darting through the water in a large school.

She blinked and paused, hiding behind a half-submerged boulder to keep out of sight. How did she know whether those were seals or selkies? Then one darted close by her and she saw a small satchel tied around its neck, the fabric bottom bulging with its contents.

That had to be selkies, she thought. Seals had no trinkets or valuables to carry with them. She watched, feeling suffused with excitement, as the large group passed her. Then, as the throng thinned, she swam forward and joined the end of the train.

She swam behind them, hearing the clicks and barks as they spoke to each other in the water. She'd keep quiet, observe everything about them, and hope they didn't realize she was a stranger among them. There was no telling what the Anchors would do if they found out she was the daughter of the prince.

Guilt twisted in her belly. Her father would be worried sick about her once he realized she didn't attend breakfast. An inquiry into town would reveal that she hadn't shown up for work at Madam Ruagh's shop, either. But she steeled herself. She was doing all of this for him. He would come to see that later. And once she got the Great Elder to restore his sealskin, he would be so overjoyed, he wouldn't be as angry that she'd risked herself to do it.

He will be grateful, she told herself firmly. He would be too busy changing back into a seal for the first time in over two decades to bother with punishing her.

Content with this knowledge, she swam on.

IT WASN'T LONG BEFORE she realized she was in trouble, after dawn broke and brightened into morning a couple of hours into their trek. The clan had moved into the open ocean, where darkness stretched out below her like a black curtain on the horizon despite the streaks of light breaking through from above. Her flippers were feeling rubbery, unused to such activity, and her lungs began to burn. She'd popped up to the surface with the others when she needed to, but it was getting harder and harder to hold her breath for the same length of time.

She lagged behind the others, noting with a rising worry that several selkies had passed her, each giving her a curious look as they went by. A large gray seal, a male and, she bet, one of the Anchors bringing up the rear of the train, swam up next to her, bumping her with its shoulder. It barked at her, an imperious noise that clearly meant *hurry up*.

She bobbed her head, unwilling to risk losing any breath by responding, and the Anchor swam on ahead.

A glance around told her she was alone. She watched the tails of the seals ahead of her fade from view and she fought against the panic threatening to well inside of her.

Her lungs burned, and she felt a sharp pang of pain ripple along her side. It was no good—she needed to take a break.

She swam toward the surface, up from the darkness to where the light shone through the top of the water. She broke the surface and inhaled a grateful breath. Bobbing on the surface, she watched the shapes of the seals in the distance, arcing out of the water as they swam. She'd seen them do that from time to time and had realized that they were taking their breaths of air when they leapt out of the water. It was how they kept moving without taking a break.

How did the pups make it? she wondered, as she rolled gently on her back, letting her natural buoyancy keep her afloat. The sun was warm on her face, and she closed her eyes, letting herself bask. There would be plenty of time to catch up to the others, she thought. It would be a small break only.

She bobbed on top of the water, savoring the feeling of the sun on her fur, and stayed like that for several long moments.

Something bumped her from below, bouncing off her back hard enough to push her sideways in the water.

What in the seven hells? she thought. She rolled over, letting her head dip below the surface. A long silver shape swam away from her. She peered at it, then motion caught her attention in her peripheral vision. She turned her head and saw another one close by. For a moment, the name of the creature eluded her, as her mind grasped for it.

Then she remembered the last catch that had come in off the docks, the celebration from the fishermen as they hauled the creature tail-first over the rail of the ship, its mouth open to reveal the sharp rows of teeth frozen in a permanent rictus.

A shark.

She was looking at a shark. And as she stared in shock at the one near her, she noticed more motion below her. She looked down and saw two others circling a few feet away.

Circling.

Sharks.

Circling... *her.*

Panic flooded her as she twisted away, down into the water, shooting past the creatures faster than they were prepared for. She swam in the clan's direction, her mind racing with terror as a single thought reverberated through her brain: *get away, get away, get away.*

She glanced behind her, and a ripple of fear shot through her as she saw the three sharks close behind in pursuit, their thick bodies cutting easily through the water after her. One of them had its mouth open in a grin, as if it couldn't wait to see what she tasted like.

And worse, she saw, as she gave another panicked glance behind her: they were gaining on her.

Think, Lyall, think!

If she kept on the way she was going, near exhaustion and nowhere near the clan, they would catch her for sure. She had to come up with something to get away.

What did seals in the wild do? she wondered. How did they escape predators?

She glanced around her, looking for something, anything that could hide her. But there was only the black curtain of the ocean all around, and she felt a sinking feeling at the realization that she was truly on her own.

Something grazed her tail flipper, and she twisted to the side, instinctively moving away from the danger. The shark shot past her, but the two behind it darted closer. She twisted the other way, flipping back on herself to avoid the open mouths and gleaming teeth.

This. This was how they stayed safe, she realized. They used their innate acrobatics in the water to keep out of reach.

She wove in erratic patterns, realizing that the straight path led to a quick death. The sharks stayed close behind her but couldn't keep up with her tight twists, squirting out of the way of their teeth at the right time, staying just ahead of their clashing jaws.

From the corner of her eye, she saw something dark swimming towards her, and she panicked, twisting away from it, thinking it to be another shark coming in for the attack. But it shot past her, arrowing into the gills of the shark on her tail.

The shark darted away as if in pain from the impact, as the dark shape came into clear view for her. Another seal, the large male that had barked at her earlier, winnowed past her, barking urgently, and swam again after one of the other sharks.

It opened its mouth as the Anchor came close, but the seal twisted at the last second, using its powerful tail to slap at the shark's gills in a chopping motion. The shark angled away and swam a few yards away, keeping its distance but staying within dangerous range.

Lyall saw the Anchor pause, looking for her. But he was unaware of the third shark angling up from below him. She tried to cry out to warn him, but a sharp bark came out instead. The seal turned and swam towards her, but she saw it would be too late. The shark opened its mouth and clamped down on the seal's tail. It shook its head from side-to-side, flinging the seal's body through the water like a cleaning rag.

Anger welled in her, anger at the sharks for disrupting her in the first place, for making her fear for her life, and adrenaline flooded her body. She charged downward, aiming for the shark the same way she'd seen the Anchor do, and crashed into its slitted gills with her nose.

The impact felt as if she'd struck a rock with her face, and she reeled backwards, aware of the shark twisting away from her in pain and swimming away with the other one.

She blinked, trying to clear her vision. For a moment, when she'd struck the shark, she'd seen a flash of light, like a starburst directly in front of her. It was as if there had been a shield of light between her and the shark, a flash that made her whole face feel warm. But her aching nose confirmed that she'd hit it, that was for sure.

Then she remembered the other seal. Had he escaped when she'd attacked the shark? She desperately hoped so.

She felt a gentle push against her shoulder, and she turned to see the Anchor leaning against her, bracing himself for support. It barked at her, then swam upward. With a body that felt like jelly, she followed.

CHAPTER 4

He was going to kill her.

It was unheard of for a selkie to stray away from the clan during a Migration, even the pups knew that. He'd drilled it into their heads for months leading up to this event, had even given a final, stern warning to all accompanying members of the clan about the dangers that awaited them if they left the safety of the group.

And here he had this lone idiot pulling some foolish stunt, which was bad enough without his getting injured on top of it. Well, he wouldn't put up with it, not on his watch. He fumed as they swam towards the shoreline, pausing every few seconds to glance back to make sure she was following. And to add insult to injury, the stray female was lagging behind, as if she had all day to make it to safety.

Selfish female, Ceannas fumed. He'd known which clan members might try some kind of power play like this, had pegged them weeks ago, and had tried his best to shore up those weak areas so the stragglers wouldn't be tempted to dawdle. He constantly stressed the dangers of the open water and even embellished with a few stories of his own about selkies from past Migrations who didn't return.

Glancing over his shoulder again, he saw she was still there, though lagging a bit more. He clenched his jaw, then gave an urgent *hurry up* bark.

She looked at him, but continued swimming at the same slow pace.

She had to be doing it on purpose, he thought. Nobody in their right mind would want to be in shark-infested waters by themselves. He paused, letting her catch up to him. From the labored way she moved, he had the brief thought that she might be tired. Was she exhausted? They hadn't been swimming that long, and most of the pups had remained with the clan.

Perhaps she'd been injured, he realized. Though there was no blood in the water, maybe she'd pulled a muscle or hurt herself in the shark attack.

He tried to brush the thought away, but it remained persistent in his mind. *Always assume positive intent,* his friend Ronan always told him. *You never know what someone's going through.*

Ceannas growled to himself. He didn't want to assume positive intent right now, not in the mood he was in. He wanted to rage at her when they made it to shore, wanted to shake her until her head popped off for the inconvenience she was causing him right now.

Not only was the clan now one Anchor short for protection as they traveled the open sea, but he was taken away from his primary duty given his injury. As Lead Anchor on this journey, he had greater responsibility than the other Anchors did—he handled the entire clan, down to the last pup. If any of them didn't make the Migration successfully, the king and queen would have his skin for it.

He jerked his nose towards the land they were now approaching, and he noticed with grim satisfaction that she seemed to be paying attention to his commands. She swam past him and headed for the shore. With a labored effort, Ceannas followed.

As he swam, he realized he couldn't place who she was. He knew all the selkies in Liath Clann both by their human and seal forms, and he never forgot a face. But this female was different.

The most noticeable trait, he realized, was that her pelt was all white, like that of a newborn pup. Usually that soft white fur morphed into the dark grey color of their kind after the first change. So this one was different, but how? Was she an albino?

He'd met one of those once in the Arctic. It had been another male, a castoff from his own clan. They'd determined him to be too much of a liability to the clan, since he lacked the ability to blend in with the rest of them when they swam in a group. That male had not acted normally, and Ceannas attributed it to his long isolation. It was enough to drive any selkie mad.

But was this female the same sort? Did she hang behind the others because she was ashamed of her pelt color?

He would have to find out. If she was a threat to the rest of the clan, he'd have to take care of the situation. His eyes narrowed as he watched the female's labored movements. What was this one about and why was she acting so differently from the others?

Then he had the thought that she could be from another clan. He knew of no albinos in Liath Clann and had not been warned that any would accompany them on this Migration. So she had to have joined up when they swam past her clan's location.

Probably ostracized by her own, he thought. It made more sense when he thought of it that way. It explained everything: why she lagged behind, why nobody warned him she was swimming with them, why she swam so slowly even as they headed towards the safety of the shore. Obviously, she wasn't looking forward to being called out.

But something didn't quite seem right still. He remembered Ronan's warning about sedition in the clan. Then, coincidentally, he ran into an unfamiliar selkie female on the day they left. He wasn't a fan of coincidences.

She could be a traitor, his mind whispered. *You'll have to watch her for the first sign of danger, either to herself or to the rest of the clan.* He would watch her closely. And he would get his answers in time. Once he'd dealt with her, after sending her on her way to wherever she was trying to get to, he'd return to his clan and continue his duty.

But first he would extract some information. He was adept at getting selkies to reveal things they hadn't any intention of revealing. It was a skill he'd developed during the siren-selkie war. Though he didn't like to dredge up those memories, he wasn't shy about using those tactics he'd learned to keep his clan safe. It was why King Righ had given him the promotion to Lead Anchor in the first place: he was solid. Dependable. Willing to get his hands dirty defending his clan.

He hoped he wouldn't have to deploy any of those tactics on this female to get the answers he needed. Especially since he didn't know how injured he was—he wouldn't know until he tried to change into his human form.

When they were about fifty yards from the shore, he gave several barks at her, then swam up to the surface, hoping she'd have the common sense to follow him.

Once his head was out of the water, he did a partial shift so that his head became his human form again, even while his seal form remained below the surface. It allowed him to see better in the chilly air above water. He glanced at the sky. If the clan continued at the same pace they'd been swimming when he left to help this female, he might catch up to them by dawn. It wasn't a bad plan. Assuming nothing else went wrong.

But then, he thought as he waited for her to reach the surface, *nothing ever went according to plan.* He smiled to himself. He could hope, though. And remain ever vigilant to any threats this female's situation might invoke. He would get her sorted out and on her own merry way, and then he would catch up to his clan and deliver them safely to the Great Elder. It wasn't a hard mission. And there wasn't much about this small female that posed an obvious threat.

Besides, he thought as the female's head poked out of the water a few feet away, *what's the worst that could happen?*

CHAPTER 5

Once she breeched the surface, Lyall spiraled around, looking for the seal head of her rescuer. But instead, she saw a man's face poke out of the water behind her.

"What are you doing?" he asked. "Why aren't you with the clan?"

She let out a series of barks. How had he changed so quickly? One moment he'd been a seal, and a heartbeat later, a man!

"This would be a lot easier if you'd change, too, you know," the man grumbled. He frowned at her, and she gaped at him. Strikingly handsome, he had a strong jaw and a crooked nose that spoke of having been broken multiple times. His copper-colored hair was plastered to his head, and he spit out the water that splashed over his face with an ease that spoke of long habit. His eyes were a radiant blue that seemed to leap off of his tanned face as he stared at her.

She made a small, frustrated whine, and he rolled his eyes.

"Fine. Can you make it to shore?" He jerked his chin over his shoulder, and she saw that the dark horizon of land several hundred yards away. She hadn't realized they were so close to safety.

She nodded, and his head dipped back below the water. A moment later, a gray seal arced out of the water with a sharp bark, then dove back underwater. He made a series of leaping arcs towards the shape of land, and she ducked under the water and followed.

By the time they reached the beach, Lyall's whole body ached, and her head was pounding. She saw the male Anchor dive under the water one last time, then a naked man emerged from the sea onto the sandy beach. His sealskin hung off his shoulder and dripped a steady stream of water down his muscled back. He favored his right leg, and even from her distance, she could see a garter of blood running down his thigh.

Lyall paused in the shallow water. How to turn back? And would she be naked, like he was? The thought was mortifying. Perhaps it was better to remain in her seal form and rest on the beach with him.

But there were so many questions she was burning to ask him! There was so much she wanted to know about being a selkie, things her parents always told her they'd explain later, when she was older. Well, she was older now, and still in the dark about what she was.

The man turned and planted one hand on his hips. "Well?" he demanded. "What are you waiting for? An invitation?"

If she could have blushed, she would have. She swam forward until her flippers scraped the sand. Then, using her front flippers, she lumbered out of the water until she was a few feet from him.

He looked at her expectantly.

She stared back, then barked and wiggled her front flippers.

"Are you going to stay in your seal form the entire time?" He glanced up at the sky. "It's about midday. We don't want the clan to get too far ahead of us. And if we wait until nightfall, well... predators come out at night, you know." This last he said with a wry grin.

She let out a series of barks and hopped back and forth on his flippers again.

He frowned. "What's the matter? Can't you change?"

She shook her head, as if she were human. A look of shock crossed his handsome face, and a tiny wrinkle appeared between his eyebrows. "Why wouldn't you be able to change? I didn't hear of any new members in our group. The only one who's even close to changing for the first time is..."

His face grew thunderous, and he dropped his sealskin off his shoulder. It fell with a wet splat on the beach, but he ignored it as he stalked towards her. "Are you Lyall? Lord Prion's daughter?"

She looked away, embarrassed. So the entire clan knew about her now? She felt both angry at her father and ashamed at the same time. She'd never considered her father to be anything other than a simple treasure finder. To have found out that he was a prince was an entirely new situation, one she was still growing accustomed to. But to see such deference to her father in action was unsettling, especially when directed at her.

"So you changed for the first time and now you don't know how to change back?" the man guessed.

She nodded. He let out an explosive sigh and ran his hands through his hair. With his wet hair streaming down his shoulders and his chiseled body standing taut in front of her, he seemed every inch some warrior god from a myth.

He sat down next to her, carefully maneuvering his injured leg so that it didn't bend, and rested his forearms on one knee. She noticed blood welling in the bite marks on his thigh, just above the knee, and the long streaks of it running like small, red ribbons down his calf to drip on the sand.

"I'm Ceannas," he said in a soft voice, as if speaking to a scared wild animal. He seemed oblivious to his wound. "And it's going to seem like a very scary thought to change for the first time. But it's not."

She glanced up at him. His face had lost its angry expression, and he gazed at her with a mixture of compassion and pity.

"It's going to be okay," he said with an entreating smile. "The first change is always the hardest. But once you do it, you'll always know how to."

In the span of a heartbeat? she wondered. That would be a wonderful ability.

Ceannas looked at the sand, thinking. He stayed that way for several long moments while Lyall observed him. The frown line between his eyebrows was back. She decided it was charming. It made him look younger, somehow, though he looked to be about the same age as she was.

He finally looked up at her. "You need to think of sliding out from under your sealskin," he began in a cautious tone, as if testing the words before he said them. "You're going to think of your sealskin as a blanket that's draped over you, and you have to slide out from beneath it to get back to your human form."

Lyall closed her eyes and thought very hard about becoming human again.

Nothing.

She opened her eyes, looked down at her flippers, then whined.

Ceannas grinned. "It doesn't always happen the first time. Picture yourself—your human self—buried underneath a layer of fur. Then take off the fur and let your human self slip through."

Lyall closed her eyes again. She focused on her flippers first. She pictured her hands sliding out from beneath the dried pelt she first pulled from the bag back on the beach outside her parents' house. In her mind, she saw her pale skin sliding from beneath the gray fur, of each finger wiggling as they separated from the fur glove covering them.

Her flippers tingled, like they had when she'd first changed, and she prayed she was doing it right. The sensation increased to a burning, prickling heat, and this time, when she risked a glance down, she saw her mental picture had become reality: two dainty hands peeked out from beneath her flippers. She squinched her eyes shut again, screwing up her face so she could concentrate.

Next she imagined her legs, clenched together, separating as a dark gray pelt covered them like a sheet.

The tingling sensation spread down her body to her legs, the feeling turning to the burning of a hundred bee stings. But she pushed away the pain, focusing all her mental energy on the image of her legs, whole and human again, standing upright.

She glanced down after several moments and saw two pale feet peeking out from beneath the flippers of her tail. But she could still feel the constricting pull of the sealskin across her back and shoulders, and she wriggled against it.

"Now reach down with your teeth and unfasten the hooks at your stomach," Ceannas's soft voice said, close to her ear. She reached over with one hand and felt down her belly—a row of small hooks met her fingers.

She marveled at the realization that she was almost there. But when she tried to pinch the hooks between her fingers, they slipped off the too-tiny fastenings.

"Use your teeth," Ceannas repeated. "They're more nimble than your sea-numbed fingers."

She reached down with her seal muzzle and awkwardly used her teeth to pinch and unfasten the bindings that ran down the length of her stomach. It was painstaking work, and she had to stop a few times to catch her breath—the odd angle made it difficult to breathe.

The whole time, Ceannas sat, watching as she struggled, seeming to understand that she had to work it out for herself the first time.

After what felt like years and copious false starts, Lyall got the last of the hooks to unfasten, and the sealskin fell away from her. Her skin tingled all over, rubbed raw from the chill of the ocean and the sand that scraped against every part of her.

But she was free!

"I did it!" she crowed, lurching to her feet. She got halfway upright, then her knees buckled, sending her sprawling to the beach.

"Easy there," Ceannas cautioned. He had made no move to rise when she did and made no effort to catch her when she fell. She glowered at him, and he flashed a toothsome grin. "Give yourself time to get your sea legs under you." He chuckled as if he'd made a joke.

Lyall glared at him. "And how long does that take?"

Ceannas gave a shrug with one shoulder. "As long as it takes."

She shot him a venomous look, then struggled to her feet once more, determined not to let the ocean—or his comments—get the best of her. When her legs held her weight the second time, she flashed a triumphant smile at him.

In response, he gave her an appraising once over from head to foot, then gave her a pointed look. Confused, she glanced down at herself, curious about what he saw, and realized, to her horror, that she was as naked as he was.

"Look away!" she screamed, crumpling on herself to hide her breasts and crossing her legs.

But Ceannas just grinned even wider. "Interesting," he drawled, eyeing her with open curiosity. "I'd heard you were raised by humans, but I somehow expected the selkie side of you to win out."

"What are you talking about?" Lyall hissed, looking around frantically for something to hide herself with. She spied her sopping sealskin on the ground behind her and snatched it up to drape it across the front of her.

The size of the sealskin caught her attention and she paused, looking down at it. "This wasn't this large when I first changed..." she said.

Ceannas nodded. "It starts off small, the same size as it was expelled from your mother's womb when you were born. But when you first change, it warps to fit your actual size. Though, granted, I've only ever seen it work with pups when they do it for the first time." His tone turned wondering. "I've never met a selkie born as a human before."

"They exist," Lyall snapped, stung. Her parents had told her that was the case with selkies who were born when their parents were in human form—those selkies didn't change until they reached twenty-two, if they even changed at all. That was the mystery, they'd told her: whether or not she'd ever be a true selkie. Apparently, she realized, it was more common for selkies to be born when their parents were in seal form.

Ceannas held up his hands in an *I surrender* gesture. But his grin said he wasn't sorry in the slightest.

Lyall decided that, whether he had the looks of a mythical god or not, she didn't like this fellow. Not at all.

"So now what?" she asked, taking in their surroundings. They were up against a line of trees a short way back from the waterline. But she saw a dirt path over Ceannas's shoulder that looked well worn.

"I assume you'll be wanting clothes?" Ceannas asked. At her furious glare, he grinned again and stood, brushing the sand from his backside and thighs. The motion was laborious as he struggled to keep his injured leg straight, as if it hurt to bend it. Lyall realized he had her to thank for the wound and felt a sense of guilt that he'd gotten it while trying to save her. He limped over and bent to pick up his sealskin from the beach, and Lyall looked away, a flush heating her cheeks. He'd given her a perfect view of his perfect, muscular buttocks and the view was, she had to admit, spectacular.

"I'm sorry you got hurt," she said, studiously looking anywhere but at his naked backside.

He turned back to her. "Accidents happen. I'm just glad we got away relatively unharmed." He gestured to his leg. "I've had worse before and I'm sure I'll have worse sometime later."

She turned surprised eyes to him. She knew her father to be determined and unflappable, but this was an altogether different level of stoicism. "If I had some cloth, I could bandage it for you," she offered in a hesitant voice.

Cocking his head, he gazed at her for a long moment, then smirked. "Well, thank you. Unfortunately, though, I don't have any spare clothes or bandages myself. So we'll have to get creative." He paused and turned to her, frowning. "I don't suppose you have any experience swimming in open water, do you?"

"Only how far we've come since Selbane."

His eyebrows lifted in surprise. "You've been with us since Selbane? Your father didn't warn us you were coming. We would have taken precautions."

Her cheeks heated again. "He doesn't know that I'm here... with you... on this Migration."

A series of emotions flitted across his face: admiration, then shock, and finally anger. "What in the seven hells do you think you're doing playing at being a selkie with no obvious training or protection?" His voice seemed to echo off the water.

Lyall was aware of her heart beating very fast in her chest, and she clutched her sealskin tighter to the front of her. "What do you mean 'play at being a selkie?' I *am* a selkie!"

"You're a liability is what you are!" Ceannas raged. He turned and paced, whipping his sealskin from side to side as if it were a flag flying in a strong wind. "To think you tried to make a Migration after your first change, without letting anybody know about it, and you nearly got yourself eaten by a school of—" The color drained from his face and he stopped in his tracks. "Oh gods, if they had killed you," he breathed. "If I had let sharks get the Prince's daughter..." He looked horrified.

"My father would kill you," Lyall said in a matter-of-fact tone.

Ceannas glared at her, then resumed his pacing. He didn't like this brat of a princess at all, he decided.

"Well, all that's done with for tonight. We need to get you somewhere safe until the morning. Then we can figure out what to do with you."

Lyall frowned at him. "Can't we stay on the beach?"

Ceannas glanced up at the sky, then back to Lyall, noting the shivering of her shoulders as she clutched the sealskin to her front. "I think I'd rather not have you go into shock after your first big day." Lyall noted the sarcasm in his voice and scowled at him. "However," he continued, "there is a town nearby, if I recall correctly. We'll get you something to wear and a place to stay for the evening."

He began limping towards the treeline, only to pause once he realized she wasn't following. "Well?" he demanded with open arms. "Are you coming or not?"

"I don't seem to have much choice, do I?" Lyall snapped back. She didn't like the predatory gleam that came into his eyes.

"No, princess, you don't."

"Stop calling me that," she groused as she picked her way across the sand towards him. "I have a name, you know."

"But it fits so well," Ceannas teased. He held aside a tree branch so she could walk past him. In response, she lifted her chin like royalty and strode past him, oozing hostility from her every pore.

"Where are we headed?" she asked as she struggled to wrap her sealskin around her torso to cover most of her delicate areas.

"See this trail?" Ceannas pointed to a small dirt path that wound between the tree trunks. "We follow it until we get to the town."

Lyall stopped abruptly, causing Ceannas to almost run into her. "Then what?" she demanded, ignoring his irritated scowl. "Two naked people just stroll into town and ask for a room for the night? That won't seem at all out of place?"

Ceannas ground his teeth together at her tone, then forced himself to take a single, calming breath. "Not quite." He lifted the leather pouch from around his neck. "I have some gold that will buy us some lodging. Not enough for clothes, though, so we'll have to steal those."

Lyall raised her eyes in indignation. "We can't steal clothes! The people they belong to need them!"

"I guarantee, princess, we need them more."

"But where will we find clothes to steal? Are we just going to break into someone's house?"

"Unless you have a better idea...?"

She gave him an incredulous look. "What about bartering? Work for clothes. Surely someone will take pity on our situation."

Ceannas gave her a deadpan look. "I don't suppose you're feeling energetic right now after the morning you've had. Because I am in no position to do much other than remain upright." He gestured to his thigh, and she felt another brief flash of guilt.

"Fine," she snapped. "Have it your way. But I don't like this plan."

He grinned at her. "That's the beauty of it, princess: you don't have to."

She fumed as they walked, with the cool night air drying the salt on her skin. It made her feel itchy and uncomfortable. She hoped that whatever she was feeling, Ceannas felt it a hundred times more intensely. That thought made her smile, made the fuming rage she felt towards him dim.

It was good to smile, to have those thoughts, since she knew it helped keep her mind off the terrible burning in her legs. She didn't give enough credit to her legs, she decided. They took her literally everywhere, anytime she wished to move. And now, when they were screaming with pain, she hoped they could keep her upright enough to get to shelter.

His legs seem fine, a voice at the back of her mind whispered, despite the shark bite. *In fact, they are more* than fine. She realized as she'd been walking behind the selkie jerk, that her unfocused gaze had been resting on his backside. Specifically, she realized, on his tight, muscular buttocks that flexed and relaxed with each stride.

Shame flooded her cheeks, making them burn. She was glad he couldn't see it.

"Here," Ceannas said, crouching down on the path next to a short wooden fence that seemed to have appeared out of nowhere. Lyall stood for a moment, confused, then Ceannas pulled her arm so that she crouched next to him.

"What do you mean?" she whispered, since everything about his body language screamed *caution*.

"See that?" he whispered back. She followed where he pointed to and saw a large white rectangle floating in the semi-darkness. It took a few moments for her to realize that she was looking at a bed sheet hanging on a thin line to dry. Behind it, a small log cabin squatted like a toad.

Ceannas pressed one hand to her shoulder to indicate that she should stay. Then he rose and darted forward, moving with grace and determination despite the hindrance of his injury. She saw him leap over the fence and disappear behind the large white sheet.

She'd started shivering when he reappeared moments later with his arms full of clothing. "Here," he hissed, throwing a dress in her general direction, as he pulled on the shirt and trousers he'd stolen for himself.

Lyall folded her sealskin in the satchel containing her father's, then pulled on the dress. It was several sizes too big, and, judging from where the hemline fell to her shins, made for a fatter, shorter woman than she. Lyall stared down at it in dismay. It might have been a potato sack.

If only she'd thought to bring her sewing materials from home, she might have been able to salvage it. But right now, it was altogether too much.

"I can't wear this!" she hissed at Ceannas, who was busy tying the drawstring of his pants.

He glanced up at her. "Why not?"

Lyall looked at him incredulously. "I don't want to wear this horse's blanket! It's hideous!"

"Well, it's the best we've got," he sighed. The last thing he needed was a picky princess telling him what to do. Even if she was right: the dress was unflattering. However, he noted her curves were still enticing. Though he didn't know how she did it, she still looked desirable in the ill-fitting clothing, and he found himself staring a little longer than was proper.

He tilted his head towards the area over his left shoulder. "We don't have far to go now. Can you walk?"

"Can you?" she shot back. But at his reprimanding look, she softened. "Barefoot? I won't last long."

Ceannas made a humming sound as he thought. Then he held up one finger to indicate *stay put*. He leapt over the fence again and darted around the hanging laundry to the side of the small cabin.

Lyall danced from one foot to the other, gazing about anxiously while she waited for him to return. But when he did, grinning and out of breath, he held out two pairs of shoes.

"Where did you find those?" Lyall asked in surprise. She reached for the pair of workman's boots, but Ceannas pulled them out of her reach.

"Nope, those are for me," he said. "*These* are for you." He held out a pair of ladies' dressing slippers. As Lyall huffed and snatched the slippers away, he added, "I found them just inside the back door. Silly humans never lock their doors. Too trusting a race, by far."

"We aren't all silly," she began, as she stood on one foot to cram her other foot into the too-small slipper.

"It's not 'we' anymore, princess,' Ceannas said pointed out. "Remember?"

She paused and stared at him, feeling a sudden crushing wave of loneliness and home sickness sweep over her. She wasn't human, and she never had been. As she opened her mouth to retort, grasping at some line she could use to hurt him as much as he'd just hurt her, when a light appeared in the cabin's window.

Ceannas's head jerked towards the movement, then he grabbed her hand and pulled her forward. "Let's go!" he whispered.

But Lyall paused, trying to get her other foot into the other slipper. "I can't, my shoe—"

"I said *go!*" he hissed at her and pulled her along so that she had to hop on one foot to keep from falling down. She got the slipper on, then raced after him on jellied legs that felt as if they would collapse under her at any moment.

They ran for countless minutes that felt like hours to Lyall, her hand sweaty as it clenched around his. Her back felt like there were two flaming bands of iron on either side of her spine, and it wasn't long before a stitch in her side made her crumple to a halt.

"I can't," she panted in desperation, one hand clenched on her side as if she were trying to hold herself together. "I can't make it much further."

Ceannas turned once her hand slipped out of his, and he regarded her with grim determination. "We have to keep going. The human world is just as dangerous a place at night as the selkie world. Predators come out at night to prey on the weak. We need to keep going. It's not far now."

"Predators?" Lyall gasped between breaths. Her lungs felt like they were going to burst. "You mean like thieves in the night?" Ceannas nodded his head once, then froze, realizing what she'd said. She grinned at him in satisfaction as his expression darkened into a scowl.

"Can you walk?" he asked.

Still panting too hard to breathe, she just nodded her head.

"Then follow me. And keep one hand on your bag at all times." He readjusted the bag holding his own sealskin on one shoulder. "The last thing we need is for you to turn out like your father."

Pride made Lyall lift her chin at him. "There are worse things to turn out like," she said in a prim voice. Ceannas spat to the side, not breaking eye contact with her, then turned, gesturing for her to follow.

CHAPTER 6

THE TOWN THEY CAME to a few minutes later was small, as Ceannas had predicted. A dirty sign with letters comprised of peeling paint read, "Albermarl." Practically nobody was on the street at this time of night, though they passed one cart pulled by two horses headed on its way out of town.

Ceannas was relieved to see that the first business they passed was an apothecary, whose sign showed two roses with intertwining stems.

"Stay here," he told Lyall, as he pressed her shoulders up against the coolness of the building's stone wall. "Don't move." Lyall gazed at him but nodded assent. Ceannas noted the dark bags beneath her eyes, clear indicators of how exhausted she was.

He darted inside, found the small jar he was looking for on one shelf, then grabbed a pair of thin leather gloves. As he paid for the items, he ignored both the flirtatious grin of the young woman behind the counter and her offer to show him how to use the jar's contents.

Then, a moment later, he was back on the street next to Lyall, who was gazing around the street with dazed interest. *How is she still standing?* Ceannas wondered to himself. He felt as if the day had wrung him out like a washrag—how was she still able to remain upright after her own ordeal? It was a puzzle to him, but he knew he needed to find them shelter soon. He didn't like the way she kept swaying from side-to-side as she stood there.

They moved on down the street.

After several more minutes, they found the town's inn, a ramshackle building with bare wooden boards that looked weather-worn grey. The sign hanging above the entryway read, "The Suckling Pig" and had a painting of a spitted pig on it with an apple in its mouth. Lyall shivered at the image, and Ceannas placed a comforting hand on her back to propel her onward.

As Ceannas opened the door, light and music and laughter leaked out into the quiet corners of the street. Inside was warmth and liveliness and the rich smell of barley soup. He liked it immediately. It was dingier than other human taverns he'd been in before, but he didn't care. All he wanted was a bite to eat and a place to sleep.

As they stepped across the threshold, Lyall shrank back at the volume of noise, but Ceannas grabbed her hand and held it in a vice-like grip.

"Remember, we're on our honeymoon," he growled over his shoulder as he swept them inside. It was the story he'd concocted as they crested the town limits, and Lyall appeared too tired to suggest otherwise.

Ceannas dragged Lyall to the worn and dirty bar and slapped a hand down on it. The surface was sticky, and

Ceannas didn't want to entertain what substances he was touching. The barkeep, a slight man wearing a stained cotton shirt, sidled up. Ceannas didn't like the way the man's eyes glided over Lyall's curvy form next to him.

With a growl in his voice, Ceannas stepped between them so that Lyall was out of sight behind him. "We need a room."

Without removing his eyes from Lyall, the barkeep said, "Fourteen coppers."

Ceannas gritted his teeth and tried to manage something that passed as a friendly grin. From the way the barkeep straightened and took a step backwards, Ceannas supposed he wasn't quite successful.

"It was only seven coppers last time I was here." He could feel Lyall trembling at his back and he resisted the urge to strong arm the barkeep into letting them stay. *No need to get violent,* he told himself. *Not yet.*

The barkeep reached underneath the bar and retrieved a worn beer stein and a dingy looking rag. While making eye contact with Ceannas, the man spat into the stein and wiped small circles in it with his rag. "That was when it was only yourself." The barkeep jerked his chin to indicate Lyall. "Now there's two of you. Doubles the price."

"That better include two meals and a wash basin," Ceannas grumbled. Both men knew he was going to pay the extra money—Ceannas could practically smell the desperation leaking off of himself and Lyall, and from the bartender's smug expression, Ceannas knew he could, too.

"One bowl of soup. No wash basin. You'll have to visit the bathhouse up the street." The barkeep's tone was one of smug satisfaction, and Ceannas wanted nothing more than to pull him over the nasty counter of the bar and beat his face to something unrecognizable.

But he could feel Lyall's trembling body pressed against his back. A quick glance around the bar told him others were noticing the pair of them, and that was attention Ceannas couldn't afford.

He dug into his coin pouch and slammed the coins on the bar top. He leaned forward, indicating with one finger the bartender should come closer. With a small frown, the man leaned in, still wiping absent-mindedly at the dirty mug.

"Anyone who tries to get in my room tonight will not walk out of it alive," Ceannas murmured, low enough that only the two of them could hear. "Be sure to spread the word. I'd hate for you to have to clean the blood off the floor."

The man straightened with a scowl. "Wouldn't be the first time I had to do so." He gave a wary look around the tavern with an expression more shrewd than Ceannas thought him capable of. "But I'll make sure you're undisturbed for the night. Tomorrow though?" He gave a small shrug. "I can't promise anything past tonight."

Ceannas glanced around the room over his shoulder, noting the way several of the men in their vicinity were watching them with appraising looks. Ceannas didn't bet the promise of safety would make it past the night either.

"Second door on the right," the bartender said as he put down the stein and swiped the coppers into the pocket of his dirty apron. He fished around beneath the bar and pulled out a single key on a black ribbon.

Ceannas nodded at the bartender, then led Lyall across the room towards the stairwell.

They trudged up the stairs, Ceannas leading the way down the small hallway to the door to their room. He opened it with a flourish and gestured for Lyall to step inside. She glared at him as she passed, and he grinned. It was too easy to get under her skin.

But she stopped just inside the threshold, and he bumped into her. "What's the problem, princess?" he snapped.

She turned and gestured to the room. "There's only one bed."

Ceannas peered around her and took in the room. To the left, there was a small desk with a single wooden chair in front of it, sitting beneath the window against the short wall of the room. The wall was barely wider than the desk. Four strides away, on the opposite side of the room, was the bed. It looked as if it had been made in a hurry, with lumps and wrinkles on the bed cover as if someone had made it, then slept on top of it.

He leaned forward and sniffed it, detecting the musky scent of previous occupants. He wrinkled his nose, then glanced at Lyall. She stood with her arms wrapped around her body, as if she might break into tiny pieces if she didn't hold herself together. She was shaking.

"Here," Ceannas said in a rough voice, and gripped her upper arm, leading her towards the bed.

"What do you think you're doing, manhandling me like that?" Lyall squawked, pulling away from him. But his hold didn't break as he pulled her forward until her knees brushed the edges of the lumpy bedspread.

"Lay down."

Her look was apoplectic. "I will do no such thing!" she hissed. He thought he detected a thread of fear in her voice. He looked more closely at her, noting the shaking shoulders and the panicked look she cast between him and the bed.

Ceannas rolled his eyes. "You're barely standing as it is. Lay down before you fall down."

Lyall stiffened her spine and leveled an icy look at him. "I'm fine."

Ceannas suppressed a sigh of irritation. *As stubborn as her father,* he thought. *And twice as prideful.* But he let go of her arm and gestured towards the bed. "There is no reason to be scared."

She flashed him a quick, wide-eyed look, as if he'd caught her doing something wrong. "I'm not scared," she said, and he knew they both could hear the tremolo in her voice.

"I know how to help you feel better," he coaxed in what he hoped was a gentle tone.

"By getting me in bed?" she snorted. "Unlikely. There is no way I'm getting in there with *you.*" She cast a desperate look around the room, as if looking for a different bedding arrangement.

Ceannas gritted his teeth and forced a grim smile. "You're about to collapse. It's all over your face. Either you can get in bed yourself, or I can pick you up and throw you there. It's all the same to me."

Lyall's panicked expression shifted at his words, and she snorted as she gave a pointed glance to his injured leg. "Not with that you aren't."

Leaning a shoulder against the wall, he crossed his arms. He knew it didn't take much to look imposing—he'd been told he was often enough. And now he let all his intensity leak into his expression.

She glared at him for several long seconds, then glanced at the bed. He saw longing flash across her face, and it reminded him of the first time he'd changed as a pup. His sire had been less forgiving of his weakness then. He'd been shaking and crying on the floor, barely able to stand, when his sire had looked down at him with a sneer.

"Pick yourself up. There's chores to be done."

He remembered how he'd looked at his bed, how it had seemed like an oasis, just the thought of resting for even a moment. But it was so far away, three feet that seemed like a mile, and he couldn't muster the energy to get to it.

Then a booted foot had crashed into his ribs, lifting him off the ground with the force of it.

"Get up, lazybones! There's no place for weaklings here!"

He'd stumbled to his knees, gripping his ribs, then made it to his feet, reeling on shaking legs that felt they'd collapse at any second.

"That's more like it." His sire's voice oozed with pride. *"Now get to work."*

Ceannas shook himself, ripping his mind away from the memory that gripped him. Now was no time for remembrances. There was work to do.

He saw her face change seconds before her legs gave way. As she collapsed, he stepped forward, halting her fall so that she didn't hit the floor. He lifted her up, one arm around her ribs, sliding her other arm over his shoulders so he could help her ease herself down on the bed.

She groaned as she sprawled out, her feet hanging off the edge of the bed. With her arms spread out to either side, she took up the entire sleeping space. Ceannas sighed. This was going to be a long night indeed.

He knelt at the foot of the bed and eased the shoes off her feet, wincing as he saw the broken blisters along the backs of her heels. *Why hadn't she said anything about the pain?* he wondered, then glared up at her. Of course Lord Prion's daughter wouldn't have said anything.

Though, he had to admit, he admired her tenacity. Few newly changed selkies would have managed a swim like hers and still had the reserves to make the trek through the city to find shelter. That she had remained standing at all was a testament to her iron willpower. It was a trait he respected.

She whimpered as his strong hands massaged the tender sole of one foot. Her toes curled as his thumbs rubbed gentle circles along her arch, then slid upward to flex each toe and stretch it away from her heel. While his thumbs rubbed along the bottom of her foot, his fingers wrapped around to rub small circles along the bony top of her foot. He slid a finger gently between her toes, spreading them slightly, and she groaned in pleasure.

"Why are you doing that?" she asked, her voice muffled against the bedspread.

"Because I know what it feels like after your first change. Your entire body was one huge muscle in the water, and now it's not. You have to take care of yourself the first few times you change until your body gets accustomed to it."

Her answer was a deep groan as he switched his attentions to the other foot.

His hands worked their way up her legs, gently rotating and stretching the small muscles of her ankles, then massaging her calves, one-by-one. But when his hands slid up the backs of her knees to her hamstrings, where he knew she'd be tightest, she pulled her legs up to her stomach and raised up to look at him over her hip.

"What are you doing?" she asked in a sleepy voice. He knew she'd been dozing under his ministrations and he'd let her, keeping quiet and monitoring the change in her breathing that told him she had started to drift off.

"Helping," he murmured. "Though this would be easier if you were naked."

Her face darkened, and he knew he'd been careless with his words. She had some bizarre sense of human propriety about her, and he kicked himself for forgetting it.

"I will not be naked in front of a strange man," she said haughtily, all traces of sleep gone.

"You mean for a second time?" Ceannas joked, grinning as she scowled at the memory of the beach. His grin deepened at the flush that worked its way up her cheeks.

"When my father finds out that you—"

"Helped his daughter when she could barely move?" he quipped. *Get your mouth under control!* he reminded himself. *This would be so much easier with her cooperation.* He schooled his expression into one of rueful appeal. "Look, I get that you don't know me. But I'm here to help. I'm one of your father's trusted advisors. And I'm going to make sure you get back safely. But for now, you can't continue with your body so wrecked. Let me help you." He held up his hands in a surrender gesture. "I promise nothing untoward will happen without your permission." But as her face softened, he couldn't resist adding, "And I don't bite... much."

Her mouth twisted as if she'd eaten a lemon, but she eased herself to the edge of the bed and sat up. "What do you want me to do?" He could tell from her voice she didn't enjoy acquiescing to him.

"Get undressed and lie on your stomach."

"Why?" She eyed him warily.

He forced himself to speak with patience as he answered, "So I can rub those aching muscles. If I don't, you'll be too sore to walk in the morning, much less swim. And we are a long way from Selbane."

"I'm not going back to Selbane," she blurted. "I'm going to see the Great Elder."

Ceannas's mouth twisted in scorn. "No, you're not. You're going to get home as fast as we can. It's not safe for you out here."

"I can take care of myself!" she retorted.

"Like you took care of those sharks?" he countered.

She lifted one eyebrow and crossed her arms. She gazed at him coolly. "Yeah, like I took care of the one about to eat *you.*"

He scowled down at her. "You almost got yourself killed."

"I saved your tail, and you know it!"

He gazed at her, marveling at the determination and confidence in her voice. She really believed she had the situation under control, he realized. And she had no idea how dangerous that was.

"I'm taking you home."

Lyall cocked her head and gave him a sly grin that he didn't like the looks of. "Are you, though?"

He gave her a suspicious sideways glance. "What do you mean?"

"Aren't you duty-bound to help other selkies? To take care of them at all costs?"

He nodded with a wary expression.

"And doesn't that include selkie royalty?" she cooed sweetly.

"Of course. Which is why I'm taking you back, princess."

"But that would deny my father the ability to change back into a selkie again. How do you think he'd appreciate that gesture?"

Ceannas froze, staring at her. "What do you mean? He can't change back. His sealskin was damaged. Nobody can fix it."

"The Great Elder can."

He gaped at her. "Is that why you're so intent on going? To get the Great Elder to heal Lord Prion's sealskin?"

She nodded. "That's why he sent me," she lied. "And I don't think he would take it well if you brought me back empty-handed."

"He sent you?" Ceannas said in a disbelieving voice. "Why didn't he tell me you were coming, then?"

She smiled at him and it was full of evil sweetness. "Apparently you aren't as trusted an advisor as you thought." She brushed an invisible speck off the lumpy bedspread.

Ceannas's face darkened. But he paused. If she was right, Lord Prion would end him for ruining his chance at shapeshifting again. He knew it was how he himself would act, at least. And that was without the reality of not being to change. Now add a few decades of time to that timeline—he couldn't fathom the horror of it.

"He really sent you to repair his sealskin?" he asked, gazing at her with narrowed eyes.

She bit her lip and nodded.

"Where is it?"

She pointed to the bag she'd been carrying. He stood in a graceful movement and stalked over to it. Opening it, he withdrew her sealskin, then fished around the bottom. His hands felt something soft, and he paused.

There was another skin in the bag.

He withdrew it, noting the tears in it, the gaping mouths of grey blubber that shone like rubber lips in the dim light of the room. This had to be the fabled skin, the one all selkies had been told the story of. To actually touch it, hold its ruined beauty in his hands...

He let go of it and dropped it back in the bag, resisting the urge to wipe his hands on his pants legs. His hands felt dirty, as if he'd touched something he shouldn't have. He glanced at Lyall and noted with surprise the bare expanse of perfect skin that ran along her back.

While he'd been occupied with the sealskins, she had unbuttoned her dress and peeled it back to her waist so that the back of her upper body was exposed as she lay face-down on the bed.

"What are you doing?" he asked in a harder voice than he meant to. He cleared his throat.

"You said to get naked," she said, turning her head so that her cheek lay on the bed. "This is as comfortable as I can manage."

He noted a blush in her cheeks, and the heady scent radiating off of her. It was sweat and fear and dried ocean water and something musky he couldn't quite place. *She's nervous*, he realized. *Of being exposed to me.* The thought filled him with a primal sense of satisfaction and the immediate urge to comfort her, to assure her he meant her no harm. Though he was one of the more hardened Anchors in the clan, he didn't want her to fear him. He wondered if she'd heard any of the war stories his clan liked to pass around. He knew himself to be in several of them, especially over the last few years of the war, when he'd risen to the rank of Commanding Anchor among his contingent.

But he knew words were fine, but actions were better. So he set to work. He strode to his pack and pulled out the small jar of salve he'd purchased for this very reason. Pulling loose the top, he lifted the pot to his nose and inhaled. The acrid scent of liniment burned his nostrils, along with the soothing scent of lavender and oats. He dipped a finger in the salve, hoping it was as potent as the merchant had promised.

Immediately, his fingertip went numb, and he smiled. This would do just fine.

He plucked a glove from the bag, put it on, and used his gloved fingers to smear a great glob out of the pot. Crossing the few steps to the bed, he knelt on it next to Lyall.

He eased his gloved fingers down her spine, coating her skin with the salve. Seconds later, he grinned as she let loose an audible sigh of relief as the mixture burned its way into her skin.

"What is that?" she asked in a surprised tone.

He half-grinned down at her face, turned towards him on the bed. She watched him from the corner of one eye. "Like it?"

"It's like... ice and fire all at once. Like it's burning and soothing at the same time. How is that possible?"

"It's a special mixture. All the Anchors use it—it helps with the muscle ache after training or a fight. And it's handy for newly changed... individuals." He had to catch himself from saying "pups."

"Well, I love it," Lyall sighed with satisfaction.

Ceannas concentrated on the feel of her muscles beneath the glove. As he spread more of the mixture down one side of her ribs, he watched her back muscles flex in response. The sight of them caught his attention, and he paid closer attention to the movement of her body as he rubbed small circles into her skin.

His thumb found a knot along her shoulder blade, and he pressed more firmly into her skin. She moaned into the bed sheet, in pain and pleasure both, and he found his stomach tightening at the sound.

Stop that! he told himself. *She's Lord Prion's daughter, not some female that caught your eye!* That should have made all the difference, should have dashed his arousal like a splash of cold water.

Yet he found his tongue slipping along his lower lip as he rubbed more circles over the strong bone of her shoulder blade. She moaned again, and it was like she had a direct line to his more intimate areas the way they jerked in response.

He found himself timing his breaths with hers, inhaling as she did and exhaling on her small whimpers of pleasure.

His hands worked harder and deeper into her muscles, enjoying the noises he could elicit from her.

Suddenly, the feeling of the leather glove on his hand was too restricting, too bulky. He needed to touch her, needed to see if her skin was as soft as it seemed to be.

He set down the pot of salve and worked the glove off his hand with his other hand, trying to be as careful and quick as possible. The last thing he wanted was for her to move away, thinking he was finished.

He tossed the glove over his shoulder, not caring where it landed, and dipped his fingers into the salve again. His skin tingled. Heedless of the numbness spreading across his palm, he smeared more salve over the other side of her ribs.

Her answering sigh made his rising erection throb in response. He traced his hands down her ribs, letting his fingers linger in the shallow grooves between the bones, savoring the feeling of her muscles rippling under his touch.

"That feels amazing," she murmured.

"Do you like it?" His voice was husky, even to his own ears. He wondered if she noticed.

"I love it."

He grinned at her, noting that her eyes had drifted shut in pleasure. Working his way down the long muscles on either side of her spine, he let her moans seep into his brain to fire his arousal into a burning flame.

He was nearly panting by the time he made it to her lower back, his erection throbbing in time with his movements. She writhed as he hit a particularly tender area and he had to bite his lip from moaning in response.

She pressed her face into the bedspread and mumbled something.

Afraid he'd hurt her, he lifted his hand, ignoring the tingling burn that seared its way along his whole hand. "What was that?" he managed hoarsely.

"Harder!" she cried, and he closed his eyes at the way his body leapt in response. He fumbled the salve pot onto the bedspread and applied both hands to the motions as he rubbed his thumbs along her lower back, kneading with the heels of his hands in time with the rhythm of her panting cries.

Though he knew she was responding to his expert touch, part of him delighted in the obvious pleasure he was giving her. As he pulled and squeezed, rubbed and slid his way along her lower back, he leaned his weight into his hands.

Without realizing it, he'd edged her dress further down her waist to increase the area he could massage. But when his fingers brushed the tops of her buttocks, she stiffened, causing him to freeze in sudden panic.

"Everything okay?" he asked, fighting to keep his voice neutral. If she turned to face him, she'd see the effect she was having on him, and that would out him as a liar after assuring her he was trustworthy and safe.

"Fine," she said after a moment. "Just... can you focus on my shoulders some more? They still feel tight." Her voice was soft, sleepy. There was no anxiety or fear underlying her words.

He relaxed, letting his breath ease through his gritted teeth, and moved his hands to her upper back as requested. He closed his eyes, letting his hands memorize the curve of her spine, the taut muscles that shifted and yielded to his firm touch.

Yes, her skin was as soft as he'd suspected. Though his hands had both gone numb from the effects of the salve, he could feel the pressure of the touch and savored each movement of her body underneath him. He felt the muscles in his own arms warm with the exercise of massaging her aching muscles. Losing himself to the sensations, he closed his eyes and imagined his hands moving lower on her body, pictured her flipping over and exposing herself fully to him to rub and caress and touch as he pleased. In his mind, she wore a smile and nothing else.

It was a delicious thought.

So lost in the fantasy, he didn't recognize the slight buzzing sound when he heard it. He opened his eyes and paused, waiting, and heard it again: a soft snore.

Grinning to himself, he eased off the bed, careful not to jostle her. He wiped his hands on the outside of the bag that held the salve, hoping the effects would wear off soon. He looked down at Lyall asleep on the bed, her skin pale and gleaming from the salve. Her hair had tumbled over one shoulder, exposing her delicate neck. He watched her pulse flutter underneath her jaw and felt an answering tightness in his lower body again.

Sleep had softened her features, making them younger, almost angelic, without the fierce pride and haughtiness she'd worn earlier. For a moment, as he watched her, he felt his own heartbeat pulsing at a faster rate than normal. Then, on the tail of each beat, there was another answering beat, like a ghost memory of a heartbeat that beat in a slower rhythm than his own. The ghost beat flashed with every other beat of his own heart, and when he inhaled, he felt another set of lungs expanding, too.

He shook himself and the feeling dissipated, leaving him along with only his one pounding heart and lungs. He swore under his breath. This would not do, panting after this young thing like a dog in heat. It didn't matter that she was only a few years younger than him—the gulf between them was vast, given her life experience.

He shouldn't have touched her without the glove, he decided. It had been crossing a line. Still, he glanced down at his hands as if he could still feel her muscles bunching under his palms. Could still imagine his fingers plucking at the tips of her breasts.

He glanced back at her and wondered if her hair would feel as silky as her skin. Would it tumble like water through his fingers when he ran his hands through it? Or would she gasp as her hair caught on the callouses on his fingers, her clear eyes meeting his with a challenge in them, as she had earlier?

He closed his eyes and forced his rising arousal to calm. She was not his to possess. She was part of the royal family, which put her off-limits in a hard way.

Still.

He glanced down at the tent his erection made in his pants. His body seemed to disagree with his thoughts.

Sighing, he made his way over to the bed and eased his body down next to Lyall. Though he tried not to touch, it was impossible to fit on the bed and not have his body press against the length of hers. He tucked his arm under his head for a pillow and tried to make as much space between them as possible—it wasn't easy, given that she was lying in the middle of the tiny bed.

The second his body came in contact with her, however, she wriggled backwards, pressing her body into his. He swallowed hard, trying to calm his pounding heart.

It's just to keep her warm, he told himself, as he draped his arm over her ribs. *It's nothing intimate.*

He could feel the bottom of her breast on the back of his hand. The touch burned like fire, so intense he wondered how she didn't wake from the contact.

"Ceannas," she murmured.

He raised his head, looking to see if she was speaking to him, but her eyes were closed. The eyelids were lavender with exhaustion, and there were dark circles under her eyes.

He lay his head back down and pressed his arm more firmly against her ribs, pulling her closer to him. At her satisfied sigh, he swallowed again, feeling his throat clench.

It's just one night, he thought, and closed his eyes. *Never again.*

He let his breathing even out, unaware of the way he began to inhale on her exhale so that their lungs moved back and forth in tandem with each other, pushing and pulling in an easy rhythm.

His last thought was of his fingers, covered in soft blonde tendrils that gleamed in the sun like molten gold.

CHAPTER 7

SHE WAS GETTING USED to the walking, she decided. She could already feel her legs getting stronger and thought her muscles were looking more defined as well. It was a small vanity she allowed herself, given that any overt interest in her looks would earn no end of derisive comments from Ceannas.

It was bad enough that she had to walk with him, but knowing that he was playing babysitter was downright insulting. Though, she had to admit, as she took in the sight of him walking in front of her down the dirt path, the view was spectacular. The pants they'd stolen several nights ago were too small for him, giving her the perfect view of his muscled ass as they walked. She let herself drink in the moment, savoring the sight of his shirt straining across his broad shoulders, the hair that curled just above his collar, the thinly veiled limping stride as he sauntered along. Everything about him screamed warrior, and even if he was an uptight jerk about just about everything, she could at least admire the view of him.

She'd seen him naked, back on the beach, though she was grateful he'd taken up a temporary vow of modesty for her sake while they traveled. Still, a part of her wished she could catch another glimpse of his muscled body, down to the areas she had only dreamed about touching. In her dreams, she roamed his body with more than her eyes, letting her fingertips imagine what firmness his chest would have, how the hair there would slide through her fingers like silk. Often in her dreams, she was the aggressor, taking charge of him by pushing him down on the bed and straddling the top of him, staring down into his face while he looked up at her in worship.

Yes, that was her favorite dream. Getting to drag those ill-fitting clothes off of him, peeling them away like a second skin while he watched, unable to move without her permission, surrendering to her touch with reckless abandon.

It had been hard enough waking with tangled limbs, with their legs intertwined and him snoring in her ear. She had awakened before him, thank the gods, and had eased herself out of his grasp, flushing with the embarrassment of being so brazen, so open to this stranger who made her feel emotions she'd never felt before.

As strange as it sounded, she had to admit that not even Lucas Hew had made her feel so safe. Despite their interactions never having reached the bedroom, she still had never felt so secure in Lucas's arms as she had during that one night with Ceannas. She could remember the feel of his body snaking along hers from neck to toe.

She licked her lips at the memory and sighed. Immediately Ceannas pivoted on his heel to walk backwards while regarding her with a skeptical expression. "What's the matter, princess? Tired already?"

His voice taunted her out of her daydream and back to the reality of her situation. They were, according to Ceannas, only a few days behind the clan, and if they made good time to the next town, they might tag back up with the group before it stopped following the shoreline and headed westward towards the vast uncharted territories of the ocean. But they needed to be in town tonight if they were going to catch up by morning.

Lyall scowled at him. "I could do this all day," she scoffed with a haughty tilt of her head. Of course she was tired, though nowhere near as tired as she'd been the last few days. But it wouldn't do to let him know that.

He grinned at her, as if her statement were amusing to him, then pivoted back around to face the front again.

Lyall glared at the back of his gorgeous head, wishing she could wipe the smug smirk off his face. He knew exactly how tired she was, and he kept pushing her endurance on purpose to see if she'd crack. Well, she'd show him. She'd walk until her feet were rubbed down to boney nubs before she'd give him the satisfaction of asking for a respite.

She tried to picture the last image she'd had in her head, the part where her hands were gliding down the muscled plane of his stomach, down below his waistband to where that perfect V-shape rested. In her mind, she leaned down, preparing to lick one side of that V. He would tense in anticipation beneath her hands, and she grinned at the thought. One more inch and she could almost feel the hard length of him against her tongue and—

"So, Lyall, how do you plan on convincing the Great Elder to help you, anyway?"

His voice, pitched to the perfect timbre to shatter her thoughts like glass, broke her reverie. She blinked a few times to come back to reality, then she gave him a cool appraisal. While she'd been daydreaming, he'd slowed his walk to keep pace alongside her instead of in front of her.

Her cheeks flamed with the thought that he might have somehow realized what she was thinking about, and she pressed her palms to her cheeks to hide it. When she glanced at Ceannas, she noticed him watching her with open interest.

Strange, she thought. He'd never used her name before. The sound of it on his lips made her stomach flip with desire.

Stop that! she demanded of herself. *I will not run after this arrogant creature like some lovesick hound!* With a huff, she took her hands off her cheeks and straightened her spine. She imagined stone walls, like a fortress, rising around her as she built her mental armor up piece-by-piece.

Though there was nothing antagonizing about his expression, she regarded him warily, expecting some sarcastic comment. However, gone was the smirk and the twinkling mirth in his eyes that seemed ever-present when he spoke to her. It was almost as if he were asking her a real question he wanted a serious answer to.

Like she was a real person. Like she wasn't some young charge he was unwillingly responsible for.

She considered the question. What *was* she going to do when she met this Great Elder? Beg on her knees? Offer all the gold her family had? Barter some kind of service? She was forced to concede that she had very little to negotiate with, other than her clothes, which she didn't figure someone with the title "Great" Elder would want; her seamstress skills, which may or may not be useful to someone who could change shape at will; or her body.

The thought that this Great Elder might want her body as a bartering tool made her face drain. She had no idea what this creature was like. Was he kind or cruel? What if he wanted more than she could give? What if his physical tastes ran to the extreme? What if the price was for her to stay with him forever?

A violent shudder ran through her, and Ceannas immediately placed his arm around her shoulder, pulling her close to his side. "Hey," he breathed. When she refused to look at him, he stepped in front of her and pressed both hands to her shoulders to stop her.

"Look at me," he commanded. With hesitation, she raised her eyes to meet his gaze. "I don't know what you were just thinking about, but I want you to know that you're safe with me. I won't let anything happen to you. Whatever's got you so scared, tell me and I'll take care of it for you."

His face, inches away from hers, was filled with concern. Even his beautifully striated eyes seemed to bore into hers, as if he could read her thoughts. She became acutely aware of the warm puff of his breath on her face, and the fact that he was close. So, so close. If she angled her head to one side and leaned forward, she could easily press her lips to his.

What would he do if she dared?

The thought was like a dash of cold water over her. He'd probably stop the concerned protector act and would storm away, leaving her on her own to find her way around. She knew how he saw her: as a weak, sheltered pup barely able to survive on her own. He would never respond favorably to her advances.

She let loose a deep sigh, and Ceannas frowned down at her.

"Tell me," he urged in a low voice. "Let me in."

She examined his eyes for several long moments. Then she remembered that time was precious. Every second they wasted standing here were seconds the clan gained to get away from them.

"It's nothing," she lied, forcing a weak smile. "I guess I'm more tired than I thought. Let's keep going."

Ceannas continued to frown down at her, seemingly unwilling to let the issue go. Then, as she forced a bigger smile, he stepped to the side and gestured for her to continue on the path. "If you're sure, then lead on, princess."

Some part of her was glad that he gave up pursuit of this issue, that they were back on familiar ground with the nickname and the self-confident persona. But another part of her, as she stepped forward past him, felt let down. She didn't know what she expected to have happened, but she knew the moment had passed without it happening.

"I'm not entirely sure how I'll get the Great Elder to help me," she admitted as he stepped into place next to her so that they walked shoulder-to-shoulder. "I suppose I'll have to find out what he wants first. I've found that people act in predictable ways when you find what motivates them." Ceannas gave her an appraising look. "What?" she said. "It's not a hard problem to figure out. You just have to know what questions to ask."

"How will you find out what the Great Elder's motive is?" His voice was curious, though his expression held a bit of wariness.

Lyall thought about it for a moment. "I'm not sure just yet."

Ceannas frowned in thought, idly scratching his cheek. "Ok, new subject. Tell me something: how did a seamstress learn so much about managing people and their expectations?"

Lyall cocked her head with a quizzical expression on her face. "What better area could I have had to learn it? My father taught me a lot about offering people what *they* want in order to get what *you* want. And there's no better place to figure that out than when you're trying to sell something to someone."

She paused, with a glance at Ceannas, and almost lost her train of thought at the intensity in his gaze as he watched her. She cleared her throat, feeling a suddenly dry mouth, and looked at the path ahead.

"For example," she continued, as if she wasn't aware of the fact that she had his full attention. "Most of the people that came into Madam Ruagh's shop didn't know exactly what they wanted. They knew they wanted a dress or a suit, but they didn't know what color or style or fabric they wanted. They just wanted to walk out looking nice. So that's where I come in: I talk with them to figure out what they're looking for, what they like, and what they don't like. Then I make educated guesses based on the resources that are available.

"If they are on a budget, I know that offering them the pricier options might lose me a sale. So I have to work with mid-range fabrics. If they're trying to impress someone in particular, I try to offer different styles to flatter the figure or highlight their hair or eyes. It's all about knowing your customer better than they know themselves. Often they don't know what they want until it's right in front of their faces."

She paused and risked a peek at Ceannas. He was still staring at her, but his expression had lost its former intensity. Instead, it held a curious frown, as if he were thinking very hard. She allowed herself to meet his eyes for two heartbeats, then looked away again. Now she thought she knew what the rabbit felt like in the presence of the wolf.

"So you have to be good at reading people," he said.

Lyall nodded. "You have to be good at reading the *right* person," she corrected with a small grin. "The one who controls the money is the only one that matters."

"Hmm. So, I ask again, how are you going to find out what the Great Elder wants?"

She shrugged. "I suppose I'll have to ask him."

Ceannas stopped and brayed laughter toward the sky, his head thrown back, exposing the tanned, vulnerable expanse of his neck. Lyall had the sudden irresistible urge to lick it.

"What's so funny?" she demanded, stopping to plant her fists on her hips.

"It's just… you can't just…" Ceannas was laughing so hard he couldn't get the words out. His face turned purple. "Don't you know that selkies from all over the world come to see the Great Elder every fifty years? That's hundreds of creatures who all want an audience with him, to ask for favors or to deliver offerings and gifts. Kings and queens will be there, with their entourage, all of whom have greater social standing than the newly turned daughter of a banished prince. And you want to just…"

His laughter burst forth with renewed mirth.

Lyall turned her back to him and began walking, striding ahead with no concern for her aching legs and hips. She let her anger pound down into the earth of the pathway, imagining that each foot was planting onto Ceannas's laughing face. She watched her feet as she went, aware of a pounding noise in her ears that coincided with each step.

Laugh at me? she raged in her mind. *We'll see who has the last laugh. My father will rip you to shreds after he finds out how you treated me. He'll find out and you'll wish you'd never met me.*

The pounding of her feet was loud enough that she didn't hear Ceannas call her name at first. Such was the thudding of her own heartbeat in her ears. It wasn't until his hand clamped on her upper arm and spun her around that she realized he was coming after her.

"What are you doing?" he cried as she spun around to face him.

But she swallowed her sharp retort when she saw the urgency in his expression. "What's wrong?" she asked, frowning.

"Didn't you hear those noises?" he asked as he scanned their surroundings with a sharp, alert gaze. In an instant he had shifted from concerned friend to trained warrior.

"What noises?" She pulled her arm from his grip, still ready to continue the fight.

"Those thuds. It sounded like the earth itself had a heartbeat. Then it stopped."

His eyes were like chips of ice in his stern face as he looked around them. His entire body was taut, ready to fight or flee with her in tow if the situation required it. She saw him straining to listen in the surrounding silence. She paused, too, and cocked her head to hear better.

Nothing but the sound of their breaths surrounded them.

After several long moments, Ceannas relaxed, like a bow returning to its starting place: still ready to explode at any moment, still wound under great pressure. When he spoke to her, he didn't look at her and instead scanned their area. Without asking permission, he grabbed her arm again and marched them along the path.

"Hey!" Lyall exclaimed. "I can walk perfectly well, thank you!"

He let go of her arm but moved his hand to the small of her back to urge her forward. "I don't know what that was, but I don't like it. We need to keep moving." His voice was tight with concern.

Lyall, still trying to piece together his heartbeat comment, let him usher her along without complaint. She had heard nothing strange, but then, she'd also been raging mad at him and only concentrating on her own feelings. Her feet felt warm, as if they were held in front of a fire. She wriggled her toes in the slippers, trying to get the heat to leave them. It took a few minutes before the blood flow to her feet felt normal again.

They moved down the worn dirt path until the trees around them began to thin. Lyall realized she could hear the faint crash of waves against rocks, could smell the tangy brine of the ocean on the air. The scent was tantalizing to her, calling her with each swooshing wave to *come home, come home.*

She glanced at Ceannas and saw he had stopped to savor the feeling of the air on his skin. He stood with his eyes closed, face turned upwards to catch the sunlight, a slight smile on his full lips. He looked like a figure carved from marble, a fairy prince who could cast spells and trick naïve human girls into joining him in his underground kingdom.

Lyall watched for several long moments, ignoring the pull of the sea to admire the physical perfection in front of her. She'd never noticed how attractive he was before, during the few times they'd met. But now, she found herself unable to turn away. The breeze off the ocean whipped at their clothing, making the chiseled planes of his body visible. She was well aware that she was staring at the firm chest, the rippling stomach muscles, the thick slabs of his thighs in his too-small pants.

The sight made something low in her stomach tighten in response. She couldn't deny that he was attractive, couldn't pretend that he was anything other than perfectly proportioned. She bet he'd look very fine in a suit tailored especially for him. How she longed to kneel before him and take his inseam measurements.

She closed her own eyes and pictured what it would be like. In her mind, she was on her knees, face close to the junction of his thighs, staring up at him as if she were worshiping at the altar of his body. He would be shirtless, with those amazing muscles on display right down to the dangerous V-shape hidden by the waistband of his pants. Unconsciously, she licked her lips at the thought of running her tongue down the sides of that V.

His amazing eyes would stare down at her with the intensity of a thunderstorm as she ran the measuring tape from his ankle up to his groin. Her fingers would brush gently against his manhood, only to find the length of him straining against the waistband.

"You'll have to take off your pants," she'd say in a modest voice. "So I can hem the legs." He wouldn't break eye contact as he untied the fastening at his waist. He'd hook his thumbs into the loosened waistband and slide them slowly, ever so slowly down, over his buttocks and down further until she could see his impressive—

"So, are we just going to stand here and appreciate nature, or are we going to stick to the plan?" Ceannas's vexed voice broke through her daydream.

She blinked and looked over to find him staring at her with open irritation written across his face.

"I... ah, sure. Yes." She brushed her hands down the front of her dress to smooth invisible wrinkles. She risked a glance at him and saw that he was staring out at sea with ferocious concentration. It gave her a few extra moments to compose herself and rub the flush from her cheeks with the heels of her hands.

"The mission, right. Of course." She stepped closer to the edge of where the land banked steeply downward, earthy clay giving way to sand and small gray and tan pebbles that lined the beach. She saw nothing but the expanse of blue sea before her, the white-capped waves sliding into the beach with a foamy chaos before sweeping back out to the rest of the ocean. The beach was empty near the water.

We missed them, she thought in dismay. Her shoulders slumped in defeat.

"Do you see them?" Ceannas asked. His voice held an electric excitement that she hadn't ever heard before.

She shook her head and glanced at him. To her surprise, he was grinning, a wide, open smile that showed his very white teeth in contrast to his tan skin. He met her gaze and pointed out toward the sea. "Look down."

She edged closer to the embankment and peered over the edge. In shock, she took in the group of seals lounging near the embankment wall. There had to be over a hundred selkies resting there. Some were in their seal forms, basking in the sun, while some of them were in their human forms, their naked bodies looking pale and innocent in the sunlight. To one side, she saw a pair of pups playfully swatting each other with their flippers and tails. Many of the humans were in pairs, draped over each other, the picture of lazy indulgence. Their nudity shocked her more than the fact that they'd caught up to the selkie clan in the first place, and she averted her eyes when she realized she'd been staring.

Ceannas grabbed her hand and pulled her back. She followed as he led her to one side of the embankment towards a thin, sandy path that led down to the beach. Her feet slipped on the shifting sand, but she stayed upright as she followed him. He took them on an unerring path through the group of selkies, ignoring the curious looks and hailed greetings thrown his way.

He finally came to a halt in front of a naked man who was speaking in animated fashion to a large grey seal with a small burlap sack tied around its thick neck. Lyall watched, intrigued, as the seal bobbed its head once in what appeared to be agreement, then turned and waddled to the waterline where it disappeared into the sea.

Beside her, Ceannas dropped to one knee, a fist clapped to his chest over his heart. Surprised and feeling that she was missing out on some important ritual, Lyall stood there, trying not to show her discomfort at Ceannas's action or the open nudity of the male figure before her. Pursing her lips, she cast her gaze around the wall of the embankment they were next to, as if it were the most interesting thing in the world.

After a nod from the naked male, Ceannas rose, still holding her hand. "My Lord Trian, please forgive my disappearance. A new development has kept me busy—"

"Too busy to protect your clan?" Trian asked. Though his voice sounded innocent, Lyall detected an undercurrent of threat in it. His long black hair hung like a sheet down the front of him, hiding his chest. He was slender, with small pale lines running down his forearms. After a moment, Lyall realized those must be scars. But received where? She didn't suppose selkie lords fought enough to get battle scars. But the man's eyes were an icy blue, devoid of warmth as he regarded the two of them.

Lyall decided she didn't like this man.

"As a matter of fact," she broke in, overriding Ceannas, who had opened his mouth to speak. "He was busy protecting me."

Trian's gaze sharpened as he focused on Lyall. "Yes, little Lyall. I hadn't hoped to see you on this Migration." Trian cocked his head. "But I don't remember your father requesting permission to send you this year. How did you come to be here?"

Lyall cocked her head, confused. She cast an uncertain glance at Ceannas, who frowned at her. "I'm sorry," she said slowly. "I'm not sure we've met before. I'm—"

"Lyall, daughter of Prion and Leannán. Yes, we've met."

Lyall's eyes widened in shock and she took a step forward, despite Ceannas's hand clenched on hers to hold her still. "When? When have we met?"

"I've visited your house many times when you were younger." Trian examined his fingernails with a small scowl. "But my duties have called me away for some time now." He flicked away an imaginary speck of dirt, then met her gaze with that icy stare. "I wasn't impressed."

Sensing there was an insult there, Lyall narrowed her eyes. "Why should I care what you find impressive?" she shot back. Ceannas's hand tightened on hers in warning.

"Because we have a greater tie than you know."

"Who are you?" she asked in a soft voice. There was a roaring silence building in her mind, one that wiped out the other feelings and thoughts she'd been processing, one that left no room for anything other than his answer to her question.

The man's gaze narrowed as he smiled at her, and his teeth reminded her of the shark attack from a few days ago. "I am Trian, the youngest of three brothers and the last in line for the throne. Am I supposed to believe that you have never head of me, not even from your father?"

"He's never said a word about you," she said, gathering herself and straightening her back. She was the daughter of a prince. She would not be intimidated by the creature before her.

Trian watched her gather herself as if for battle and his smile widened in predatory fashion. "Well, my dear. Let me assure you that I've heard an awful lot about *you*. In fact, I've kept tabs on you for some time now." He stepped forward until he was close enough to reach out and stroke a lock of her hair.

His touch was clammy against her face as he trailed the back of one finger down her cheek. She couldn't hide the shiver that ran through her at the contact.

"As I'm sure this is your first Migration, let me congratulate you on getting this far. And let me offer my formal welcome."

He reached down, holding her eye contact as he wound his long fingers around her free hand. Bending at the waist, he gave a mock bow and pressed his cold lips to the back of her hand. But his touch repelled her, and she snatched her hand back to hide it behind her.

Trian's grin widened as he straightened. "Greetings, niece. Welcome to Liath Clann."

CHAPTER 8

CEANNAS WATCHED THE INTERPLAY between Trian and Lyall and fought to calm the rising rage inside himself. He could tell Trian was playing with her, just as he could tell that Lyall didn't know how to react. He wanted to step in front of her, to place himself between her and Trian. But he knew one step in that direction, showing a splinter of affection for her, would be twisted and used against him by Trian.

So he schooled his face into the calm mask he wore in battle and concentrated on keeping his breathing slow and steady. Meanwhile, his heart thundered in his chest at Trian's audacity. To toy with Prion's daughter was to tempt death.

Ceannas cleared his throat. Neither Trian nor Lyall looked his way. Each was staring daggers at the other, waiting to see who would break first. Ceannas had his money on Trian, but time was short, and he needed to brief Trian on the latest development, not wait around for a pissing match to end.

He cleared his throat again, longer and louder than before. Trian gave a small upward quirk of his eyebrow to Lyall, a gesture that seemed to say *we'll come back to this later*, and turned to Ceannas with an irritated expression.

"What?" Trian snapped.

The second Trian's attention came off her, Lyall sagged in relief. Ceannas noted the gesture out of his peripheral vision.

"Lyall's presence here complicates things, my lord. How do you want to handle this?"

Trian narrowed his eyes. "Why did she choose to come on this Migration? Why be so secretive about it? If Prion had known, he would have warned us not to let his precious darling out of our sights. So I can only assume he is unaware of her little adventure."

He cocked his head as he regarded Lyall, who became very busy looking anywhere but at him. "What's in your bag?" he asked in a hard tone. "Show me."

Lyall flushed and her hands clenched the strap holding the bag to her body. She glanced at Ceannas with wide eyes, silently asking what she should do.

Ceannas nodded at her to go along with Trian's demand. "There are two sealskins in the bag, my lord," he answered for her.

Trian glanced back at him, then snapped his fingers at Lyall. "Two? Why two? Open it, girl! I haven't got all day!"

Flushed with anger, Lyall jerked the bag over her head and reached in. She pulled out a dark gray pelt and gazed at it in shock. Ceannas knew she was surprised it wasn't the white lunago that she'd worn at first. *Why didn't I explain to her then that it changes color after your first change?* Ceannas thought.

Trian held out his hand for the sealskin, but Lyall pulled it close to her chest. Ceannas stepped around Trian to join her. "It's ok," he murmured in a low voice so that only she could hear it. "He can help us."

He took Lyall's sealskin from her and stepped to the side so that she could present the other to Trian. Lyall reached in and withdrew her father's damaged skin. Ceannas glanced over at Trian and was surprised to see the eagerness on his leader's face. But when he noticed Ceannas looking at him, Trian schooled his expression into a more neutral one.

"Ah, the famous pelt. Damaged by a siren princeling and never repaired." His voice was reverent as he held out his hands and let his fingers dance over the tears in the skin. "We went to war over this skin," he murmured. "Because of my brother, lives were lost. Some would say it never should have happened..." His voice trailed away. For several moments, he stared at the damaged pelt. Then he seemed to shake himself out of his reverie. He looked around at the others waiting in a loose circle around him. Lyall watched his face harden as he recomposed himself.

"This complicates things," Trian said in a firm voice. He handed Prion's sealskin back to Lyall, who stowed it back into her bag along with her own.

"I now see why you abandoned your duties," he said to Ceannas. "This changes everything. Obviously, we must protect this skin and its carrier at all times. Can she travel with the clan?"

Ceannas thought for a moment, then shook his head. From the corner of his eye, he saw Lyall bristle.

"I can keep up, if that's what you're asking," she said in a firm voice.

Trian ignored her. "Then you'll have to travel by land until our next meeting. I'll need to know where you are at all times. You must stick to the plan and never deviate from it." He glanced down the length of Ceannas, for the first time taking full note of him. "You're injured." His voice was clipped, brusque. "I will send along another Anchor—"

Now it was Ceannas's turn to bristle. "I can keep her safe by my—"

"—*just* to keep an extra set of eyes on my niece." Trian spoke over him with a disarming smile. "I can't have anything happening to her under my command for this Migration." His voice dropped to a low, intimate tone as he stepped towards Ceannas. "And if anyone damages a hair on her head, they will answer to me. Got it?"

Ceannas swallowed back the cutting retort he wanted to make and nodded.

"Good." Trian turned and scanned the sea of bodies behind him. "Garach!"

Lyall and Ceannas turned to watch as a dark-skinned, naked man stood up from his lounging spot and stalked towards them. Ceannas knew of him, but only tangentially—Garach was typically stationed as Trian's bodyguard and seldom deviated from that role. As the two approached, Ceannas made out further details. Garach had a strong jaw that looked like stone and a long, aquiline nose set below a pair of close-set eyes.

The overall look reminded Ceannas of a pig, but he could see crystal clear intelligence blazing from the other's eyes. *This one's not to be tangled with,* Ceannas thought. He looked like he would fight dirty.

"Garach," Trian said, as he jerked his chin in greeting, "I've got a special mission in mind for you. You are to see my niece here, and her companion, to safety."

Ceannas flexed his jaw. Not even worth the name? Just "her companion," as if he were a lowly servant? He gritted his teeth and lowered his shoulders away from his ears. Taking a deep breath, he inhaled for four seconds, held it for two, then exhaled for eight. He would not let anyone provoke him into a fight. Not here. And especially not with a bully like Trian.

As if he could read Ceannas's thoughts, Trian flashed him a sly grin before turning back to Lyall and Garach. "Now go," he said in a bored voice. "Ceannas, we will rendezvous in two days at the Cape."

At Lyall's confused expression, Trian's grin widened. "It's the last land-bound respite we have until we head straight west to the island of the Great Elder. It's not a long swim, but it will be worse by having to drag you along with us." At Lyall's furious expression, he added, "Because you aren't used to it, my dear! There was no offense meant." He chuckled, and behind him, Garach smirked at her.

"Besides," Trian said, his grin fading, "The swim there isn't hard. You'll just have to keep up. We don't dawdle in the open ocean. Too many dangers in the deep."

Then he turned and waved them away with a flick of his wrist. "Grab your bags and let's go. I want them on the road with at least a few hours' head-start on us." Garach turned and walked over to fetch the bag containing his own sealskin.

Trian turned to Ceannas and when he spoke, his voice was devoid of any laughter. "The last thing I want on this mission is to be waiting for you at the Cape. Should anything happen to her while you are traveling, don't bother meeting up."

Ceannas gave him a puzzled expression even as his stomach churned. "What are you saying, my lord? To meet you at the Great Elder's caves instead?

Trian's eyes were like blue ice chips in his face, and Ceannas had the random thought that he was staring into Lord Prion's face instead. "I'm saying," Trian said in a low voice, "if you fail to bring her to safety, there is no place for you here. So don't come home expecting one."

Ceannas stared at him in shock. The message was clear: bring Lyall safely to the Great Elder or face exile from the only home he'd ever known. His throat felt thick as he swallowed hard. Unable to speak, he nodded.

"Good," Trian drawled. "Then we're on the same page." He glanced over his shoulder and Ceannas looked over, too. Lyall was standing next to Garach, looking uneasy as she clenched her hands around the cross-bodied strap of her satchel. "Better not keep them waiting," Trian murmured.

Ceannas swallowed again, then stepped forward towards Lyall. He jerked his chin to one side to indicate they were traveling back the way they'd come. Garach led the way, threading them through the throng of bodies. Next came Lyall, and Ceannas brought up the rear.

He cast one look back over his shoulder as they began climbing up the pathway to the top of the bluff. He could make out Trian standing in the same place they'd left him, with his arms crossed in front of his chest, watching. A shudder rippled across Ceannas's shoulders, and he rolled them to make the feeling go away.

There's nothing to be concerned about, he told himself. *Everything will turn out right in the end.* But as they crested the bluff, shutting off their view of the rest of the clan, he worried over the meeting in his head. He knew Prince Trian had the weight of the entire clan on his shoulders with this Migration and that it was a heavy burden.

But something about the whole thing seemed odd, and it started with the male assigned to help Ceannas keep Lyall safe. Not just some other male, but an Anchor? Trian wouldn't leave the entire clan defenseless just for one selkie. But maybe there were other issues at hand that Ceannas wasn't aware of. Perhaps Garach was an expendable Anchor, and this was a simple task to keep him out of Trian's hair.

At that thought, he stepped to one side so that he could take in his companions. Lyall still had a tight set to her shoulders, which Ceannas knew meant that she wasn't comfortable with the situation. But Garach moved with a warrior's grace. Who had he studied with? Ceannas wondered. And how much could he count on Garach if they all ended up in a tight spot?

He shrugged and let out a deep sigh to relieve the tension creeping across his own back. It wouldn't do to dwell too much on how helpful this male would be—Ceannas knew he could handle any situation that befell them. He just hoped Garach didn't get in his way.

He let his gaze wander, taking in their surroundings and letting his subconscious Anchor training take over. But he found his eyes straying back to Lyall's figure as she walked. Her hips swayed from side-to-side in a saucy way he rather enjoyed watching. It matched her temper when she was fired up about something. He grinned at the memory of her indignation on the trail earlier that day. Yes, she could be feisty when the situation warranted it.

Her shoulders lost their hard-set edge as she relaxed into the rhythm of walking, and he was glad for it. She carried the weight of her family in that side satchel she wore, and he knew it had to be a heavy burden.

I should offer to carry it for her, he thought. But as soon as he thought it, he could clearly imagine the scenario in his head: her clamping down harder on the strap pressed between her breasts, scowling in anger at him for daring to suggest she might not be strong enough to carry it, the fire in her eyes as she glared daggers at him...

He grinned. It might be worth it just to see the fire in her eyes when she looked at him. Fury looked good on her, and he wasn't above provoking her for next to no reason.

He knew that if it were just the two of them, he'd have done it for no other reason than to bask in her rage, to push her buttons just to see her rise to the provocation. But not with the other male here. He scowled at the broad shoulders of Garach in front of him. He was built sturdy, like the broad side of a barn, and looked just as immobile. Even while walking, his body moved very little, as if he were saving all his energy for some unknown thing.

It made Ceannas curious, if not a little worried. What sort of event was this unknown warrior waiting for? Any decent fighter knew to conserve his energy when possible, but this was a little extreme. And, Ceannas noticed, the male never looked around them. How could someone with warrior training not have been taught to take in his surroundings at all times?

The extra Anchor was a source of irritation inside of Ceannas. But he decided to let it go. He'd monitor everything around them and be willing to strike when he had to. He just hoped Garach wouldn't get in his way when the time came to act.

CHAPTER 9

THEY HEADED DOWN A well-worn cart path. Lyall wanted to ask Ceannas how he could have such an unerring sense of direction, but Garach's presence gave her pause. She didn't trust the pig-faced Anchor. He made no attempt at conversation, and she didn't press it. But she was aware of Ceannas at her back, staying uncharacteristically silent for the better part of the day. Even when they stopped to share the stale loaf of sweetbread and jerky the innkeeper sent them off with, nobody spoke. They ate in silence, each stuck in their own thoughts. And when they were done, they moved off without a single word.

Finally, as dusk settled around them, she couldn't stand it anymore.

"How much longer are we going to be on this road before we meet a town? I'm ready to find a bowl of soup and a halfway decent bed to sleep on." For a moment, she caught herself, knowing that Ceannas would jump on her loose words and crack some joke about sleeping together.

"You sure are eager to get me back in bed," he might tease. Or, perhaps he'd respond, *"Well, princess, if it were up to me, you'd already be in my bed."* Or something. Anything except the total silence that met her words.

She glanced over her shoulder to see Ceannas perusing the forest around them with the utmost of somber expressions. "Ceannas?" Her voice was soft-pitched so she could have an interaction between the two of them that didn't include Garach, the intruder.

But it wasn't Ceannas who answered her.

"I think we'll be having to camp here tonight." Garach's voice was nasal and unpleasant to the ear. "Ceannas? What do you think?"

Lyall watched as Ceannas surveyed the clearing area, seeming not to have heard the other Anchor. Then he nodded. "This will do." He gave a half-hearted shrug at Lyall's incredulous expression. "Sorry, princess, but we're another day's walk from the nearest town. We'll have to make do with this tonight."

"But... but..." Lyall couldn't make the words come out. "But it's so... rough." She spat the word.

Ceannas cracked the first smile she'd seen since they left the clan on the beach. "Some like it rough. I know *I've* always been a fan."

Lyall pursed her lips and shook her head, as if disgusted. But inwardly, she was glad for the levity. Maybe her playful Anchor was still there under that warrior's exterior.

"Here," Garach said. Lyall turned to see his large hand reaching for the satchel she wore.

"No!" She spun away with indignation. "Nobody touches this bag but me!"

Garach growled at her and took a threatening step forward. "We need to bed down for the night. I was going to keep it safe for you while you slept." He turned to Ceannas. "I've got first watch."

Ceannas nodded, then limped over to peer into the edge of the trees surrounding them.

Lyall fought the wave of fear that washed over her as he moved away from her. "Don't leave me alone with him," she wanted to shout. But, as she gathered herself together, she reminded herself that she was the daughter of a prince. No mere Anchor could boss her around.

She straightened her spine and gave Garach a haughty look. "I'll sleep with it like it's a pillow. It will be safe with me."

But instead of nodding in agreement, Garach's scowl deepened. "I am under strict rules to keep you and that skin safe." He closed the gap between them and gripped the strap of her satchel with one beefy hand.

"Stop it!" Lyall exclaimed, trying to wrestle it away. But Garach's grip was strong and immobile.

"Give it to me," he growled, stepping close enough for her to smell his breath. It was briny and sour, and she cringed away from it.

Then suddenly there were hands between them, pushing them apart. Ceannas slid into the gap, using his body as a shield. He rounded on Garach.

"What do you think you're doing? She carries the satchel. She keeps track of the skins. You are a bodyguard. Nothing else."

Lyall cringed back from Ceannas's expression, noting the fury in his eyes and the hard, unyielding face that was set into a scowl. This was a man carved from stone, and Garach's anger was nothing more than a wave crashing against the granite that formed Ceannas.

For several seconds, the men's eyes snarled at each other. Then Garach took a step back, holding up the palms of his hands.

"Well met, brother," Garach said in a disarming voice. "She can keep the pack. I have orders to keep it safe and I was just doing my job."

"You're under orders to keep *her* safe, you mean. Right, *brother*?" Even Lyall could hear the way he stressed the last word, spinning Garach's phrase back at him.

Garach smiled and nodded at Lyall. "Of course. I misspoke."

Ceannas made a noncommittal grunt, then pointed to one end of the clearing. "Garach, you bed there to watch the northern part of the trail. Lyall, you can bed down here, next to the fire. I'll man the southern end of the trail."

Lyall flashed him a panicked look. Her immediate reaction was to ask to sleep curled up next to him, as she'd awakened to find themselves at the last inn they'd slept in. But Ceannas was already moving away from her, limping over to the southern-most tip of the trail. He turned a corner and disappeared out of sight.

She sighed and gave a mistrustful look at Garach. But the Anchor was settling down several feet away with his back against a tree trunk. His own satchel carrying his sealskin lay next to him.

She set her satchel down on the ground and tried to fluff it up to resemble a pillow. Lying down, she found it wasn't a terrible resource, if that was all she had to work with.

She rolled over on her side, putting her back to Garach, and thought about how uncomfortable the ground was that she lay on. No matter where she positioned herself, there was some stick or pebble or leaf poking her, keeping her awake.

She sighed, wishing she was back at The Suckling Pig. Even despite the grimy accommodations that had been the best sleep she'd ever had.

Wonder why that is? a small voice in her mind spoke up. She paused, considering. She had been bone-tired that night from swimming so far. And she'd had that lovely massage from Ceannas, the kind that made her melt into a useless puddle on the bed, though she'd never admit as much to him. And then, to have fallen asleep, only to wake with one warm hand covering her bare breast and a warm wall of comfort spooning against her back.

She'd slid out of his embrace and watched him sleep for a few moments, savoring the unguarded expression of peace on his face, which made his features even more handsome without its stern arrogance. And that muscled body that had pressed against the length of her... part of her wished she could have taken advantage of the situation to match the sultry dreams she'd had all night, staring him.

The memory made her smile to herself. Though she was sure that kind of intimacy would never happen again, it was a cherished moment in an otherwise turbulent set of events.

She re-situated herself from one uncomfortable position to another one just like it. Her hand crept up to cup her own breast over the material of her dress, and she closed her eyes, pretending it was Ceannas's hand from the night before.

SHE WOKE CHOKING.

One minute she was dancing at a ball with a masked man whose hair was the color of fire, and the next, she couldn't breathe from the death grip of something around her neck. She opened her eyes to see a wolf's face above her, lips back and snarling with effort just inches away from her own. Then her mind made sense of it all and she realized it was Garach's face contorted with rage as he choked the life out of her.

Her hands scrabbled for purchase at the iron bands around her neck. She heard herself gasping and wheezing as she tried to take enough breath to cry for help. But no air could escape the confines of Garach's grip.

She flailed, trying to catch his face in her hands so she could gouge at his eyes, but he leaned away from her fumbling fingers, evading her easily.

Stars danced in front of her eyes, and she knew her window of opportunity was getting smaller by the second. In desperation, she brought her knee sharply upward, driving it into Garach's groin.

He let out an explosive *oof,* and, for a moment, the bands around her throat loosened, allowing her to take in a single, deep breath.

"Stop," she managed. Her voice was a whisper, and she knew she'd have to do better to save herself. She inhaled again, but his hands tightened again, cutting her off.

"Don't do this!" she gasped with the last of her breath, pouring all of her desperation into the words. The stars in her vision turned into lightning bursts that exploded before her eyes. Darkness seeped in around the edges, obscuring Garach's snarling face.

Then, to her surprise, the hands around her neck loosened. It wasn't much, just enough for her to take a whooping, gasping breath, but it was enough. She tried to pry the fingers from her neck and found them to be as immobile as if they were stone.

"Ceannas!" she screamed, as she tried to shove and pry her way out of Garach's grip.

But Garach, while he wasn't still squeezing, wouldn't remove his hands from her neck, even as he sat back on his haunches, his face calming into a smooth, expressionless mask.

She had a brief moment, the span of a heartbeat, to recognize that Garach was no longer attacking her. Then he rolled off her to one side as Ceannas drove his shoulder into Garach's ribs.

The action ripped his fingers from around her neck, and she cried out in pain. But Ceannas didn't seem to notice. He had straddled Garach's body and was pummeling the other Anchor's face with one strike after another.

"Ceannas," Lyall ground out, but her voice was too soft. "Ceannas!" she tried again, with more effort. "Stop, please! He's not even fighting back!"

And it was true. Garach lay on his back, making no effort to dodge or evade Ceannas's blows. It was as if Ceannas were attacking an unconscious man who lacked the ability to defend himself.

She struggled to her feet, wincing at the burning in her throat, and stumbled over to the two Anchors. She caught Ceannas's hand as he pulled back for another hit and held tight, preventing him from landing the blow.

Ceannas turned, his face contorted with fury and rage. But when he saw it was her, his expression softened. "He deserves this and anything more that I can think of," he snarled.

Lyall crouched next to him, cradling his fist in her hands. He was trembling, barely keeping his anger in check. But as she stared into his eyes, the tremors subsided. He stared at her for a long moment, then threw a disgusted look back at the bloody face of Garach.

"Let this be a lesson to you and whoever sent you," he growled. "Mess with her and you'll get more than what you bargained for. Understand?"

Garach gave a weak nod. Ceannas glared at him for a few heartbeats, then stood. He didn't offer his hand to Garach as the Anchor stumbled to his feet. His face looked like a tomato had exploded where his nose should have been, and one eye was swelling. He avoided their gazes as he re-slung his pack containing his sealskin.

The entire time, Ceannas kept his body between Garach and Lyall.

"If I ever see you again," Ceannas said in a matter-of-fact voice, "I'll kill you on site, whether she's around or not."

Garach paused without meeting his eyes, then nodded once, and made his way back down the path they'd traveled from.

Ceannas and Lyall were silent as they watched him leave. The air felt heavy and oppressive, despite the cool breeze blowing past. Lyall thought she could still smell the copper tang of blood.

After several long moments passed, Lyall felt the air lighten, as if Garach's absence was a burden that had been lifted from the clearing.

"Do you think he'll be back?" she asked in a low voice.

Ceannas sighed. "Not if he's smart." When he realized Lyall was staring at him, he amended with a rueful twist of his lips, "I wouldn't think so. He was unarmed, and I bested him. I doubt he'll be back to finish the job soon." He glanced around the clearing. "However, I think we need to be on the move. I don't want to risk misjudging him. There are few provocations worse than a warrior humiliated."

"But he didn't even say anything," Lyall said, casting a nervous glance back the way Garach left. "It was like he was a puppet."

"And where there's a puppet, there's a puppeteer," Ceannas growled. "It was odd the way he just lay there, taking it." He rubbed his chin with one hand as he spoke. Worry lines wrinkled his forehead. "That reeks of a conspiracy, which is something your father warned me about."

"He did?" Lyall said, surprised. "What kind of conspiracy?"

He thought in silence for a moment, then glanced at her as if just remembering she was there. "It's nothing you should worry about. I'll take care of it."

He walked around the corner to get his bag. "I'll tell you what, though," he tossed over his shoulder, "this changes things. I can't help but wonder why there's an attack on you when you weren't even supposed to *be* on this Migration."

He came back into view, pulling his bag over one shoulder. "If I ever thought you were safe on your own, now I know that's not the—"

Glancing up, he saw Lyall rubbing her throat. Immediately, he was by her side, touching her neck with sure hands.

"You're hurt." His voice was husky with worry. The sound of it made things low in her stomach tighten. She looked into his eyes and read the concern there. For once, there was no mocking, snide tilt to his mouth, no reprimand in his voice.

"I'm fine," she responded with a similarly husky voice. His nearness was intoxicating, and she stared at his lips, unable to look away.

"You aren't fine," Ceannas growled as he touched the purple banding already forming on the tender skin. "I'm going to kill him for this." He turned towards where Garach had strode off, and Lyall caught his arm to stop him.

"It won't make any difference," she said in a matter-of-fact voice. "What's happened has happened. We just make sure it won't happen again." She hoped she sounded more confident than she felt. She had to fight the urge to press her body against his and wrap his arms over her shoulders like a blanket.

Ceannas gave her a rueful look, then nodded. "You're right. Besides, once I get word back to Prince Trian what has happened, Garach's life will be forfeit, anyway."

"Do you think it has something to do with my father's sealskin?" Lyall asked.

Ceannas pursed his lips in thought. "Possibly? But I'm not positive. It's certainly a coincidental set of events, and it's hard not to suspect a correlation. But the clan only just discovered you were on this Migration. Did you tell anybody back in Selbane that you were coming?"

Lyall shook her head.

Ceannas ran a hand through his hair in frustration. "Then I don't know how someone could have amassed a personal attack on you in the short time we were with the clan."

They both stood in silence for a few moments. Finally, Lyall couldn't stand the silence.

"I'm sorry you're caught up in this," she said in a soft voice.

Ceannas looked at her in surprise. "You have nothing to be sorry about. This is my job."

She stepped closer to him, feeling shy as she tried to convey her feelings. "Actually, so far I've been the reason you aren't with the clan doing your job." She found she couldn't meet his eyes, and she wrapped her arms around her middle to hug herself.

To her surprise, he stepped forward and cupped her elbows in his hands. "Listen to me." His voice was soft, intimate. "You have done nothing wrong. You are doing this to save your father, and there is nothing more noble than risking your life for someone you love." He squeezed her elbows until she risked a glance up at him. He stared at her earnestly. "*Nothing.*"

She risked a tentative smile at him, which he returned.

They stared at each other for several moments. Gradually, Lyall realized a shift in Ceannas's expression. A hunger that lent an intensity to his expression that hadn't been there before. She recognized that look—it mirrored the feeling inside her: a desire to press forward, to step into the warmth of his gaze and see if she would drown in the depths of it.

In response, she closed her eyes, feeling as if she were about to fall forward into a deep chasm. After a moment that felt like a year, she felt his lips touch hers. The kiss was hesitant, almost chaste, with no presence of the warrior behind it.

She leaned into the kiss, opening her lips more to allow him better access. In response, his tongue slipped past her lips and slid down the length of her lower lip. The movement drew a moan out of her, a small, needful noise of desire she couldn't help but express.

Instantly, the pressure changed, becoming more demanding and forceful. His lips pressed and slid over hers as if he were hungry for everything she had to offer. Her arms snaked up to wrap around his neck, pulling him closer so that their bodies pressed together. She felt one arm grip her waist, pulling her in, as his other hand wrapped itself in her hair at the base of her skull. Both actions drew her closer to him, and she let out another moan of pleasure.

The kiss was nothing like what she'd experienced with Lucas before. Where Lucas had been tender and hesitant, Ceannas was all fire and demand. His lips mapped hers as if he owned them and encouraged her to respond in kind.

Matching him breath for breath as they clung together, she let her desire pour into the physical connection at every point of contact. She became aware of her heartbeat galloping in her chest, then another phantom heartbeat that ran just slightly out of rhythm to her own. She had the sensation of two sets of lungs expanding, of filling and expelling in opposition to each other, so that one filled while the other exhaled. The tandem feeling of another's body was intoxicating, but she had no room for conscious thought outside of the points of contact between her body and his.

Finally, he pulled away and looked down at her. She reluctantly opened her eyes and unhooked her arms from his neck, but his arms still held her in place against him.

"That was..." she began, but she couldn't find the words to complete the thought. Her lips felt swollen, and she resisted the urge to put her fingertips to them to see how large they were. She found she couldn't meet the intensity of his stare, so she looked down at his chest. She made a circular motion with one hand to indicate the enormity of her emotions.

Ceannas seemed to understand. He let go but stayed with his body pressed against hers. "I agree." His voice was husky with desire. Then he moved away, and Lyall felt a whoosh of air come between them. The experience was a cold chasm where his body had been, and she wished he were back in her arms.

He moved around the clearing, picking up their satchels while she watched. He handed hers over with a gentle smile, and she couldn't help but smile back at him. Then he turned and began limping away down the trail. She watched his stilted progress for a few moments, struggling to process what had just occurred.

She felt as if she were standing on the edge of a precipice. There was an attraction there, that much was obvious. But could anything come of it? He had sworn to protect the clan. She was determined to save her father's life. There was no room in either of their goals for anything intimate.

It was a mistake, she thought. One that she'd never allow to happen again. Despite the attraction between them, she could not let herself be distracted from her mission, especially given what was at stake should she fail.

She straightened her shoulders. She wouldn't let him divert her gaze from her goal. Regardless of her attraction towards him, she would make sure not to let another slip up happen again.

With her emotional armor firmly in place, she followed him, one hand clenched on the handle of her satchel where it rested between her breasts, feeling only her thudding heartbeat like a drum against her knuckles.

CHAPTER 10

As they walked, Ceannas limping in the lead with Lyall following behind, he fumed. Garach had gotten too close to her, and it almost turned out badly. He couldn't afford to be that lax again. Garach was probably gone for good, but that still left Ceannas injured and with a new selkie that didn't know the basic defense strategies.

Hmm, perhaps he could remedy that? Maybe teach her some minor things that could come in handy during a pinch? He liked the idea of getting physically close to her again, though he would have to watch himself after what had just happened.

How could he have let his desire get the best of him? Taking anything from the daughter of Prince Prion was well past his respectful boundaries. And to take *a kiss* of all things? He wiped a hand down his face in frustration.

He wanted to turn around and look at her, to see how she was processing this new development. The impulse was like ants walking over the back of his neck. It wouldn't take a lot of effort, just a quick turn of the head.

But he couldn't bring himself to do it.

What would he see if he met her eyes? Condemnation? Judgment? Cool detachment, as if it hadn't been one of the most earth-shaking kisses of her life, as it had been for him? Or worse, what if she wanted more? What if he turned around and saw the same desire burning in her eyes for him? She had responded ardently.

The thought stopped him in his tracks. He was an Anchor, a seasoned warrior, who had taken his vow to his clan seriously. It was the entire moral compass he devoted his life to following. And it left no room for mates or dalliances or impromptu kisses he couldn't risk happening again.

"You all right?" Lyall asked from behind him.

Without turning to look at her, he nodded. "Fine." His voice came out more tersely than he'd intended.

"How far is the nearest town?" Her voice held no traces of anger or sharpness, no goading undertones or breathless entreaty.

Maybe it didn't affect her the same, he thought. *Maybe she was used to that sort of thing.* The moment he considered it, it seemed like a very plausible idea. That had to be it! She'd had her share of romantic entanglements, surely, and so a kiss from a nobody like him must barely have registered with her.

The thought relaxed him and took away the tense set to his shoulders. If that was the case, then he was free to act in whatever manner he pleased. She had been very clear that she thought very little of him, especially when he made joking advances. And she was stubborn as the day was long—she wouldn't interrupt her personal mission to engage with him further. She'd probably just been overcome after being attacked. It was reasonable to assume that she was feeling the desire for physical safety and comfort more than was normal for her.

The fact was, he was her guardian, and she was his ward. If he wanted to claim the moral high ground, then there shouldn't be any intermingling of the relationship. He knew how it would look for him to engage in a physical relationship with her; that he'd coerced her using his position as protector to leverage her natural feelings toward him. That alone should put her off-limits, regardless of any other details.

No, he wouldn't let anything like that happen again. The thought made him smile. At least it had been worth it, he thought. The feel of her lips pressed against his as she answered that hunger that seemed to linger in him while he was around her. The pressure of her curvaceous body against his...

"Hello? Is anybody home in there?" Lyall poked his shoulder for emphasis.

He turned to her with a grin. "Just reminiscing."

"About what?"

"How good it felt to tackle that idiot, Garach." It wasn't *quite* a lie. "But," he said with a more serious expression, "I think it's time to teach you some basic self-defense."

Lyall scrunched her mouth to one side. "Whatever for? Why do I need to learn to fight when I have you around?"

Her words made him feel warm inside, a smugness that spread throughout his whole body. She may not have realized it, but her words showed a level of trust that he found deeply satisfying. Maybe even *too* satisfying, if he was being honest with himself.

He shook himself. *Focus!* he demanded. *Her safety is the priority here.*

"Plenty of reasons," he went on in what he was relaxed tone of voice. "First, I may not always be around. Something might have incapacitated me first, or killed me, or I might be off washing my hair." Lyall rolled her eyes. "Point is, you need to learn how to defend yourself if you get attacked alone."

"So you want me to be a fighter like you?" Skepticism dripped from her voice, such that Ceannas had to choke back a laugh.

"Nobody gets to be like me—I'm one of a kind. But self-defense isn't always about fighting. Sometimes it's a matter of being able to read someone's weaknesses so that you can exploit them and get away to safety."

Lyall raised her eyebrows in a doubtful expression.

Ceannas sighed and thought for a moment. "It's like you said about knowing your customers at your job, right? You learn what they're after and you respond accordingly to get the maximum desired outcome. At your job, that's money. At life, that's your body, safe and secure."

Lyall cocked her head, considering his words. Then she nodded. "All right. When do we begin?"

Ceannas glanced down at his injured leg, then at the darkness surrounding them. It was still a few hours before daylight, and the nearest town was another four hours away. He sighed. Neither of them would sleep tonight, that was for sure. He might as well use the time wisely.

He gave her a mischievous sideways look. "You sure you're ready, princess?"

Even in the dim light, he saw her square her shoulders. "Ready when you are."

Grinning, he stepped towards her.

This was going to be fun.

THREE AND A HALF hours later, Ceannas had to admit that she was tougher than she appeared. They had sparred for over a half hour, working on basic head control movements. The exercises were simple and designed not to require a lot of legwork on his part to execute.

She was a surprisingly fast learner, evading his quick grabbing hands, twisting out of his control when he had her by the hair, and even mastering a technique that would allow her to gauge out the eyes of her attacker.

And, as they walked into town—another small hamlet called "Connacht"—he'd been proud to see that she retained the movements he'd shown her. He'd been surprising her with different scenarios on the road, alternating between gentle conversation and surprise attacks. He'd slow his pacing so that he edged closer and closer to her without her realizing it, then would reach out, fast as a snake, and snatch a handful of her hair while she twisted and fought to break free. Or he'd whirl on her and take a pretend swing at her face, which she always dodged just out of reach.

And even as his injured leg screamed in protest at some of the movements he'd used, he was still proud of how much she'd mastered in such a short time. They arrived a few hours past dawn and made their way to the town hostel, casting curious glances at the banners and ribbons that decorated many of the town's buildings. It looked like a silent party had been held or was about to be held—Ceannas wondered which it was. The former didn't worry him as much as the latter—more people meant more opportunities for attack, and he wasn't in top fighting form at the moment.

Connacht's housing was much more upscale than Albermarl's had been—the paint on the sign above the door wasn't peeling in thin strips and the people inside looked cleaner than Ceannas expected.

Though they were hungry, Ceannas felt the strong need for sleep to help heal.

"Can we get a meal here?" Lyall asked as they walked across the room towards the innkeeper on the other side of the bar.

"We need sleep first. Then we eat." He pitched his voice low so that only she could hear. "I'm ready to drop. If I don't get proper sleep soon, I'll be useless to either of us."

Lyall frowned as Ceannas waved to get the innkeeper's attention. The innkeeper was a slight man, with a halo of greying hair that left a bald cap on the top of his head. His face was droopy, like a hound's, with long jowls that hung off his face and large, sad eyes that seemed to be on the verge of tears.

Ceannas asked about the room situation and was pleased to find out that all the other lodgings with single beds were taken and only one suite, which held two beds, was available.

"I sure am sorry," the manager said.

"Oh dear," Lyall said with mock worry, overriding Ceannas when he opened his mouth to speak. She'd agreed to be the blushing bride once more, and this time she wasn't ready to faint from exhaustion. She turned to the manager. "We're actually on our honeymoon right now." She leaned close, using one crooked finger to invite the manager to do the same. "Isn't there *anything* you can do to help us out?" She flashed her winningest smile on him, the one she used to close sales at the dress shop, and he smiled back.

"Well, since the two-bed suites are the only rooms we have left, I'll tell you what I'm going to do: I'll only charge you for a single-bed room instead of the two." He flashed a kind smile at Lyall. "Happy honeymooning to you both."

"Can you believe it, darling?" she gushed to Ceannas, who gave her a wry look. "And you said Connacht was a dung-heap of a town."

Ceannas froze, his warrior senses aware of the sudden pause of the room's occupants at her words. "It's time to get you to bed, my dear," he said through gritted teeth. He gripped her with a firm hand on her upper arm.

Lyall flashed him a satisfied smirk as she let him lead her towards the stairs and up to the lodgings.

Upstairs, the rooms turned out to be semi-furnished, with a few pathetic paintings on the walls to encourage a "homey" feeling. The beds were both made with goose-down pillows and large patchwork quilts for covers.

"At least these folks understand what it's like to be married," Lyall said, gesturing at both beds.

Ceannas grinned to himself. For all her saucy remarks, she was rather funny to travel with. He peered through the tiny window at the corner of the room. "It's only just light. I'm going to sleep for a few hours—I'm beat." He gestured to the opposite bed. "You should do the same. Once we're rested, we'll head out. We should be able to meet up with the clan by tomorrow night, if we're lucky."

"And if we aren't?"

He began to pull off his clothes, starting with his shirt. It was an itchy thing, and he didn't see how humans wore them all the time. He felt as if little spider legs were prickling his shoulders.

"What are you doing?" Lyall demanded behind him.

He turned, halfway through the motion of taking off the offensive garment. "Getting ready to head to Tír na nÓg. What do you think I'm doing?"

"At least give me some warning before you just strip!" she cried, averting her eyes. Ceannas was pleased to see a flush dappling her cheeks. *So there is an attraction,* he realized. He flexed his arms so that his muscles would stand out. With a flourish, he removed his shirt and flung it through the air. It landed on her head, and she let out a shriek. Pulling it off her head, she turned to glare at him, freezing in place as she realized he was partway out of his pants as well.

Grinning mischievously, Ceannas let his pants slide lower down his hips so that she had a clear view of the V-shape of his lower abdominal muscles. "Care to help?" he teased, enjoying the blush explosion on her bright pink cheeks. Even as he spoke, a small voice in the back of his mind was screaming at him to at least pretend he had some propriety and to treat her with the distance their relationship deserved. But the curious reactions she kept putting off intrigued him. It pressed a button deep inside him that wanted to keep pushing the line, to see how far he could go with her to get more reaction.

"I've seen enough!" she declared and turned her back to him.

He stepped forward until he was close enough to whisper in her ear. "Princess, you haven't seen anything yet." Her nearness tantalized him, and he realized he was crossing a line by being that close to her. But the other part of him craved her nearness, craved being close enough to her to feel the heat coming off her body.

She shivered, as if the breath from his words were a chill breeze down her spine. Then she straightened her shoulders, turned, and marched towards the door. "I'm going downstairs to get some breakfast," she said in a prim tone. "You're a fool if you think sleep is more important."

Ceannas chuckled, and she shivered again. "I think sleep is best when done with the right partner."

Lyall paused, and he wondered if she was remembering the last time they shared a bed. He certainly remembered it, the sensations from touching her skin and the longing he'd felt to do more. He wondered if she wanted the same things.

She is your ward! The voice inside his head spoke up. *You are her protector. You are duty-bound to honor that relationship, not ruin it!* The thought was like cold water splashed over his body.

I can't pursue this, he reminded himself, *regardless of any desire on her part. She is off-limits.*

To regain control of himself, he shook his head. He took a deep breath, then another, aware of her watching him. With intense regret, he forced himself to take two large steps backward, away from her.

"Lyall, you don't need to be going out by yourself. Not without me."

She turned and scowled at him, one hand holding the door cracked open. "I can handle myself, thank you very much."

"Not when someone is trying to kill you."

She shrugged. "That was just Garach. And you took care of him."

Ceannas shook his head. "He might have trailed us. Or there might be someone else. It's not safe for you to travel without me." He tried to convey with his expression how serious he was. He held out a hand, indicating her bed across the room. "Look, stay until I wake up. Give me a few hours to sleep, then I'll show you everything Connacht has to offer. Besides, you must be worn down, too. Aren't you the least bit tired?"

Lyall rolled her eyes at him as she closed and locked the door, then glanced towards the bed. She stifled a massive yawn. "I'm definitely tired, but I still feel anxious for some reason. I feel like my brain is a beehive where thoughts are flying all around and refusing to settle down."

Ceannas nodded in understanding. "I feel that way sometimes. It's normal, especially given the latest turn of events. But I've found that when I lay down, my brain slows down eventually." He jerked his chin towards the other bed. "Why not try it?"

She pursed her lips, glancing between him and the door. Then she nodded once. "You get an hour. Then I'm going without you."

"Two hours and we'll spend the entire morning here."

She narrowed her eyes at him. "30 minutes then."

Now it was his turn to glare. "That's not how bargaining works."

"It is where I come from."

From the set of her shoulders, it was clear she wasn't willing to budge on this. He ran a hand through his hair with a deep sigh. He was tired to his bones. "I need at least an hour and a half, or I won't be of any use to anybody, let alone you."

She opened her mouth to reply, and he held out his hand. "Please."

The word stopped whatever she'd been about to say. For a moment, she stared at him and his outstretched hand. Then she rolled her eyes and nodded. "Fine." She spat the word. Then she held up one pointer finger. "But that's all you get!"

He managed a grin, then cocked his eyebrow at her. "Then you'd better turn around or you'll get an eyeful of what physical perfection looks like."

She made a derisive noise but turned her back.

He shucked out of his pants, then slid naked under the quilt. "It's safe now," he teased.

She glanced over her shoulder, as if expecting to see him standing there fully nude, then sat on the edge of her bed. "An hour and a half," she reminded him, letting loose a mighty yawn.

He smiled in response, then turned on his side. "Aren't you going to avail yourself of the fine furnishings in this room, too?"

For several long moments, there was silence. Ceannas was tempted to turn over and look at her, but the bed was too comfortable and laying down was like a full-bodied hug all over. Finally, he heard the scuffling of her slippers on the wood floor as she approached the bed.

"I'll sleep on one condition," she said.

Was that a hint of uncertainty in her voice? he wondered. "What's that?"

"I sleep with you."

Now Ceannas sat up in the bed and regarded her with surprise. "In my bed? I thought that was the last place you said you'd ever end up." Though he was grinning at her, his voice was all serious.

Lyall shuffled from one foot to the other, unable to meet his eyes. "I just... it feels safer... there... with you."

At the long silence that punctuated her statement, he realized she'd said all she was going to. He nodded with a deep sigh. "All right. Come here."

He lifted the corner of the quilt so that she could slide underneath the covers with him, but she put out her hands. "No! Not like that!"

She walked over to the side of the bed and lay down, fully clothed, on top of the quilted comforter. She positioned her body so she spooned his back and lay one arm over his ribs.

"And this is comfortable for you?" he asked, perplexed. *Shouldn't I be the one covering her?* he thought. But he felt her nod as her chin brushed his bare shoulders. "Care to tell me why?"

But she just pressed herself closer to his quilt-clad body and remained silent. Ceannas marveled at the sensation of being the comforted one, the one on the inside of the embrace. It gave him a sense of peace, that was sure, but it also made him aware of her well-curved body pressing against his, even with the quilt between them. He felt desire stirring in his lower belly and took several deep breaths to hold the feeling at bay.

She is the prince's daughter, he told himself. *Which means off-limits.* It was a line he'd oft repeated to himself on this trip, though it didn't seem to work. *She's just scared and tired and I'm the guardian-figure. That's all.*

Still, the imagined heat of her body next to his was intoxicating, and he felt himself rise to his imagination's visualization of what it would feel like to be skin-to-skin with her instead of having these damned sheets between them.

After several minutes of fantasizing, his mind began to wind down. The even breaths on the back of his shoulders told him she was already asleep. With that knowledge, he closed his eyes and waited for sleep to claim him.

CHAPTER 11

SHE WOKE BEFORE HIM two hours later. Her arm was still thrown across his body and she'd hooked one leg over his as well. Lifting her leg over to her side of the bed, she extricated herself from laying over him like a blanket. She took a deep breath, taking in the scent of him: cedar wood and the sea and fresh fall air. She'd never smelled anything like it, and she inhaled deeply to savor it.

Despite not wanting to move, her stomach growled at her relentlessly. She rolled off the bed, careful not to jostle him, and headed for the door. She'd grab a quick breakfast downstairs and wake him afterward.

Lyall stepped down the stairs, feeling like a young girl sneaking out without her parents finding out. She felt a thrill down her spine with every step that took her further away from the sleeping guardian upstairs.

She knew he was overreacting to the threat Garach posed. And in fact, the way he treated her like some fragile doll was a little galling, now that she'd had time to think on it.

"I can take care of myself," she muttered as she took a seat at the bar downstairs.

"Did you say something, lass?" a voice asked from behind her. She turned to see the hound-faced manager peering at her through rheumy eyes.

"I said I could use some breakfast," she said.

At her grin, he smiled back, and let himself behind the bar through a side-door. "Coming right up, my dear!" He paused, thinking. "As long as you don't mind lorne sausage and tattie scones…?" He looked at her hopefully.

Her smile widened. Something that wasn't ocean- or fish-based? Count her in! She nodded at him, and he turned and stepped through a small doorway into what she assumed was the kitchen. Glancing around the small bar area, she saw five empty tables waiting for occupants. She detected a slight hint of soap and wondered if he wiped down the bar with it every night or just some nights in particular.

The thought reminded her of the fact that she hadn't bathed in two days while they'd been trekking across Scotland. It was a disgusting feeling to have days' worth of sweat clinging to her skin. She made a mental note to ask the tavern owner where she could find a bathhouse. Or maybe, if she was lucky, she could get a wash basin in their room.

But then she'd have to share the warm water, she thought. And Ceannas was already too comfortable being naked around her. Worse, she realized, she'd have to be naked in front of him, too! Because, of course, he'd refuse to leave if she asked him.

She could picture it: her in the nice, warm water, surrounded by white suds that kept her modesty intact. And him standing in nothing but a thin pair of pants, laughing at her as she demanded he give her some privacy. Then, to make matters worse, he'd decide to join her in the tub, despite the lack of room. He'd shuck off his pants, revealing a perfectly chiseled body and a large erection. He'd look down at her with a smug smile and say—

"Here's your sausage, my lady!" The tavern owner slid a plate of food down before her with a flourish. She startled back into awareness of herself and managed a thin smile at him.

"My thanks, sir."

"Oh, call me Thomas," he said with a flap of his hand. "Everybody else around here does."

She gave a more realistic smile in acknowledgment. "Well, Thomas, I meant to ask you a question. What are all the banners for outside? We saw them coming into town, my... husband... and I." She choked a little on the unfamiliar word but recovered quickly. "Is there something special going on?"

Thomas's face lit up, and he leaned his torso backwards as if blown away by her question. "Something special, lass? *Something special?* It's only the town's one hundred and seventy-fifth birthday!"

She raised her eyebrows in surprise. "That sounds promising."

"Oh, my dear, it is! Vendors line the streets, selling all manner of things, from fruits to fabrics to furniture. There's a farmer's market that sells produce picked fresh from the fields. And some of the town's best seamstresses turn out to take custom outfit orders. They do the most amazing things with clothing! Mark my words, lass: you'd turn from a dandelion to a rose garden in the span of a day's work!" He leaned forward and winked at her. "Not that you need any help, my dear."

But Lyall found herself intrigued. "When do the events start up?"

"Oh, you're bound to see a handful of them out now. But things don't get going until after lunch, when everybody's awake and all."

"Hmm," mused Lyall. "I'm not sure I have the time to wait for all that. My husband's going to be awake soon, and he'll want to get going, I'm sure..."

Thomas's eyebrows raised to his hairline. "Well, I'll tell you what! Why don't I wrap up this food in a handkerchief and you can walk and eat and shop at the same time? Get a little taste of Connacht while you can."

She thought for a moment, then nodded. "That sounds lovely!"

Thomas grinned wider and took her plate back to the kitchen. Moments later, he returned with two cloth-wrapped parcels. "This one's the lorne sausage," he said, handing her a triangular, blue wrapping, "and this green one's the tattie scones." He held them out to her, and she took them with a grateful smile.

She stuffed the blue package in the waistband of her dress and strolled out of the tavern and onto the street, unwrapping the green parcel as she went. There were two scones inside, still warm, and she took a tiny bite of one to see how it tasted. It had a pleasant, savory taste and she could tell the potato cake was fried in bacon fat, which was her favorite way to prepare them.

This day's starting off right, she thought happily to herself, and she headed up the street to see what she could see.

A MERE HOUR LATER, the entire town had transformed itself into an explosion of brightly colored ribbons and banners and flowers. Enough people had appeared, as suddenly as a summer rainstorm, that Lyall didn't notice, at first, that she wasn't alone. It was as if she turned around after finishing the lorne sausage, and the entire town had turned out to celebrate.

She saw the same design painted on several signs and part prints at the vendors' booths: a single red rose with a curving stem and three sharp thorns sticking out along it. She finally got up the nerve to ask one vendor about it, an artist who was selling her canvas prints and who introduced herself as Annis.

"It's because we formed the entire town around a single rose bush," she explained. When Lyall frowned in confusion, the woman chuckled. "The story goes that once there was a pragmatic king who ruled his subjects with a firm hand and a knowledgeable heart. His tuath spread far, but he lacked the resources to spread it further. So he sent his best knights, one at a time, to claim the land beyond the eastern edge of his territory. 'Bring me back a token once you have succeeded,' he told them.

"But one-by-one the knights left. And one-by-one, they failed to return. During this period, the king's health failed, and he began to fade from it. His young son, Conn, a slight young man who had inherited his father's sensible temperament and heart, went in search of a healer who could help his father. He traveled wide but not far—he knew his father lacked the strength for him to be gone long.

"So the boy made it to the edge of his father's kingdom, following the rumors of a healer nearby, and there he found a hut in a clearing, exactly one step beyond where his father's kingdom ended. The hut was inconspicuous, with a mud-thatched roof and spindly wooden support beams that kept the house suspended above the earth. Clustered beneath the bottom of the house and under the staircase leading to the front door, a thicket of thorny rose bushes grew. A strong river gurgled a few feet away, the likes of which the boy couldn't remember from any map of his father's kingdom.

"He knew the stories of creatures in the forest, knew the games they liked to play with unsuspecting travelers. Not to be outsmarted, he used his knife to pluck and de-thorn a small bouquet of roses. He knew the value of arriving with a gift. He also remembered rumors of a healer, the ones that said she dabbled in both light and dark magics, and which suggested she was capable of shapeshifting, when the moon was in the right position.

"So he was especially on his guard when he stepped up the stairs and knocked on the door. It swung open, as if prompted by his touch. And in the doorway stood a small, frail-looking old woman. Her hair was silver and hung to her waist. Her gown was simple homespun, with an assortment of pockets on the front.

"He introduced himself as Conn and presented the rose bouquet as a token from His Majesty the King. When the woman asked what he wanted from her, Conn told her of his father's ailing health.

"'Ahh, the king who would attempt to rule me via his errant knights. Why should I help him?'"

"'I promise you,' cried young Conn, 'if you heal him, we will never set foot on your lands again!'

"The woman smiled and told him she would heal the King on three conditions: first, that Conn present the bouquet of roses to his father instead; second, that Conn return to be her apprentice for the rest of his natural life, and third, that his father let her keep her land for as long as she lived.

"Shocked, the boy asked why he must deliver the roses to his father, and the woman replied, 'So that he regains the great soldiers he previously sent.'

"You see," Annis said with a cunning smile, "she had turned each one into a rose for daring to force her off her own land."

"But what happened to Conn?" Lyall asked, entranced. "And the town?"

"Well," Annis said, with the relish of someone telling a secret, "he returned home to his father, just as she had commanded. And the second the king's fingers touched the rose bouquet, his illness disappeared. And so, because the sorceress had kept her part of the bargain, Conn returned to her side to learn the ways of magic that she possessed.

"Over time, the pair of them developed a reputation throughout the land. People with chronic illnesses sought her out for her restorative potions and stayed so they were near her. Couples unable to bear children came, too, and with her help grew families that thrived and played with the others living there. The town grew up around them, and soon there were enough people living there that they decided upon a name. 'Connacht' means 'descendants of Conn.'"

"What a lovely tale," Lyall said. "I wish I were as brave as—"

A hand clamped down on her arm and spun her around.

"Hey!" she shrieked. She opened her mouth to tear into whoever had the gall to touch her, when she recognized the furious expression on Ceanna's face.

"You couldn't wait an hour!" he growled in her face.

Lyall felt her shoulders sagging in guilt, then she straightened. "You have no right to keep me cooped up in that room!"

"I would have taken you anywhere once I woke up!" he exclaimed. "Do you realize what could have happened while I was asleep? Do you have so little self-preservation that you couldn't have waited?"

Annis spoke up. "Do you know this man?" she asked Lyall. Her voice was hard and firm, as if she were ready to come to Lyall's defense if required.

"He's my... husband," she ground out between clenched teeth, as Ceannas turned to Annis and yelled, "I'm her husband!"

"I can see why you went out on your own," Annis said dryly. Ceannas shot her a warning look, then turned back to Lyall.

"Our things are waiting for us in the hotel room. We need to get them before we leave."

Lyall pouted and waved farewell to Annis. As she turned, with Ceannas's death grip still on her arm, she gave him a mulish look. "I was fine," she groused.

Ceannas didn't look at her. Instead, he kept the hard line of his jaw clenched, making tiny muscles in his temple flex. "The fact that you—"

He stumbled suddenly, his injured leg buckling underneath him. His grip on Lyall's arm pulled her down with him, and she found them tangled in a heap on the dirt road. A group of people rushed over to see if they were all right. Ceannas brushed them away with a wave of his hand and tried to stand.

His leg buckled once more. Two men stepped forward and each slung one of Ceannas's arms over their shoulders and lifted him up so that he could bear weight on his good leg.

"You need to see a healer," one of them commented to Ceannas.

Lyall, who had stood and was brushing her dress clear of soil, noted the paleness of Ceanna's skin and the circles under his eyes as he nodded his head in agreement.

He really had been on his last leg, she thought with a surge of guilt. And because of her, he'd had to run all over town, making the injury worse. Shame filled her, and she followed in silence as the two men supporting Ceannas helped him up the road to the healer's building.

To Lyall's surprise, the inside of the healer's building was more like an apothecary than a doctor's office. In Selbane, there was a waiting room and individual seeing rooms. But this healer had rows and rows of tinctures and potions and salves lined up along the shelves. And there were no patient rooms that she noticed. So how did this healer handle injured people? she wondered.

The two men supporting Ceannas took him to a long wooden counter that sat on one side of the room and sat him down in one of two chairs behind it. At Ceannas's assurance, they left, casting dubious glances over their shoulders at Lyall.

After a moment, a large woman appeared from a doorway neither Lyall nor Ceannas had seen. "Hello, new friends. How can I be of service?"

Her voice was low and melodic, and Lyall instantly liked her. She put back the small vial she'd been peering at and walked over to where the woman knelt next to Ceannas behind the counter.

"Shark bite," Ceannas said, pulling up the leg of his pants to reveal a line of raw-looking puncture wounds just above his knee. The surrounding skin was an angry red and some of the punctures wept a yellowish, creamy substance.

"Well, that's pretty infected," the healer said in a matter-of-fact voice. "I can mend it somewhat, but you'll have to give it about four hours for the salve to take effect." She cast a wry look at Lyall. "I doubt he'll give it the rest it needs. So you'll have to convince him to wait four measly hours." She chuckled at that, and Lyall smiled at her infectious laughter.

"I'll do my best to keep him off his feet," Lyall promised. "But it'll be hard."

The healer gave him an affectionate glance, then got to her feet, bracing her hands on her knees. "Oof! This gets more difficult by the day." She turned, glancing around the floor as if looking for something she'd misplaced. "Now, where is that healing salve?"

Lyall noticed a small grey jar sitting on the edge of the counter behind her. "Is that it?" she asked.

The healer scowled at her, then looked at where she was pointing. "There's a lass! That'll do just fine. Now I'll get some bandages and wrap up that nasty bit there, and you both'll be ready to—"

"—do absolutely nothing," Ceannas groused.

The healer grinned at him again, then disappeared below the counter to rummage through her bins of supplies.

While she searched for the bandages, Lyall wandered down the closest row of shelves. This shelf had several trinkets on it, which Lyall found curious, given this was a healer's station. On the shelf, she saw a series of colored jars with cork stoppers in them and other bowls filled with a clear liquid, but which preserved small animal fetuses inside. She gave a disgusted look over her shoulder, but neither Ceannas nor the healer were paying her any attention.

As she moseyed along, she trailed her fingertip through the slight film of dust collecting on the shelf. She heard the healer say something to Ceannas, and the two erupted into gales of laughter. The sound made her smile. It was good for Ceannas to get out of his own head for a while. And if it took a small injury to do it, more the better.

She wandered back to them and heard the healer murmur, "You two are a far way from the sea to have a shark bite."

You have no idea, Lyall thought with a smile.

After a few more minutes of idle chatter as the healer finished tying the bandages on his leg, she retrieved a wooden cane for Ceannas to use and sent them on their way.

They stepped out of the shop and paused in the afternoon's sunlight, letting their eyes adjust to the brightness.

"Ready to go rest now?" Lyall asked in a bright voice.

Ceannas flashed her an irritated glare. "I've got a thousand more important things to do than rest. But," he glanced down at the cane, "I suppose I can take a few hours to let the medicine do its job."

Lyall scowled. "Four hours. Not a few. We can't have you collapsing on the road just because of your pride."

"*My* pride!" Ceannas cried with a laugh. "You're one to talk!"

But Lyall glowered at him. "Regardless of how you feel now, imagine how much better you'll feel in four more hours." Though she kept the banter light, she watched him carefully, looking for more signs that he might fall over.

Though it would take a village to lift him up again, with all that muscle, she thought. "Come on," she said, placing a hand on his shoulder. "Let's get you to bed."

She pretended not to see the mischievous expression on Ceannas's face at her words. *Let him take innuendo where none was meant,* she told herself, bracing for the crude joke she knew he was readying to say.

She was surprised, and a little concerned, when he nodded in agreement and hobbled his way back to the tavern inn.

Four hours of bed rest. She could manage that. Though keeping him busy was going to be a great deal harder than with anybody else, she figured. So she squared her shoulders and marched after him, keeping pace with his limited progress. Let him rest for a while longer—the trip would take care of itself.

CHAPTER 12

ONCE THEY HAD RETURNED to the room, Ceannas collapsed on the bed with a loud groan. Scowling, he threw his cane to the floor, ignoring the loud noise it made as it spun across the floor.

This was weak. He felt disgusted with himself. To get attacked was a job hazard, something he acknowledged happened, but the fear of which didn't rule his life. He knew how to work through pain, and he knew how to doctor most injuries that befell him.

But being this weak while on duty was unacceptable. He could almost hear his father's voice needling at him, wearing him down with insidious words.

You aren't enough. You'll never be enough. She's going to die because you aren't strong enough to protect her.

The words replayed over and over in his mind until he shook his head to clear his thoughts.

"Are you okay?" Lyall asked. She perched on the opposite bed, hands wringing in her lap like small birds.

Ceannas glowered at her. "Now what makes you think I'm not?"

Lyall gave him a deadpan look. "Because you haven't said two words to me since we left the healer's place. And we both know you're incapable of keeping that big mouth of yours shut for any length of time when you're feeling well. So your silence makes me think you're not doing well."

"My big mouth, huh?" Ceannas snorted. "Look who's talking, miss 'you said Connacht was a dung-heap of a town.'" His voice was high-pitched in mockery of her voice. "Do you really want to pick a fight here with the locals? Or are you just set on making my life more difficult?"

Lyall smiled at him. "I was just having a bit of fun, is all. Nobody got hurt by it."

"*This* time no. Next time? Next time you could start something I'm not able to finish, given my leg." He gave another disgusted look down at the bandages. Even the short walk from the healer back to the inn had opened some of the wounds she had cleaned. The bandages were spotted with blood, indicating they still weren't healed.

"Here," Lyall said, rising and moving over to the bad of wound care materials the healer had sent them home with. "Let me change that strip out."

Ceannas rolled his eyes, then nodded. "Fine. If you have to." He watched Lyall pull out the roll of cloth and the numbing salve and sighed in relief. He'd forgotten about that tincture and was grateful for the pain relief it would bring.

"I don't want you walking around with a bloody leg, advertising your weakness to anybody with a decent pair of eyes," Lyall continued as she knelt down in front of him on the floor.

Ceannas snorted. "Well, if they come too close, I'll just whack them with my cane until they run away."

Lyall grinned up at him. "My hero. In the meantime, I'll try that leg-sweep maneuver you taught me yesterday. Together, we can take on anybody."

Ceannas felt a blush of pride. She felt confident enough to use those techniques he'd taught her, which was good. But the sentiment of them doing it "together" made him feel warm inside.

"We are a formidable force," he agreed, leaning forward to prop an elbow on one knee while she unwound the bandage from his other leg. The movement put his face very close to hers, such that he could smell the fresh scent of her hair, which smelled like outdoor air and lilacs.

She glanced up at him and smiled without showing her teeth. It was an adorable smile, a secretive smile, and he had the sudden urge to kiss it off her face.

"What do you plan on doing for the next four hours?" he asked instead, his voice deeper and more gravelly than before. He winced, hoping she didn't notice.

"Aside from taking care of you?" Lyall pursed her lips together as she pulled the blood-stained bandage away from the wound. "I'm not sure. I might go back out to the festival and see what else there is to see."

For a moment, anger filled Ceannas at the disregard she was still showing for her safety. He opened his mouth, ready to let fly a hot retort, when he noticed her sideways glance and the tight set of her lips, as if she were struggling to hold back laughter.

He deflated and stared down at her. "You think you're funny. But you aren't. Not in the slightest."

She grinned up at him, her eyes dancing. "I'm hilarious. You're just too stuck in the sea to notice."

Ceannas appraised her for a few moments, while she bent her head to rebandage his leg. As the bandage came away from his skin, he expected a cool sensation as she bared the flesh to the open air. But as her hands moved over the wound, reapplying the healing salve and caressing the skin above and below the circlet of teeth marks, he felt a warmth flowing from her hands. The heat increased from a vague warmth to the feeling of sitting close to a fire—the flesh felt singed but not painful. If he touched it, he imagined he'd feel extra heat radiating off the injury.

"What are you doing?" he asked, perplexed.

She jolted a little, as if she'd been lost in thought. "Oh, nothing. I guess I was just woolgathering." She smiled at him. "For a moment, I thought I could picture the internal parts of the bite marks, like a fabric I could weave together to make it healed again. Isn't that silly?"

With her head so near and those golden locks brushing his kneecap, he had the sudden urge to reach out and run his fingers through her hair. It was probably as soft as a bird's feather. And it shone like molten gold.

"It's not silly at all," he murmured, entranced.

Without realizing it, he reached out a hand and let his fingers slide through the soft locks.

She froze at his touch, and he cursed himself. *Too far!* his brain cried. *Too far!*

But when she looked up at him, there was no fire in her eyes, no indignation or anger. Just surprise.

"Did you... did you just touch my hair?" she asked, perplexed.

Ceannas's mouth went dry. He tried to speak, but his racing brain couldn't come up with anything clever to say, nothing that could take back the fact that he'd stepped over a boundary without her permission.

"I've been wanting to do that for days." The words popped out of his mouth, and he stared at her, horrified that he could blurt out something like that.

She cocked her head, then gave a tentative smile. "I've wondered the same about you."

Ceannas felt his heart thundering in his chest. "You have?" All complex speech abilities seemed to have frozen, so that he was only capable of single-syllable efforts. There was a thudding in his head, like a thousand horses galloping over the earth, that threatened to overwhelm his senses.

Get yourself together, fool! he thought. *You aren't some moonstruck pup with his first partner.* He shook himself, taking a deep breath to get control of the shallow breaths he'd been taking.

"Here," he said, dipping his head in silent invitation for her to touch. There was a moment's hesitation, where he wondered how foolish he must look to her, then he felt tentative fingers run along his scalp, flexing like a massage.

He moaned, losing himself in the pressure, longing for the touch to deepen, to make a fist full of his hair and pull it backwards in ownership. But the fingers were already retreating, leaving him aching for her touch once more.

"It doesn't feel like normal hair," she said in soft wonderment, and he picked his head up to look at her.

"It's like… like there's oil in it. I don't remember feeling that earlier."

He grinned at her. "It's waterproof like our pelts. Yours will feel like that soon, I'm sure, the more you change."

Her eyebrows rose in surprise. "You think so?"

He nodded. "They always do."

"Even the late bloomers, like me?" She cast her eyes downward, as if ashamed, and fidgeted with the tie on the bandage.

He bent a finger and hooked it under her chin, forcing her head up to meet his gaze.

"You aren't a late bloomer. You're a selkie. And you are exactly how you were meant to be."

As she stared at him, a single tear welled and spilled over her lashes, making a crooked path down her cheek. He used his thumb to brush it away, but the movement made him cup her cheek in his palm. She leaned into the touch, and he stared down at her, holding her face as if she were the most important thing in his world.

Her eyes were like twin moons as she stared up at him, and he'd be a fool not to see the desire in her eyes, the loneliness, and the wistfulness of wanting to connect with someone, anyone, who could make her feel as if she mattered.

He lowered his face towards her, making his intentions clear, giving her time to pull away if she didn't want him.

His lips touched hers, pressing into them with confidence. She answered his pressure, moaning into his mouth as one of her hands crept up and made a fist in his hair, as he'd hoped she would. Pulling him closer, she widened the kiss until he scooped her up beneath her armpits and hauled her to her feet. From there he pulled her forward, so that she was lying between his legs on her stomach, still kissing, still scrambling for purchase on the other's body.

She pulled back long enough to gather her skirt and pull it up to the top of her thighs so that she could more easily straddle him. His hands roamed over her rib cage as she tried to pull the dress off over her head. Slowly, he became privy to the glorious image of her body as she struggled to get the dress up her stomach, then over her ample breasts, and finally over her head.

She tossed the dress behind her on the floor, and he gazed in wonder at the vision in front of him. Sure, he'd seen her without clothes before, but he'd never seen her truly naked in the way of lovers, the baring of oneself both within and without. She looked down at him with hooded eyes that shone with dark desire.

"I've dreamt of this view," he said in a husky voice. "But I never thought I'd be lucky enough to actually see it."

Lyall chuckled, a low, sexy sound. "Luck has nothing to do with it. Now get your clothes off."

Grinning, he sat up, letting her move off of him to give him room. He lifted the shirt off with a casual grace, then staggered to his feet. He unfastened his pants and pulled them down past his throbbing manhood. But when he got to his injured knee, he paused.

"I can't get these pants down around the bandage," he said in sudden realization. He turned to her with an anxious expression. "I don't know that I can... I mean, maybe I could if I just..." He let out a frustrated groan and collapsed back on the bed.

But Lyall just giggled. "Leave the pants where they are." Her hand trailed light, teasing paths across his chest and stomach. He looked over at her and saw her wide, easy smile, and it was infectious, impossible not to smile back at her.

Her hand trailed lower down his stomach, teasing its way down the sharp V-shape of his lower abdominal muscles. He sucked in a breath as her fingers skipped across the juncture of where his manhood met his body, the back of her hand brushing against the intimate area.

He felt himself throb with the slight touch, and he ached for her to take him fully in her hand. But instead, her fingers wandered over to the V-shape on his other side, trailing her way south like she'd just done.

Ceannas groaned in anticipation, and Lyall's grin widened.

"Like this?" she teased. Ceannas closed his eyes and nodded, unable to speak. "Do you want more of it?" He nodded again, even faster. But her fingers hesitated.

"What do you want me to do?" Her voice lacked the sultry confidence of a moment ago, but he pushed the idea aside.

"Take me in your mouth."

With his eyes closed, he couldn't see when she lifted her hand from his body. But there was a moment when the absence of her hand felt like a physical punishment before the warmth of her mouth closed around his erection and his mind went blank.

He craned his neck to see her bobbing up and down on him, taking him into her mouth to the hilt before sliding back up to the tip.

She gazed at him from the corner of her eyes, smiling as she worked him over.

"Oh, Lyall!" he exclaimed, grabbing a fistful of the bed sheets in one hand.

He felt his excitement rising, the wave of desire coming in to crash on the shore. But right before the wave could crest, it went back out again as she removed her mouth from him.

He sat up on his elbows, frowning. "Why did you stop?" He felt disoriented and bereft. "Is everything okay?"

Lyall nodded with noticeable hesitation. He noticed, for the first time, her body language: the bashful set to her shoulders, the hands fidgeting in her lap, the difficulty meeting his gaze. It was as if she had no plan, no idea of what to—

Oh. The realization struck him like a punch to the fact.

"Have you ever been with a man before?" He was careful to keep his voice pitched neutrally so as not to make her feel ashamed.

She shook her head, looking everywhere around the room but at him. Her hands increased their wringing motion as she frowned.

"I've gotten... close... a few times. With Lucas. But I've never actually gone..." Her voice trailed off. He felt an irrational jealousy steal through him at the thought of her being with another man from that small town. No local fisher's son could give her what she needed. And she deserved more than being some sea captain's token wife.

Though he'd had plenty of lovers over the years, it had been a long time since he'd been with a virgin. And from the way Lyall remained on the other side of the bed but didn't try to cover her nudity, he surmised she wanted this as much as he did. She just didn't know where to start.

He felt a little guilty at having focused on his own pleasure first. But now that he figured out her history, he could make it up to her.

"Come here," he said in a soft voice. She glanced up from watching her hands to see his gentle smile. She answered with a hesitant one and crawled over to him on her hands and knees.

"I'm sorry I rushed things a moment ago. I want this to be especially wonderful for you. So I'd like to try a few things. You tell me the second I try to do something that makes you feel uncomfortable, okay?"

She nodded with another shy smile. He reached for her, drawing her close so that her breasts crushed against his chest. He wrapped both hands in her hair on either side of her face, letting his mouth remain neutral, allowing her to set the pace.

Like a cat, she pounced on him, devouring his mouth as if she couldn't get enough of him. He matched her ardor taste by taste, letting his tongue slide along her lower lip. In response, she moaned into his mouth, so he did it again.

She straddled him again, so that his erection pressed between them. Unconsciously, she rocked back and forth, increasing the pleasurable pressure on him. She leaned back, taking a gasping breath, and he was delighted to see her lips swollen from his kisses, the dazed expression on her face.

He used the distance between them for his hands to grasp her full breasts. He wondered what they would look like bouncing up and down while she rode him into oblivion.

She gasped when he pulled one nipple into his mouth, then cried out with pleasure when he flicked his tongue over it. Meanwhile, his other hand kneaded and lightly pinched the other nipple.

Lyall's back arched as he groped and squeezed and licked and sucked on her body. But the pressure around his erection was getting too strong to ignore.

"Lyall," he ground out, "I need you."

"Same," she breathed into his ear as she sucked on his earlobe.

"No, I mean..." He trailed off, trying to think of how to explain himself. But Lyall's hand crept between them to grasp the length of him in her hand and squeezed, and he nearly lost all his control.

"Ride me, princess. Stick me inside and I'll make you see stars during the day."

She drew back enough to put some distance between their hips, then guided him inside her. Easing downward, she let her body weight determine how deep and fast he entered her.

She made a curious squeak, and he clasped her face in his hands to meet her gaze. "Everything all right?"

Lyall nodded with a smile. "It feels... so thick. And so full. Like there should be no way for you to fit inside me, and yet there you are."

Ceannas laughed, a deep belly laugh that drew a like smile from her, too. "And yet there we are."

He reached down to cup her buttocks in each hand and pulled her closer, deepening the penetration. Lyall's back arched towards him as she cried out, and he drew one nipple in his mouth again.

He sucked her as she began moving back and forth on him, grinding deeper and deeper into the pressure. Her cries came more frequently as she leaned back and rode him hard, her hands on his shoulders for balance.

"Ceannas," she cried. "Oh, gods!" Then she was convulsing around him, clenching and releasing with the force of her climax. Her body shuddered in his arms as her movements slowed.

He gritted his teeth against his own tidal wave of pleasure, holding her close as hers died down. Then, when she relaxed against him, he rolled her over so that she was on her back on the bed with him on top.

"I think I really did see stars," she murmured, spent.

Ceannas grinned down at her. "I guarantee none of them hold a candle to you."

She smiled up at him. But as she closed her eyes, he shook her so that she looked at him.

"Oh, it's not over yet," he promised with a smile.

At her confused look, he began to pump his hips, using a slow, steady rhythm to get her back in the mood. His manhood, which had wilted slightly, now felt firm as ever as he plunged into her depths, going deeper and deeper as she cried out below him.

At first, he paused. "Are you all right?" he asked. "Is it too soon?"

Her only response was to clench both hands on his backside and cry out, "More!"

More he could handle.

He drove himself deeper inside her, dimly aware of another set of heartbeats pumping just out of sync with his. It was like a ghost feeling, a fleeting half-sense that something was doubled in effort.

Then his climax was upon him, and he forgot everything except for the name he cried out as he released. His voice was breathless as he called her name. She held him close as his body's convulsions subsided, stroking her nails along his back as he finished.

"That was..." He couldn't find the words.

"Amazing?" Her voice was playful.

He nodded his head. "Very."

"Not good for your leg?" she asked in the same playful tone.

He glanced down at his injured leg. It didn't hurt at the moment, but he was sure it would creep back in after the afterglow faded. But for the moment, he ignored it. He pulled Lyall over to him so that her head pillowed on his chest. The pain could come later. For now, all he wanted was to hold the most incredible creature he'd ever met.

He stroked Lyall's hair, marveling that he could touch such a one as her. He had never taken a lover that matched him as well as she had. She'd taken him stroke by stroke despite her lack of experience, and dear gods, did she learn quickly!

He thought again about the way he'd felt that separate heartbeat pumping out of sync with his own. Where had *that* come from? And what did it mean? He'd felt closer to her afterward and holding her through the afterglow made something pull inside his heart that he'd never felt with anyone else. It brought him closer to her, even though he knew now, in his emotionally sober moment, that this had just complicated things for both of them.

She's out of your league, son, his father's voice whispered in his mind. *This better be one and done, or you're in a whole ocean of trouble.* This time, the voice sounded more like his own. And he couldn't help but think it was correct.

And that feeling of dual heartbeats... He wasn't a fool. He'd heard the lore, of finding the other half of yourself in someone else, some connection that's stronger than a normal mating. He'd heard of True Mates finding each other and remembered that the bond solidified when the two partners climaxed together. But that wasn't something he could allow to happen, as amazing as others rumored it to be. He had a duty to his clan and had sworn a vow to never take a mate.

He would just have to keep his wits about him and never let this happen again.

Her breathing eased into gentle snores and his arm began to fall asleep. But he kept replaying the scene in his mind, turning it over like one might a shining jewel looking for imperfections: her riding him, taking the full length of him inside her, the wild beating of both their hearts, the unspoken realization that this couldn't happen again.

The thought made his stomach turn over sourly. This wasn't supposed to have happened, and now that it had, they were both worse off for it. He knew she'd feel more emotionally attached after their lovemaking, especially since she'd lost her maidenhead. So it would be up to him to remain steadfast to the commitment to never slip like this again.

He nodded once, nearly asleep himself, in affirmation.

Never again. His heartbeat seemed to pulse in time to the words as he drifted off.

Never again.

Never, he promised himself.

Again, his mind whispered.

CHAPTER 13

THEY SLEPT UNTIL THE sun began to set from the view of their room's small window. Lyall woke first, snuggling into the warmth of Ceannas's side with a satisfied smile on her lips. But when he woke, he moved away from her almost immediately, rising quickly and setting about the room, putting their belongings back in their respective bags.

Lyall watched him putter around the room with a half smile on her face. "I could watch you do this all day."

Ceannas paused and took a steadying breath. "You should get dressed. We need to get going." His voice was reserved and detached, and she got up rolling her eyes.

He's changed overnight, she thought. *The perfect lover one moment, the cool commander the next. How mercurial.* She could sense there was a conflict going on in him, but she didn't feel close enough to ask him about it. *He'll tell me when he's ready,* she decided, and resolved to be receptive when he did.

"How is your leg?" she asked, biting her tongue against what she wanted to say about last night.

"It's... better," he said, without looking at her. "Between you and the healer, I think the bandage job is helping a lot."

She nodded, then got up, redressed, and pulled her own satchel across her body. But as he watched him prepare for their departure in silence, the quiet became too much for her to bear. It was like a weight in the room hovering above them, and she felt she had to say *something* to break it.

When Ceannas gave a final once-over of the room, she raised her eyebrows. "Well?" She placed one hand on her hip.

Ceannas paused his movement, midway through pulling on his own shirt. "Well, what?"

"Aren't you going to say anything about last night?" She felt a blush rise in her cheeks at the mention of it, but met his gaze.

He pursed his lips. "It was..." He trailed off. To see her standing there, in all her bold glory, demanding an answer from him. His blustering wouldn't put her off, he knew. She was stronger than that.

A smile twitched on his face, a betrayal of emotion he couldn't help. "Amazing," he finished in a soft voice.

Lyall felt a rush of warmth through her body. She'd felt the same way and didn't know what she would have done if he'd answered negatively. "I thought so, too."

Ceannas held up a finger in warning as his face turned sober. "But this can't happen again. You know that, right?"

Lyall cocked her head. "I don't see why not." Her voice was indignant. "I had fun, you had fun, and together we were untouchable." She lifted her chin and tossed a lock of hair over her shoulder, daring him with her eyes to refute it.

A rueful grin spread over his face. "Right, but we both have duties to uphold. You're the daughter of a prince—" Lyall opened her mouth to argue, and he spoke over her, "—and I'm lead Anchor for our clan. I took a vow to protect and serve my clan by excluding all other relationships. We don't get mates or make our own rules. We each have our own responsibilities to shoulder. This cannot be a regular occurrence. Understand?"

Lyall pursed her lips, eyes shining with amusement. He seemed so comical, trying to lay down the law on their activities as if he were in charge. Though they may have started this journey with her as his ward and him as her guardian, last night changed all that. So she nodded in acquiescence, only to give him some peace of mind.

But she couldn't remove the afternoon's lovemaking from her mind. The joining of their bodies, moving as if they were one person, the timbre of his voice when he cried her name... It was all a part of a single, perfect moment that she couldn't imagine ever having again with that same intensity.

"Are you ready?" Ceannas asked, seemingly appeased. She readjusted her satchel and nodded. He picked up his cane, and they headed out the door.

THE WALK TOOK THEM the rest of the afternoon, and by the time they reached the Cape, where they were supposed to meet up with the clan, they were both exhausted and sick of the flaming beauty of the setting sun.

"Are we there yet?" Lyall grumbled. She was trailing Ceannas and trying to take in her surroundings at the same time. He'd been instructing her on how to maintain a constant situational awareness as they walked.

At first it had been fun: calming her inner self enough to hear her heartbeat, using her ears to catch the softest of nature sounds, stepping lightly over fallen leaves instead of trampling them like a herd of horses. They were as much mental exercises as physical, and the beginning of them had seemed easy.

But now that they were hours into the journey, with no real end in sight, she was tired of hearing her heartbeat thudding in her ears and jumping at every broken branch that snapped nearby.

"Close now," Ceannas called back over his shoulder. They weren't anywhere near a town that Lyall could see, and she wondered, not for the first time, how good Ceannas's sense of direction really was. Had he been leading them in circles this whole time? Would they meet up with the clan at the right time, or would they be left behind to fend for themselves?

She could tell from the thinning trees and briny scent on the wind that they were getting closer to the ocean. But she had yet to see it.

Ceannas paused his limping progress. Lyall was glad he did so, since she'd noticed him leaning on his cane more than when they'd left Connacht. But she knew better than to say anything or remind him of his weakness.

"Do you hear that?" he asked, turning to her.

She stopped and listened. There was a slight swooshing noise that came and went in a rhythmic manner and on the tail end of it, a bark of noise.

"The ocean?" she asked Ceannas, and he nodded with a grin.

"And the clan?"

"Already there!" He picked up his pace, angling to the left of where the trees gave way to a sandy outcropping of land. His progress became more painful to watch as his cane sank into the sand instead of supporting him.

After several more minutes, they crested a hill and saw the wide expanse of the ocean spread out before them. At the base of the hill was the clan, spread out like pebbles on the beach.

It took them ten minutes to make their way down the hill and over to where the seals lounged, basking in the dying rays of sunlight.

Unerringly, Ceannas marched them right to where Trian waited.

As they came near the group of people clustered around her uncle, Lyall wondered how Ceannas always knew where to find the person or direction he was looking for.

"Ah, Ceannas!" Trian cried, with outstretched arms and a wide, expansive smile as they approached. "Good to see you made it after all."

Ceannas went to one knee with his fist clasped over his heart. "My lord."

Trian ignored him as he took in Lyall with narrowed eyes. "And kept my niece safe as well. Commendation is due, don't you think, Trodaire?"

He turned to a naked man standing next to him, who nodded. Out of the corner of her eye, she saw Ceannas flinch. But when she glanced at him, he was still kneeling.

"Well met, Ceannas, well met." Trian's voice was cajoling, as if Ceannas had done something humorous. "I'm sure you are pleased to see my second-in-command. I know you must have missed him when he ceded the Lead Anchor role to you and graduated to being a valuable asset among my protective retinue."

Lyall watched as Ceannas labored to his feet with the help of the cane. He gazed at the two males in front of him. But something was off.

She narrowed her eyes as she looked at Ceannas. Then she realized why he looked different: gone was the levity that always lurked behind his eyes or the wide, easy smile that hovered under the surface of his expressions. This was a different Ceannas entirely, one chiseled from stone and as impassive. Every inch of him radiated cool composure, and she realized she was seeing the warrior Ceannas, not the friend or lover that she'd known.

It put her on her guard, if he was giving off body language that was carefully neutral. She straightened her shoulders and re-situated her grip on her cross-body satchel strap.

The man called Trodaire was heavily muscled, with raised veins banding across his forearms and thick biceps. His stomach seemed carved from granite, giving him a waist that was wide from muscle. His shoulders were broader than any she'd seen before, and he appeared to loom over the others around him. She pegged him to be about her father's age.

Trodaire's face was not attractive, with a crooked nose that obviously had been broken several times, like Ceannas's. His eyes were chips of glaciers on his tanned face. His dark hair had fat streaks of grey running through it and was cut ruthlessly short to his head, setting off his strong jaw that looked made of bricks. He stood with his hands clasped in front of him, obscuring his groin area.

Lyall scowled at him. Something about him seemed familiar, but she couldn't tell why.

"Well met, Ceannas," Trodaire said in an amused drawl. "It's been a while." He looked amused as he took in Ceannas.

"Too long," Ceannas replied in an oddly stilted voice. "How is Isla?"

Trodaire shrugged with a wry twist of his lips. "I got bored with her. She's with another clan now."

Ceannas's lips pursed into a tight line. "Two decades is a long time to be together."

"She wanted a mate, someone she could settle down with. I didn't. It was meant to fail from the start." Trodaire's voice was casual despite the blows Lyall could tell were landing on Ceannas's tense shoulders.

"That's unfortunate," Ceannas said. "I liked her."

"You liked her because she was a substitute after your mother died," Trodaire sneered. "You were always too soft when it came to relationships." He cast an appraising glance over Lyall.

Lyall bristled. She would not let this stranger use their relationship as a weapon. "How do you two know each other?" She pitched her voice to sound bored, as if the conversation had included her from the start.

"How do we know each other?" Trodaire asked with a laugh. "Yes, Ceannas, why don't you enlighten the young lady!" He grinned at Ceannas, and the look was all teeth.

"He's my father," Ceannas said in a soft voice, not looking at her.

"Surely you can muster more emotion than that," Trodaire teased. "Though, I have to admit, I'm *much* more interested in how you know this beautiful lady." He stepped forward and held out his hand to her.

She glanced at Ceannas, but he still refused to look at her. A small muscle twitched at his temple. Cautiously, she held out her hand, letting Trodaire bring the back of it up to his lips.

His kiss was chilly, as if he'd just come out of the ocean, and lingered too long for her to feel comfortable. When she jerked her hand back, she resisted the urge to wipe her hand against her dress. Trodaire's grin widened as if he knew exactly how she felt.

"Yes, yes, this is all very fascinating," Trian broke in. "But where is Garach? Is he still with you...?" He looked at Ceannas expectantly.

"About that," Ceannas said in a rumbling voice that held an audible note of anger. He explained what happened with Garach, from the attack to the rest of their adventure up to the present. For the entire story, Trian kept his gaze affixed on Ceannas, sometimes nodding his head as if this all made sense to him. Trodaire, Lyall noticed, never took his watchful eye off her.

After Ceannas finished, Trian was quiet for several long moments.

"This disturbs me greatly," Trian said. "Not only that the attack happened, but that I could have someone so close to me be a seditionist. I thought I had weeded out all of those."

"Apparently not," Trodaire chimed in.

Trian gave him an irritated glare before turning back to Ceannas. "Obviously there are bigger issues here than just keeping Lyall safe. Trodaire, I want you to accompany them on the rest of this journey."

Beside her, Ceannas jolted as if something had hit him. Trian continued as if he hadn't noticed. "Ceannas, you served me bravely in fighting off Garach, but you're wounded and need help. This is too big for just yourself to handle."

"Yes, my lord," Ceannas said. Was that a hint of a growl in his voice? Lyall was certain Ceannas wasn't happy about this decision, but she wished she could get him alone and ask why; she knew she couldn't under Trodaire's watchful eyes.

Trian began walking away, throwing orders over his shoulder as he went. "Ceannas, while you're here, rally the Anchors for the morning's departure. We set out at dawn."

Ceannas nodded and hobbled after him, gesturing to Lyall to stay put when she moved to follow.

"So you're the famous Lyall," Trodaire drawled. "I've been dying to meet you ever since I heard you had snuck in this Migration. That took guts." He gave her an appraising once-over. Lyall had to fight the urge not to squirm under his gaze. She straightened her shoulders and lifted her chin as if she were a queen. "Not much to you, though," Trodaire continued in his speculative way. "Heard you made it a whole quarter of the way there on your own."

She nodded, wary about saying anything else when Ceannas wasn't around. "I managed just fine." She kept her voice aloof, mimicking his tone.

"Hmm." Trodaire's eyes sparkled with amusement. "It's interesting that he's tied himself to you. I thought he'd have more respect for his title than this."

"He's done nothing wrong!" she exclaimed, for a moment forgetting her attempt to appear unflappable. "He knew I needed help, and so he helped me."

"Yes, I'm sure he's 'helped' you plenty. And helped himself in the meantime." His grin widened as her scowl deepened. He held up his hands defensively. "Hey, I get it! A choice piece of tail; long, lonely hours spent on the road together... It's bound to bring you closer, in all manner of ways."

He stepped closer to her so that he was within kissing distance. She fought the urge to step backwards to maintain distance between them.

"But that's all gonna stop on my watch. I can't have him distracted *and* injured at the same time. That's a recipe for disaster. In fact, I'm surprised he didn't excuse himself from babysitting duty already. He must be slipping."

Fury radiated from Lyall—she could feel the fists at her side shaking from the effort of not slapping this male's smile from his face. But she knew he was goading her, pushing all of her buttons to get a rise out of her. And she refused to rise to the bait.

So she kept silent, hating the smug smirk he wore as if he saw all of her willpower on display. She met his gaze with everything she had in her and focused her energy like a single sunbeam on his face. Rage rode her as she mentally pushed her way forward, concentrating on the emotion filling her. She imagined her will like a shield pressing outward towards him.

"You'll keep a civil tongue in your head," she managed through gritted teeth. "I won't hear of you badmouthing Ceannas when he's done nothing to deserve it."

For a moment, Trodaire's expression slipped—his smirk wavered, and a shadow of doubt crossed his face. His eyes became glassy, and he nodded his head, as if in agreement with her. "Civil tongue," he said in a mild voice.

Lyall's concentration faltered in her shock. Was he agreeing with her? She felt as if she were back in her own body, instead of pushing a mental shield towards him.

Trodaire shook himself as if coming out of a trance. He looked around with a bewildered expression, then looked at her. He scowled. "Don't try any of your feminine tricks on me. It'll end poorly for you."

He stalked off, knocking his shoulder into hers so that she nearly lost her balance and fell.

She followed his progress over her shoulder, feeling a host of different emotions. She felt drained, as if she'd been concentrating on a sewing project for hours without a break. Her mind felt mushy, like it was hard to concentrate on any one idea.

But she also felt empowered. He had left the conversation, not her, which seemed like a win in her favor. Now, if only she could figure out how to manipulate that success into something tangible.

Because there, on the tail end of her emotions, she felt fear, not for herself, but for Ceannas. He obviously didn't have a good relationship with his father, and now he was going to be forced to be around him for the entire Migration. That didn't bode well for any of them. She needed to figure out how to stand between the two males, so they didn't kill each other in the process of getting her to the Great Elder.

But for now, her mind felt fuzzy and her whole body felt weak. So she made her way to the nearest stone on the beach and sat down. She sensed her challenge was only just beginning, and she'd need all her energy for it.

She looked around at all the selkies lounging on the beach, some in their naked human form and others in their seal forms. Most of them had satchels or bags tied around them, just like she did. But it didn't make her feel as if she were a part of them. She felt eyes watching her, even though she saw nobody looking her way.

Still alone, her mind whispered. *Not quite human and not quite selkie.* It was a sobering thought. Though, if she healed her father's sealskin, that would all change. It would make her a hero, and her father would get his glory back again. Not to mention the illness would pass, letting him live to swim again.

Her hands clenched the satchel strap running between her breasts. "So close now," she murmured to herself. "So close."

She gazed out to the sea, letting herself get lost in the rhythmic pull of the waves coming onto shore and rushing out again with foamy white heads. It reminded her of being in that cave near her house, when she'd tried and failed to change into her seal form.

But this time is different, she told herself. Now that she knew she could do it, she could do it again. As long as she had Ceannas beside her, helping.

She smiled to herself. He would protect her, Trodaire aside. Ceannas would make sure she accomplished her task. And everything would turn out exactly as she planned.

It just had to.

CHAPTER 14

He was burning with rage but couldn't show any of it.

Ceannas knew what his father was capable of and wanted Lyall nowhere near it. He found her again, sitting alone on a stone near the water's edge, after he rallied the other Anchors for the dawn's swim.

"Are you all right?" He didn't dare risk touching her in case his father or Trian were watching. And they were always watching.

She shook her head, not looking at him, but gazing out into the ocean.

The irritation and anger that had consumed him for the last half hour subsided as concern crowded in. Why was she so subdued? It wasn't like her.

"What did he say to you?" His voice was like gravel.

She didn't answer him for several heartbeats until he reached down and took hold of her upper arm. "Lyall! What did he say to you?"

She turned to him then, as if only just noticing he was there. "Nothing of importance." Even her voice was subdued, as if she'd been thinking deep thoughts.

"That doesn't sound like him. Surely he said something."

She gave a single-shoulder shrug. "He was not happy you were still with me. Called it babysitting. Said he knew we'd slept together. and that you were weak to let it happen."

Ceannas felt the rage inside glow brighter. How he longed to meet fist-to-fist with his sire, to settle after decades of derision and abuse his abilities and independence. He'd never felt closer to erupting than he felt right then, hearing the words from Lyall's sweet mouth.

"I'll kill him."

Lyall turned at that. "No, you won't. You won't do anything to jeopardize my mission. That's what he wants, to fight you. But he can't push against you if the wall's not there to shove against. Understand?"

Ceannas's jaw clenched and unclenched as he digested this. But words failed him, so he just shook his head in denial.

"Do you want to fight him and risk getting taken off the 'babysitting duty?'" Her voice was mocking. "Or do you want to stay by my side and help me get this done?"

Ceannas looked away from her probing gaze, instead taking in the view of the ocean's horizon in the distance. "You're right." He let out a huge sigh. "Of course you're right." He ran a hand through his hair, tousling it, and let out a guttural growl of frustration.

Lyall nodded in agreement. "Now, we have until dawn to figure out what to do. I feel safe enough in the clan's presence—it's unlikely someone would try to harm me amid the entire group, especially with you and Trodaire looking out for me."

Ceannas bobbed his head, thinking. "We'll stay in the middle of the herd, so there will be others all around you. I've alerted the rest of the Anchors to your presence, so all eyes will be on you. If you run into trouble, let me know and we'll take care of it together."

Lyall pursed her lips, which Ceannas noticed in an instant. "What's wrong?"

"Well," she said, "I'm a little afraid I won't be able to keep up."

"That won't be a problem. Given that this is the last leg of the journey, we expect the pups will lag behind. So this stretch will be at a slower pace than they've set so far. You'll be fine."

Lyall reached out to grasp his hand, then lowered hers without making contact. Ceannas noticed and ached a little inside. He understood the gesture. He wanted to do the same, to reach out to touch her, to make a solid connection, to reassure himself that she was still here, still fine.

But it wasn't safe to exhibit those signs of affection, especially under the sharp gaze of his father.

His father. The reason he became one of the youngest Anchors in the clan. Always pushed past his abilities and punished for showing weakness. But it made him stronger than the others, always ready to push himself past his breaking point. And this instance wouldn't be any different.

He'd protect Lyall with everything he had. To the seven hells with his father, if he interfered with that.

DAWN ARRIVED SOONER THAN he would've liked. Lyall had fallen asleep sitting on the stone but leaning against him for support. If he'd had his way, she would've had a proper bedroll made up of both her father's and her sealskins further inland and not next to the sea. But he didn't have a say. All he could manage was to stay awake and alert beside her, regardless of the stiffness in his injured leg.

As the sun rose over the horizon, spearing lavender and orange and pink streaks across the sky, he nudged her awake as the sounds of wakefulness stirred from the selkies around them.

"Lyall." He tried to wake her gently, by bending to whisper in her ear. When she groaned at him, he nudged her with his good knee. "Wake up! It's time to finish the last leg of the Migration."

That caught her attention as she startled awake with a snort and a gasp. "Where is it?" she cried out. A few nearby selkies cast dubious glances her way. Ceannas noticed and winced. The last thing she wanted to do was draw more attention to herself.

"It's in the bag," Ceannas said in a low voice, knowing she meant her father's sealskin.

She clawed the bag open and plunged her hand in, only to pause with a sigh of relief when her fingers met the torn edges of her father's skin. She closed her eyes, and Ceannas had to fight the urge to kiss the lids.

Instead, knowing his presence in the clan meant he was under constant scrutiny, he nudged her shoulder with one hand to urge her to her feet.

Further down the beach, Trian was already giving his rallying speech to encourage the rest of the clan to endure the final sprint that would carry them to the Great Elder's kingdom about 185 kilometers away. Ceannas didn't need to hear the speech to know what was being said: lots of encouragement for those who had never made the trek before, some basic reminders regarding rules for swimming in the open ocean, tips for the females on how to manage and protect small pups.

It was the same routine speech he'd heard at the previous Migration he'd attended. While it was all rote, he couldn't help but feel concerned about Lyall's attendance.

She's stronger than most pups on this trip, his mind spoke up. *She'll be fine. And I'll be nearby, so she won't be alone.*

And so will Trodaire, the voice added. The mere thought of his sire made Ceannas's mood plummet.

"Lyall," he began with open hesitation. "When my father appears—"

"Be ready to go immediately," a gruff voice finished for him. As if conjured by Ceannas's thoughts, Trodaire appeared at his shoulder.

He turned to see his sire giving both of them an appraising look. Unconsciously, Ceannas straightened his shoulders and lifted his chin as his sire had pounded into him over the decades.

Trodaire nodded with an approving smile when he noticed Ceannas do so. Then he turned to Lyall. "You look terrible." He ignored the withering look Lyall leveled at him. "Just make sure you don't use lack of sleep as an excuse to act like a weakling on this trip. I'll be pushing you just as hard as any other pup, so make sure you keep up."

Ceannas took a step forward, inserting himself between his father and Lyall. "She'll be fine. She can keep up."

"See that she does. I'm not saving her if she drifts off on her own and gets herself eaten."

"I'm sure my father will appreciate the effort," Lyall quipped.

Trodaire gave her a look of intense dislike. "I don't care who Daddy is. I follow Prince Trian. He listens to what I say, and I do the same. My situation is secure with him—anything that happens to you happens the way I say it did. Make sure you can keep up or you're on your own." He strode off towards Trian's direction. "And be ready in five!" he called over his shoulder.

For a moment, both Ceannas and Lyall gazed at his backside.

"We need to be very careful," Ceannas murmured. "He wasn't kidding when he said he has Trian's ear. If there was an accident on the rest of the trip, it would be his word against mine. And I don't think Trian would give me as much credibility as he'd give my father."

"But why is he so antagonistic against me?"

"I suspect it's because of a fight he had with your father a few decades ago. I was a pup then, but I know there was a fight over a female. She was with my father and Prion won her away. Because Prion was a prince, there was no recourse for my father to win her back. He's hated your father ever since.

"Plus," he added, "he probably doesn't appreciate being on baby-sitting duty anymore than I did at first."

Then Ceannas turned to Lyall. He didn't like the dark circles underneath her eyes. He looked around, seeing who was looking their way. When everyone appeared to look elsewhere, he trailed a finger down her cheek.

She looked at him in surprise, then smiled at him. "We're going to be together, right?" Her voice was uncharacteristically shy. The sound of it broke his heart.

"For the rest of the trip? Of course!"

"And after the trip?"

His heart flipped over. Did he dare say the answer he wanted to say, or did he crush her with the truth?

"I don't think now is the time for that conversation."

She put her hands on her hips. "It's just a question. An easy 'yes' or 'no.'"

He reached over and took her hand. "It's not that easy and you know it." He knew he shouldn't be touching her, even as small a gesture as holding her hand, but he couldn't bear not to feel her skin, as conflicting a message as he knew it sent.

She looked down at their joined hands and said nothing.

He let his thumb brush the backs of her knuckles, a brief caress, before letting it go. "We can't because.... we just can't."

She watched their hands fall apart, then nodded. "I suppose we'll see, won't we?" She stood and flashed him a radiant smile. "Of course, everything's going to change after all this." Ceannas nodded. He had the same suspicion.

"In the meantime, I want you to stay towards the middle of the pack while we're in the water. It's the safest position for you. I'll be on either side of you, keeping pace. I'll be switching sides to keep an eye out for dangers."

"Like what?

Ceannas shrugged. "Orcas, sharks, sirens. The occasional human fishing ship. There are plenty of things out there that can kill you, too many to name. It's why we travel in such a large group."

She shivered and Ceannas grinned. It was the first time he'd felt capable of such an expression since they had joined up with the clan. "Don't worry, princess. I'll make sure you keep your hide attached."

She grinned back and for a moment, they just stared goofily at each other. Then Trodaire's sharp voice cut through the air, demanding they get their acts together and get in the water.

Ceannas held the satchel while Lyall pulled out her sealskin. "You change first," he told her. When she gave a dubious glance around, he gripped her chin to force her to look at him and only him. "You can do this. You've already done it before. It's as easy as breathing."

"If that were true, I'd already have drowned," she lamented.

Acutely aware of Trodaire's eyes boring into them, Ceannas leaned down so that his face was close to hers, within kissing distance. "Drape the skin over you like a cape and fasten the hooks down the belly. Then imagine your body curling forward into one shape. It will happen. I promise."

Lyall looked on the verge of panic but nodded at his words. She turned so that her back was facing the rest of the clan and pulled her clothes off. He stuffed her clothes in the bag as she moved towards the water. She draped the sealskin over her shoulders and fastened the bone hooks with shaking hands. The satchel came next, hanging from her neck like a spare skin.

Ceannas wished he could speak to her, but he was very aware of his father watching the exchange and he'd already shown more affection to her than he wanted Trodaire to see.

She stepped to the water's edge, then eased her way into the surf until it was up to her waist.

"It's too cold!" She started to turn around and head back out of the water.

But Ceannas stepped forward. "It won't be that way once you change. Just lean into it!"

He prayed Lyall could do this despite all the mitigating factors. He saw her curl forward, as if diving into the waves. Then her whole body plunged under a larger wave. For a few seconds, she was out of sight, and Ceannas held his breath, uncertain whether to dive in after her.

Then a grey seal's head poked out of the water a few yards away and barked at him.

He grinned at her and gave a mock bow. The seal barked again, then disappeared below the water.

He pulled his sealskin out of his own bag and limped into the water as he pulled on the sealskin with a graceful ease borne of long practice. He looped the bag strap around his neck like she had and swam out to meet her.

In the water, his tail hurt less, and he moved with a greater range of motion than he had as a human. He didn't look back to see when his sire changed. He just assumed Trodaire would catch up when he was ready.

It took another twenty minutes for the rest of the clan to change and cluster together a few hundred feet out from the beach. The females and their pups formed the center of the herd, while the single adults formed the outer edge of the cluster, with the older selkies bringing up the rear. The Anchors dispersed themselves evenly around the perimeter of them all, staying at least twenty feet from the bulk of the group to stay fluid and able to intercept dangers before they affected the herd.

Ceannas nudged Lyall towards the females and pups, and she begrudgingly followed. He could tell she disliked the designation, but he also didn't care, as long as she was safe.

He kept a close eye on her as the herd moved out into the open ocean, headed west-bound towards the Great Elder's kingdom. At one point, a male swam up from behind her to bump her with his shoulder. When she looked his way, he blew a series of bubbles from his snout, then looked at her as if waiting for her to respond.

When she blew a small snort of bubbles back, Ceannas shouldered between them, bumping the other male away with an angry bark. The male looked startled, then swam ahead.

Ceannas turned and gave her his most withering look. Of course, she didn't know the mating habits of seals, but there was no way he was going to let some other male move in on her. He bumped her shoulder gently, and she made a pleased clicking noise back.

He glanced around, making sure the surrounding males all saw his territorial display, then moved back to his flanking position a few feet away. On Lyall's other side, a large gray seal watched the exchange. Ceannas recognized his sire and felt a brief flash of guilt, as if he'd been caught doing something wrong. He would hear about it once they stopped, he was sure.

But, a small voice spoke up, *why shouldn't he keep the other males away?* Lord Prion wouldn't want his daughter to sneak away and come back mated to some stranger. He was just keeping an eye out for Lord Prion's interests, that was all.

Ceannas felt better at the thought. *It's not selfish,* he told himself. *Not in the slightest.*

After a few initial conflicts, mostly where pups pressed the boundaries of their allotted swim space and a few single males tried to out-shoulder the Anchors for more room, the clan settled into an easy rhythm. Though the selkies normally swam several hundred feet down, the Migration protocol demanded they stay nearer to the surface so the pups could take air more easily. This meant that the Anchors clustered near the bottom of the herd, keeping a careful eye out for any dangers that might come from beneath.

He kept a close eye on Lyall as she swam, noting with pride the lengths of time she went between breaths and the strong movements of her body as she kept pace with the rest of the clan. After a time, he felt comfortable trading positions with the Anchor in the position behind him, which put him in a better flanking position behind Lyall. His father, he noticed, stayed in the same position to her left, never seeming to take his eyes off her. It disconcerted Ceannas, but he had to remind himself several times that she was safe within the confines of the clan's bulk. Besides, extra eyes meant extra help should something go wrong.

It was good, he told himself. He kept his attention split between Lyall and gauging the pulse of the rest of the clan. They all seemed to be swimming in fine form. He just hoped it lasted that way. Too many things could go wrong on a Migration.

Occasionally, he caught Lyall glancing back at him, as if reassuring herself he was still there. Each time, he made eye contact with her and jerked his chin to indicate that she keep swimming. She always gave a blast of bubbles, which he interpreted to mean some sassy response, then resumed her swimming.

Inwardly, he grinned. That she felt well enough to fuss at him told him she was well enough to swim on. Mentally, he took heart from it.

Ignoring the burning in his partially healed tail, he followed from his watchful position. If she could keep up, he could, too. Gritting his teeth, he realized he was lagging, so he put on a burst of speed to keep his pace. It aggravated the semi-healed bite wound, and he wished he'd had more time to rest it before swimming the final leg of the Migration, but he knew he had to hold on.

He could do this. If for no other reason than to keep her safe.

Pushing aside the pain, he focused on the strong silhouette of Lyall's seal form as they cut through the water.

He could do this.

He had no choice.

CHAPTER 15

THEY MADE ONLY ONE significant rest stop on the way: around midday when they huddled close together at the surface, forming a raft of bodies, much like sea lions had the habit of doing. This gave the pups some time to relax and recuperate, while letting the Anchors run diagnostics on how the clan was doing.

The answer was that everyone was holding their own, even down to the youngest pup. Ceannas kept close to Lyall, bumping his body up to hers after he'd finished doing his rounds with the other Anchors. He nudged her shoulder with his snout, dodging out of reach when she turned on him with a snarl.

He laughed, letting her see it in the way his mouth gaped open to show his teeth. She gave a haughty toss of her head, then barked at him in a way that he assumed meant something unlady-like.

Perhaps it was good she couldn't form words right now, he thought. But her attitude heartened him, bolstering his belief that she was doing fine on the trip.

After the break, they continued on. Ceannas felt when they traversed across one of the deep ocean currents that ran the length of the coast—the water was colder than the water nearer to home, and he shivered with delight when its icy chill pressed along his body. He saw Lyall shiver, too, and smiled to himself. He would be interested in hearing her complaint about the change in temperature later.

Though, if he was being honest with himself, he was more excited about the prospect of getting her alone than anything else. It was an instinctive desire, one he'd spent the last few hours of the Migration trying to guard against. He'd already told her there was no future between them. He'd done the right thing.

But she was constantly on his mind. and the desire to be close to her and get her alone was an increased, forbidden temptation that he knew he had to fight.

As they neared dusk, Ceannas had to admit that his injured tail was done for the day—the last few miles had taken just about everything he had to keep pace. He craved a rest stop, but would be damned if he was going to show any weakness to his father or Lord Trian.

He was rallying for a burst of energy when motion in his peripheral vision caught his attention.

Pausing, he looked more carefully around them. At first, he saw nothing. Then, as he was preparing to bark a warning to the nearest Anchors, he saw the motion again, only this time it was close enough to be recognizable: it was an elephant seal.

The intruder swam just close enough to the herd to be visible, but not close enough for an attack. Ceannas remembered the last Migration he'd attended as a pup, having to follow an attendant to find the inner underwater entrance to the Great Elder's kingdom. Since none of the other Anchors fell into a defensive formation, he suspected this was their guide.

As Ceannas watched, it swam in a large circle, then paused to watch the rest of the clan. It gave three loud barks, then swam another circle. Ceannas realized it was an invitation to follow, so he barked a series of orders to the surrounding Anchors.

The clan's trajectory changed to follow the elephant seal, who turned and swam ahead of them once they were indeed following. Ceannas hung back, closer to Lyall than was necessary. She bumped his shoulder with hers and he bumped her back, each trying to comfort the other with what touch was available to them.

The elephant seal led them down away from the surface, taking a scenic route through a coral reef that grew along the bottom of the ocean trench. Ceannas saw some pups weaving in and out of the reef with their friends, much as he had done at their age during his first Migration.

But, as interesting as they were to watch, there was no room for playtime now, as the elephant seal hung a sharp right towards a towering reef structure that went down further than Lyall could see and which seemed to rise all the way up past the surface.

The elephant seal led them through an opening in the reef, which turned out to be a tunnel leading to the heart of the Great Elder's kingdom. The clan thinned out to be able to swim three abreast into the tunnel.

After what seemed like ages, the trajectory of the leader seemed to angle upward, and Ceannas saw the water brighten as they came closer to the surface. He followed the bodies in front of him as they breached the surface and then leapt out of the water onto some solid land.

When it was his turn, he poked his head out of the water to take in their surroundings. It was a giant cavern lined with blue and lavender geodes that made the area sparkle from the light cast by burning torches set into the walls. The entry pool, where he floated, was large enough to fit several selkies at once, and he hung to one side and watched as the rest of the clan, one-by-one, leapt out of the water onto the stone of the cavern floor. A few of them changed to their human forms first and hauled themselves in ungainly fashion out of the water.

He floated to one side of the pool, out of the way of the rest of the entering clan, marveling at the sparkling beauty around him. It was more amazing than he remembered. He glanced around, looking for a familiar face, and saw Lyall, in her human form, sitting naked on the edge of the pool, staring in amazement at the cavern.

In the span of a heartbeat, he changed into his human form and swam over to her, holding his sealskin in one hand. "Ever seen anything like it?" She spared a glance at him in surprise, then pursed her lips, hiding a grin, and shook her head. "Trust me, it's more incredible farther in."

Unslinging his bag from around his neck, he hoisted it and his sopping sealskin on the cavern floor next to Lyall and pulled himself out of the now frigid water. He knelt next to her and offered her his hand.

She took it and let him lead her away from the pool, towards a tall, curving doorway that led further into the Great Elder's castle. He paused at the doorway and pointed out several woven baskets overflowing with various pieces of clothing.

"I assume you'll want to avail yourself of this?" he asked with a smile.

"What is this, then? Whose clothes are these?" She picked up a cotton shirt and eyed it with a dubious expression.

"Here for whoever feels uncomfortable enough to wear them." At Lyall's deadpan look, he smirked. "Not every visitor to the Great Elder's kingdom is comfortable in their own skin, so to speak. He understands that protocols vary by the clan and that there may be cultural differences that require some members to cover themselves. These clothes are here in case you feel more comfortable in them than out of them."

She nodded, suddenly eager, and began pawing through the options tossed haphazardly into the basket. After pulling on the cotton shirt, she found a pair of drawstring pants that only came to mid-shin on her legs.

She shrugged. "I'll take what I can get."

Ceannas smiled at her. "That's fine. I'll enjoy taking you out of them later." She flashed a mock-scandalized expression, then winked at him.

"You'll have to be a good boy or else you'll be alone tonight."

The reminder sobered him instantly, and he drew her close. "On that note, I need to tell you something. We won't be alone together tonight. I have Anchor duties that will take most of the evening, and you're going to be sequestered with the other special guests. Not the riff-raff like me."

She frowned at him. "That's fine. I'll just wander the area and get the feel of the place."

But Ceannas shook his head. "No, you're going to stay where I put you. No wandering around, getting lost, getting hurt by someone who wishes you harm." At her mulish expression, he frowned at her. "I'm serious. Be careful tonight."

"What am I supposed to do? Wait in my room like some kind of prisoner?"

"Wait in your room like some kind of special guest, is more like it. I will find out when our clan's turn will be to speak with the Great Elder. I imagine it'll be within the next few days and—"

"A few days?" she exclaimed. "And I'm supposed to be in my room until then?" She waved her hands through the air in a negative movement. "No way. No way! That's not happening."

Ceannas stepped forward and put his hands on either side of her shoulders, pressing her backwards until her back touched the wall. He pressed his body against hers, slowing her movements. "It'll be fine," he said in a low voice. "I'll make sure you're all right. It will be okay."

She gazed up at him. Gods, her lips were so close to his. He could feel her breasts pressed against his chest, their hips in alignment with each other. If he turned his head just so, he could press his lips to hers, could taste—

"What's this?"

Ceannas moved away from her, turning his head from the interloper so that he could compose his features. When he turned to face his father, it was with a blank expression.

"Just letting her know what to expect while she was here."

Trodaire raised one eyebrow skeptically. "Looks like a close conversation. Surely this place isn't *that* intimidating."

"What do you want?" Lyall said, making no attempt to hide her irritation.

"I came to show you to your quarters." Trodaire gazed back and forth between the two of them with a slight smirk on his face.

"I was just about to do that," Ceannas said. He hated the shame that he felt coursing through him, as if he was a pup who'd gotten caught doing something he shouldn't have. When he spoke, he hoped it sounded more confident than he felt.

"You have somewhere better to be," Trodaire said. At Ceannas's confused expression, he grinned. "Trian wants you to address the Anchors. Says it will be good for morale after the long trek from home."

"Why can't you do that?" Trodaire was Trian's right hand. It made no sense for Ceannas to address the group as a lower-ranking Anchor.

Trodaire shrugged. "Wasn't asked to." He narrowed his eyes to scrutinize Ceannas. "Why? Are you considering shirking your duties to play house?"

Ceannas felt his cheeks flush with anger. "I wasn't—"

"But you wanted to!" Trodaire interrupted, scowling. "If you'd taken five seconds to remember your vow, maybe this wouldn't be such a hard decision for you."

"I remember my vow very well!" Ceannas exclaimed. "And I'm doing it to the best of my ability. A member of the royal family needs my help, and I'm—"

"Barely a member," Trodaire broke in. "The daughter of a castaway prince who can't even manage his own sealskin. She's not worth the effort you're putting in this, son."

"Since when do you care what effort I put into things?" Ceannas retorted. His hands clenched into fists at his sides.

Trodaire leaned forward, his voice pitched low. "You have a lineage to uphold, as Lead Anchor, just as me and my sire did before you. This is an embarrassment to your name."

"I'm exactly where I need to be," Ceannas growled. "I'm following my duties as closely as I can."

Trodaire sneered down at him. "Then get your head together. You go where your prince tells you to and you don't argue! End of discussion." The cords in his neck stood out as he stared intently at Ceannas, daring his son to contradict him.

As Ceannas clenched and unclenched his jaw, the muscles at his temples flexed. The two stared at each other for several long moments before Ceannas looked away.

"I'll go."

Trodaire gave a curt nod. "Glad to see you're thinking straight again."

Ceannas glared at him but remained silent. He turned to Lyall. "I'll show you to your room and then—"

"I'll show her to her quarters," Trodaire said in a tone that brooked no arguments. "Trian wants you now."

Ceannas wanted to resist, but he could come up with no good reason for him not to. He nodded in reluctant agreement. "Fine." He looked at Lyall, who gazed back with a panicked expression on her face. It killed him to see her that way, but he couldn't bring himself to argue the case when he knew it didn't matter who showed her to her room.

"I'll see you later." He gave a last, dubious look at his sire, then turned and hurried away.

Inwardly, he seethed. What was it about his father that made it so difficult to stand up to him? Ceannas was a military leader, renowned throughout the clan for his adherence to his duties and his steely heart that had no patience for error. Yet, his sire makes a single statement and suddenly he's a pup again, cowering in the corner while his father lays down the way things are going to go.

He growled, running both hands through his hair. He stopped, feeling overcome with rage, so full of it he needed an outlet now. He spun in the hallway and slammed his fist into the reef wall. It gave with a low crackling noise, and when he pulled his fist back, he saw a cracked indentation where his fist had been.

Breathing heavily, he fought to control his emotions. This was no way for an Anchor to act. Yet he couldn't get that image out of his head, of Lyall's panicked expression as he left her with his sire.

She'll be fine, he told himself, as he closed his eyes and counted his breaths. *He'll dump her in her room, and I can see her later, after I'm done with my duties.* It wasn't good, but it was better than him reversing his direction and rushing back to confront his father now, while he was so filled with anger it was like metal on his tongue.

He was due for a showdown with his sire, he could feel it. But now was not the right time.

After a few more breaths, he felt his strong feelings thaw, so he could think rationally again. He would take care of his tasks tonight, then return to Lyall to tell her what to expect at the Gathering tomorrow.

"It can wait," he murmured to himself. "She'll be fine."

If he told himself enough, eventually he would come to believe it.

CHAPTER 16

Trodaire glowered at her as she watched Ceannas stalk away down the hallway. She cast an uncertain glance at him. "So, um, where will I be staying?"

Trodaire moved down the hallway in the opposite direction than Ceannas took without waiting to see if she would follow.

"In the reserved spaces," he tossed over his shoulder. "You should feel lucky: few nobodies get places of honor on their first Migration."

"I'm not a nobody," she seethed, clenching her knuckles white around the strap of her satchel.

Trodaire snickered. "As far as the Elder is concerned, you are. But, that said, being the daughter of a prince has its perks."

She glared at his back as they walked down the hallways. She noticed the walls appeared to be made of red coral, its porous substance rough against her fingers as she trailed a hand down the wall as they passed. Lanterns were set into the walls at intervals, but instead of fire lighting the way, they were filled with a blue bioluminescent material that gave a soft glow.

She longed to pause and examine them, but Trodaire kept a brisk pace, and she wasn't sure he wouldn't leave her there to figure her own way around. So she trotted to keep up as they wandered down endless corridors, taking turns seemingly at random and passing few others.

The only people they did pass were two servants, one cradling a woven hamper filled with clothes and the other carrying a tray with a plate of food and a goblet. The sight made her stomach rumble. When was the last time she'd eaten? She couldn't remember. On the final push, she'd been more concerned with keeping up and rationing her breathing air than she'd been about food.

Finally Trodaire stopped in front of a door made of white shale. He opened the door without knocking and gestured for her to enter. She gave a dubious look inside, but it was too dark to see much.

"I haven't got all day, princess." It was galling to hear Ceannas's nickname for her in this male's contemptuous tones.

She glowered at him and crossed her arms. "When will I get to see the Great Elder?"

Trodaire snorted his contempt. "When and if Trian decides you're worthy of his time."

"But I came all this way—"

"You came all this way on the gullible assumption that your task matters to anyone other than yourself. You are the forgettable daughter of an exiled prince. Do you know how many creatures make serious requests of the

Great Elder every year? He doesn't have time to grant his attention to just anybody. And the truth is that you are a nobody with expectations of grandeur.

"Now get inside before I throw you inside." The menace in his voice was clear, and Lyall remembered similar words coming out of Ceannas's mouth during their first night together. She shivered, and Trodaire grinned at the sight of it.

"I need light. I'll not sit in a strange place in the dark."

Trodaire watched her for several moments, weighing his options. Then, with a derisive snort, he turned and snatched one of the bioluminescent lanterns off the wall. He held it with an outstretched arm into her room, forcing her to go into the room to get hold of it.

With a contemptuous glare, Lyall walked into the room and took the lantern from his hand. Without another word, Trodaire turned and walked back down the hall in the direction they came from.

Belatedly, Lyall realized she should have asked how Ceannas would know where she was. *But,* she thought, *he wouldn't have told me that information, anyway.* Trodaire obviously thought little of their relationship, however she wanted to qualify it.

Calling it a relationship seemed premature, given their limited amount of intimacy. But she felt closer to Ceannas than she ever had to anyone else. She felt safe around him, secure, and capable of things she'd never thought herself capable of.

As she was thinking, she looked around the room, holding the blue glow of the lantern high. There was a single bed, a large pillow-looking puff that, when she pressed a hand to it, seemed to be filled with some kind of brush for stuffing. There was a dresser with a mirror on the opposite wall to the door. A small rocking chair made of driftwood sat tucked away in the corner. She saw dried starfish and shells pressed into the walls, as if they had washed up on the beach that morning.

Setting the lantern on the dresser, she looked around at its mournful glow. She hoped Ceannas would find her soon. She had to figure out how to get an audience with the Great Elder.

"Perhaps Trian can help me," she murmured to herself.

She snatched up the glow lantern and stepped towards the door. But there she paused. Ceannas had seemed worried about her going off on her own, despite them being in a safe location under the Great Elder's care. Surely she was safe here, if she was safe anywhere.

She nodded once to herself, solidifying the idea, then flounced out the door to find Trian.

AN HOUR LATER, LYALL had visited a vast area of the Great Elder's castle but had seen nobody she knew. The castle was bigger than she had suspected. She'd seen the underwater entry pool they entered from and had passed a massive Dining Hall with long planked tables and benches that selkies ate at in their human forms. The ceiling curved, as if giant hands had scooped the room from the stone.

As she continued down the halls, she noted the stone walls were prevalent in the upper areas of the castle and hard, red coral formed the walls closer to the waterline.

She favored the stone areas best as the coral walls made her worry that the pressure from the ocean would cave them in.

She passed groupings of smaller doorways, and a quick glance inside revealed rows of bunk beds lined in neat rows down each side of the rooms. Servants' quarters, she guessed, and moved on. Another hallway later, she found a room that looked like hers but which she found contained piles of sweet rushes used as bedding.

As she wandered the hallways, aside from getting lost, she made direct eye contact with everyone she passed. However, she noticed few people did the same—they all avoided her gaze or ducked their shoulders to avoid interaction. It was a curious pattern, made more difficult when she realized she was lost and needed directions.

She stopped a servant slinking past with a hand on his shoulder.

"Excuse me, what's your name?" she asked.

The man gave her a wide-eyed, startled look, then stammered, "W-what?"

"Your name?" She smiled to show she meant no harm. "What is it?"

"Reid," he mumbled. He looked as if he'd rather be anywhere than talking with her.

"Can you tell me where my sleeping quarters are? I think I'm lost."

He frowned and adjusted the hamper full of clean linens balanced on one hip. "What wing are you from?"

Lyall gave him a deadpan look. "Wing? I didn't know there were different wings to this place."

Reid looked down the hall both ways, as if looking for somebody to save him from the conversation. He huffed a sigh and re-situated the hamper. "If you don't know what wing you're in, I can't help you. Now if you'll excuse me." With that, he turned and walked down the hall, while Lyall stared open-mouthed after him.

"Rude," she murmured. She looked down either side of the hallway but saw nobody. Feeling on the verge of tears, she continued down the hallway in the direction she'd been going.

She would find someone soon, she knew. It was just a matter of time. She whispered that under her breath as she walked, fighting the tears threatening to leak from her eyes. She walked for several minutes without passing another person, always keeping to the left when the hallway split. Eventually, she knew she'd left-hand her way back to her starting point. She just didn't know how long that would take.

With this thought in mind, she turned another corner, only to run right into the immobile body of someone else. She rebounded from the impact and fell back against the wall. Steadying hands reached out to balance her by gripping her shoulders.

"Hello, niece. What a surprise to see you." Trian peered down at her while she tried to compose herself.

"I'm so glad to see you!" she exclaimed. "I don't know how long I've been walking."

"Let me guess, you got lost?" He sounded amused. "And here I'd thought you had a superior sense of direction."

She realized his hands were still gripping her upper arms, and she shrugged out of the contact. "I guess I got turned around."

"I instructed Trodaire to keep after you. Yet I see neither him nor Ceannas. Why would they let you out on your own?" Trian's voice oozed concerned solicitation.

Not wanting Ceannas to seem negligent, Lyall raised her chin and explained how he'd gone to help with the other Anchors. "I thought you called for him?"

Trian raised his eyebrows. "I haven't seen him. But then, I'm sure he's where ever he needs to be."

Lyall didn't like the speculative gleam in his eyes. He almost looked as if he were plotting something, though Lyall didn't know why that thought would pop into her head.

"I was looking for you," she said abruptly. When Trian looked surprised, she plowed ahead with the speech she'd practiced on her wanderings. "When will I get to see the Great Elder?"

Trian drew back in surprise, one hand on his chest. "My dear, why would you think you'd get to speak with the Great Elder?"

Dumbstruck, Lyall stared at him. "Because you said I could!"

"I don't recall promising anything like that."

"You said he might help me heal my father's sealskin. It wouldn't take long for me to ask him, mere minutes even! But he's the only reason I came on this Migration in the first place."

Trian cupped his chin in his hand as she frowned in thought. "I don't know..." he drawled. "Getting an audience with him is a difficult task. But perhaps I could make the request for you?" His face lit up, as if he was just struck by the idea. "Of course! That's what we can do! Give me the damaged sealskin and I will make the request of the Great Elder on your behalf. I'm scheduled to meet with him tomorrow night."

Lyall frowned and tightened the hand on her satchel strap. "Why can't I make the request myself? There's no need for you to do it when I'm quite capable—"

Trian leaned towards her with a conciliatory smile. "My dear, I understand your reticence. This is a very sensitive issue, of course. But we must handle it with a certain sense of decorum. It would not do for just anybody to make a request of the Great Elder. That's not how things are done. But I promise I'll get the issue resolved once I get my audience with him."

Lyall didn't like the oily feeling she was getting from the interaction. How did Trian expect to articulate the request when he'd only just found out about it days prior? And who better to argue her case to the Great Elder than the one who was closest to the issue?

But she could sense that she was in over her head. She was not only physically lost in the Great Elder's kingdom, but she was metaphysically lost as well. She didn't know the first thing about sealskins and their powers. What if she asked the wrong thing to the Great Elder, and he declined to help her? Maybe someone with more clout, like Trian, would lend gravity to the request.

She met his eyes squarely. "I'm sorry. But I can't give it to you. It stays in my possession."

Trian's eyes gleamed as he watched her. "I'll tell you what: how about you keep the skin and I'll bring the case before the Great Elder? That way, we both get what we want."

The compromise was like a physical thing lifted from her shoulders, and it made her sag with relief. She gave Trian a winning smile, which he returned serenely, then straightened her shoulders.

"It's a deal. Now, can you take me back to my room?"

"I believe I remember where you were sequestered," Trian said. He tucked one of her hands in the crook of his arm and led the way back towards the direction she'd come from.

In much faster time, she spied the white shale door and smiled gratefully to Trian. His returning smile was warmer than before, and she had the brief thought that perhaps she'd misjudged him from the last two times they'd met. This Trian was warm and welcoming, significantly different from the cold, detached leader from the beaches.

Perhaps it was the mantel of responsibility, she thought, *turning him into a machine that had no room for hesitation or interruptions.* Now that the clan is safely at their destination, he can relax a little, show more personality.

With those thoughts in mind, she stepped past him over the threshold.

"You'll take extra care with that, right?" he asked in a solicitous tone.

She gave a warm smile. "With my life."

Trian glowered at her. "So be it."

She nodded, then closed the door.

Once inside and alone, she cast a dubious glance around the room. There wasn't much to do other than lie down and wait to be summoned for dinner. She put the lantern in an empty holder by the door and eased herself onto the pillow-pad that served as a bed. To her surprise, it was fluffy, like a full-body hug.

She'd just begun to doze off when she heard a knock at the door.

Easing off the bed, she walked over and opened the door, expecting a servant to be there announcing dinner time.

Instead, she found Ceannas.

"I wondered when you'd be by. I wasn't sure you knew where I was."

He frowned at her, then gave a pointed glance down each end of the hallway, as if making sure nobody was around to overhear. Then he stepped past her into the room and shut the door behind him.

"You can't be too careful here," he murmured, as he pulled her into the circle of his arms for a hug.

Though the move surprised her, she rushed into the embrace, feeling, for the first time that day, as if she'd come home.

The embrace felt too short when he broke contact moments later. He held the points of her shoulders and put her at arm's length to study her. "You're all right? No injuries? Everything is okay?"

She gave him a bewildered smile. "I'm fine! Now that you're here, that is." She flashed him a flirtatious grin, but he didn't rise to the bait.

Once assured that she was well, he stepped over to the door and engaged the lock. Only then did he seem to relax, letting loose a deep sigh as he turned to her.

"There are those in this palace that would cause you harm. I don't want you to go out by yourself while we're here. At least not until you make your request of the Great Elder."

Lyall felt guilt wash over her. She winced. "About that..." she began.

She informed him of her sojourn through the palace and getting lost and being found by Trian. "And so he agreed to petition the Great Elder tomorrow on my behalf."

Ceannas's face grew more sober as she spoke, only fracturing into a grimace of surprise at her last words. "So Trian let you keep the skin?"

Lyall nodded. "Did I do something wrong?"

Ceannas passed a hand over his face. "Well, that could go either way. I'm not sure what his motives are. Until I knew, I had hoped to keep him away from you and the skin. But this can't be helped, I suppose." He managed an encouraging smile. "How are you doing? I had hoped to help doctor you after the strain of the swim in."

Lyall blushed at the memory of the last time he'd doctored her body, after her first leg of the Migration, back when they'd met. From the dark depths of his eyes, she could see the desire and knew he was remembering the same.

He reached down and took her hand and pulled gently to bring her closer to his body. She let him reel her in and reached up to cup his cheek with one hand.

"I have a request," she breathed. His eyes drew her in, making her feel as if she was going down into very dark water.

"For you, anything." His voice was husky with desire.

"Stay with me tonight." When he frowned and pulled away, she held him fast. "I know you can't break your vow," she said. "But stay with me one more night."

Ceannas turned his head away from her, frowning in thought.

"Please, Ceannas. I need you."

His expression softened as he turned back to her. "I need you, too." His voice was guttural and made things low in her stomach clench. "But we shouldn't be doing this. This will only make it harder to stay away from each other."

"Well," Lyall said tentatively, "maybe we shouldn't try to avoid it."

"We risk both of our futures if we don't," he said in a soft voice. "There's no way we could make it work."

"I think there's already some precedent for it to work," she said with a small smile. Taking his hand, she pulled him towards the bed, then turned him so that he was facing her and his back was to the pillow-puff of the bed. She shoved his chest, and he let her push him down to sit on the edge of the bed with her standing in front of him. Slowly, she removed the shirt and pants she'd been wearing, baring herself to him.

"What precedent do you mean?" Ceannas asked, willing his eyes not to devour the sight of her naked in front of him.

"Una and Ronan," she said with a smile.

"But—"

"No buts. He was a sworn Anchor, one of the best of you, Una said. And he gave up his vow to be with his True Mate." She saw Ceannas swallow hard at the mention of the True Mate bond as if she'd triggered some memory for him. But she pushed the thought aside as she let her hands rove over the planes of his muscled chest.

"I know you don't *want* to give up your vow. It's an intrinsic part of you, and I know you take it very seriously. But I just mean that there might be another option we haven't considered yet."

Ceannas held himself rigidly as her hands moved over him. "And that would be..?"

"The king and queen allowed it for Ronan. Why wouldn't they allow it for you?"

Ceannas looked down with an expression of true shock. "Sure, they let that happen once. But there's nothing that says they'll allow it again..?"

She smiled down at him. "There's nothing that says they won't, either."

For a long moment, he stared up at her in surprise. Then, reverently, he reached around to her backside and squeezed her buttocks, pulling her close so that he could suck on one nipple. She arched into the touch, one hand reaching up to grab a fistful of his hair and pull him closer to her.

His other hand rose to knead and pluck at her other breast, and her breath came in quick pants. His hands slid down her sides, branding her with fire at the touch.

It wasn't enough. She pulled his shirt over his head and gestured for him to shuck out of his pants. He did so, and she gaped at the sight of his erection straining upward.

"Gods, you're so big," she panted, wrapping her hands around the base of him. He let out a groan of need.

"I need you, Lyall," he said. In a quick movement, he reached behind her and pulled her onto his lap, while positioning his manhood to slide inside her as she came forward.

She slid down the delicious length of him, moaning at the pressure.

"How do you want me?" he murmured in her ear as she pressed her breasts against his chest.

"Hard." Her voice was breathless, and even though he was as deep as he could go, she still craved more of him.

He withdrew from her, and she gasped in surprise as he gently pushed her aside so he could stand. With careful hands, he positioned her so that she was on her knees on the bed with him standing behind her.

He took a moment to glory in the sight of her bared to him with her buttocks in the air, the pink sight of her exposed to his view. *Gods, she is amazing!* he thought.

He positioned himself behind her, guiding the length of him to her entrance, one hand braced on her hip to hold her in place. She made a shocked noise as he entered her.

"What is this?" she asked.

"Something different," he teased. Gripping both of her hips, he thrust in and out of her slowly, giving her time to acclimate to the deeper position. He kept it slow until she urged him faster with her panting cries.

He leaned forward and put a hand on her shoulder, pulling back to bring her upright so that his chest brushed her back with him still inside her. With one hand on her hip, the other hand reached around to fondle her breasts, gently pinching one nipple, then the other.

"Ceannas!" she panted as he moved faster and faster, feeling the rising tide in herself.

"Say my name again," he ground out as he held her bucking hips and matched her movement with his own.

"Ceannas," she whispered.

"Tell me what you want." He paused his hip motions, stalling the wave that threatened to crest over her.

"Ceannas, please!" she groaned. "I want you!"

"You want to come," he corrected in a hoarse voice. "Tell me you want it."

"I want it!" His hips moved again.

She reached around to grab one of his hips, trying to encourage his participation and growling with frustration when he controlled the movement.

"Again."

"I want you to make me come!" Her voice was barely loud enough for him to hear. "Ceannas, make me come!"

He unleashed himself, letting her desperate movements come faster and faster. "Take me, princess."

He reached around the front of her and rubbed the small bud at the apex of her sweetness as he thrust faster and faster behind her.

"Oh, gods, Ceannas, I'm yours!" She shattered around him, driving him closer and closer to his own breaking.

She shuddered and slowed her own movement.

"Not yet, princess." He put a hand between her shoulder blades to indicate he wanted her on her hands and knees. She obliged, leaning forward so her breasts rubbed against the bedding, her backside exposed to him as he remained inside her. "Are you ready for it?"

"Ready for what?" she whispered, still riding the aftershocks of her climax.

"My turn." He grinned at her as she smiled over her shoulder at him.

"Take all that you want." She braced her forearms against the bed, inviting him.

He began thrusting again, starting slower, being mindful of her sensitivity, and then moving faster and faster as she cried out to him.

"Faster, Ceannas! Give me more!"

He needed no further encouragement.

Pistoning his hips, he drove into her sweetness over and over again, roaring his climax when it came. She felt him shudder from the force of his release.

He relaxed and withdrew to lean on one elbow to the side of her, so he didn't crush her with his weight. He placed a chaste kiss on her forehead as she grinned at him.

Gazing into her eyes, he leaned in for a deep, slow kiss.

She kissed him like she didn't want to let him go, letting her lips linger against his until he pulled back.

"I think I can read your mind," he said playfully.

She cocked an eyebrow at him. "Oh, can you?"

He nodded. "I know what you're thinking right now."

As if on cue, her stomach rumbled audibly. She giggled as a pink flush blossomed on her cheeks.

"I think we want the same thing," he said with a laugh.

"Another round?" she asked hopefully.

He grinned at her. "Maybe after I get both of us dinner."

She rolled her eyes in mock defiance, then smiled at him. "Sounds like a plan. As long as you promise me one thing." He cocked his head and raised his eyebrows. "That I fall asleep in your arms tonight."

He regarded her with a sober expression for a moment. Then a slow smile spread across his face as he nodded. "Deal."

He rose and began dressing, with Lyall making mock disappointed noises when his shirt was back in place.

Lyall followed Ceannas to the door, pulling him into a final embrace once it was open, unmindful of who might pass by.

CHAPTER 17

As soon as the door shut and he heard the lock engage, Ceannas turned and walked down the hallway towards the Grand Hall, where the food was, in the east wing of the palace.

A heavy hand descended on his shoulder as soon as he made the first turn in the hallway.

"Walking a fine line, aren't you, son?" Trodaire's voice was honeyed and intimate.

Ceannas schooled his face into a blank expression as he turned to regard his sire. "I don't think so." He tried to pitch his tone as aloof as possible, as if he didn't care what his father thought.

Trodaire squeezed his shoulder hard enough to pinch the nerve cluster there, and Ceannas shrugged him off with a quick movement. "Sleeping with that little thing might make the trip more interesting, but what's going to happen when she's got to return to her world, and you have to return to yours?" His voice was oily and oozed into Ceannas's ears against his wishes.

"It's just a onetime thing." Ceannas's voice was hard, the same voice he used with soldiers that brooked no further discussion.

But Trodaire just smiled and gripped the back of Ceannas's neck. It brought back a flood of memories: hundreds of times Trodaire gripped his neck in the same fashion, the iron band of his fingers at the base of Ceannas's skull, the ducking of his head when he'd done something wrong.

He fought the urge to dip his head in shame. There was nothing to be ashamed of. Whatever he and Lyall had together was his own business, not his sire's. He thought of Lyall's trusting gaze as she pulled her dress over her head. There had been nothing shameful about their union. He wouldn't let his father ruin that, too, just like he'd ruined all his other relationships.

He straightened his shoulders and brushed off Trodaire's hand.

His sire raised his eyebrows in surprise, then put a hand on Ceannas's chest to stop him in his tracks.

"You don't get it, boy," he growled. "You play a dangerous game playing with that princess back there. She doesn't know our world and you don't know hers. This is going to end poorly, and you're going to suffer for it."

"Since when do you care about my feelings?" Ceannas shot back. "You've affected every relationship I've ever had, and I let you. But I won't let you affect this one."

Trodaire's eyes bored into Ceannas's. "You're mistaken if you think you and her are alone on this. This affects the rest of the clan." At Ceannas's quizzical expression, Trodaire grinned. "Ah, see there? I know something you don't. She's the daughter of a prince, which makes her royalty. Do you think royals get to make their own decisions? No! They decide based on the welfare of the rest of the clan.

"And you. You've taken the Anchor's Vow. You know what it says about relationships like this."

Ceannas looked away, clenching and unclenching his jaw. He didn't want to hear what his sire was saying, but he had to admit the male was right so far.

"The physical aspect of this tryst is one thing," Trodaire continued. "The emotional aspect is another. What will happen if one of you falls in love with the other? How do you cut it off then? She's new to everything about our world. It's only natural for her to bond that much more with her mentor..."

Ceannas jerked at the realization that his sire was right. He'd be blind to see the way Lyall looked at him, ever since the first time they'd slept together. There was a softness in her expression when she looked his way, a gentleness that spoke of deeper emotions than just friendship.

"I've told her nothing can come of this," he said roughly. "She knows the risks—"

"Does she, though? Really?" Trodaire cocked his head to one side. "Or is that what you've been telling yourself so you can continue to dip into that honey jar?" His smile was sly as he paused, letting those words sink in.

Ceannas looked down at his hands and clenched them into fists. To himself, he had to admit he didn't know the answer to that question. Was he being selfish with this?

Had he been forsaking his vow to the clan? He was too close to the issue to tell.

"What makes you so interested in me all of a sudden?"

Trodaire smiled and pulled Ceannas's neck so that they were face-to-face. "I want to make you a deal." Ceannas tried to pull back, but Trodaire kept a tight hold on him. "I know you think you serve the throne equally. But what if you had to pick just one to follow?"

"What do you mean? Like, taking sides against the other members of the royal family?" It was an absurd question, and Ceannas couldn't foresee where it was going.

"I'm looking out for your future, son. If you were to choose one brother to follow, I would hope you'd choose the right one. The one that makes the most *practical* sense..."

Ceannas understood the point he was getting at. He straightened quickly, pulling himself out of his sire's grip. He stared at him in shock. "You'd have me going against Lord Prion to follow his brother, Trian?"

Trodaire eyed him skeptically. "Think about it: what sense does it make for one brother to control a fighting force he cannot even swim into battle with? And who sides with sirens when we are at war?" He smiled, showing many teeth. "I'm just looking out for your best interests."

"Since when?" Ceannas spat. "You've only ever cared about yourself."

"I care about our family's reputation. How would it look for a son to reject his sire's wishes? Together, we could be formidable. You just have to do what I say."

"You sound like a traitor."

"I sound like a realist." Trodaire shook his head, disappointed. "You're only making it harder on everyone involved. Break it off tonight or you're just stringing her along. And remember," he leaned close to Ceannas's ear, "Our clan cannot survive if clan members don't keep their oaths. The whole system of protection relies on this."

With that, Trodaire stepped away, clapping one hand to Ceannas's shoulders. As if they were equals. As if they were friends.

Ceannas stood there long after his sire had gone. He could still feel the oily slide of his sire's words in his ear.

You're only making it harder on everyone involved. Break it off tonight or you're just stringing her along.

That was a hell of a blow. To imply he was shirking his duties was one thing, but to assume love was involved? He'd made it very clear to Lyall that they could not continue on their current path. Hadn't he? Now he wasn't so sure he had...

He remembered that he was supposed to be getting food for both of them. And when he returned, she might have more of an appetite than he'd bargained for. For a virgin, she had jumped wholeheartedly into a physical relationship with him. Was she developing more feelings for him than he wanted?

He had to admit, he felt a certain softness towards her, too. A carefulness that hadn't been there, even when he'd just met her off the beach after her first change. Shouldn't he have felt the maximum connection to her then, as the daughter of a price?

With a shake of his head, he cleared the thoughts away. He felt much stronger for her since she'd become his lover. And he'd be a fool to ignore that hint of a deeper connection, that of a True Mate. That was the unacceptable line he must not cross, letting that bond solidify.

He made his way to the Grand Hall, acquired two plates of steamed fish and vegetables off a servant, and returned to Lyall's room.

But when he arrived, she had already fallen asleep on the bed, her arms spread wide to either side. She had put on the other pair of trousers but left her torso bare. One hand covered a breast, cupping herself in her sleep, while a tendril of golden hair obscured the other breast.

He smiled at the sight, then placed the food down on the dresser. The discussion with Trodaire had killed his appetite. He undressed and slid into the bed beside her.

When he touched her skin, she murmured his name and rolled over, pressing her chest against his arm. He sighed. This was getting more complicated the longer it went on. He wondered what she'd say if he recounted Trodaire's conversation. Would she be indignant and offended, or would she be rueful and agree with what he said?

He fell asleep thinking about it, which led to an uncomfortable night tossing and turning next to her.

CHAPTER 18

THE NEXT MORNING, A sharp rap at the door woke them. Lyall scrambled to get dressed, then cracked the door open to receive the visitor.

"Meet in the Grand Hall in one hour. The Great Elder will see your clan today."

Lyall nodded, and the servant vanished down the hall. She closed the door to find Ceannas, still reclining on the bed and half-covered with the quilt, regarding her with a serious expression.

"Things are going to move quickly today," he said in a solemn voice. "And I won't be able to be near you to help."

Lyall reached down and snatched up his clothing from the floor, then tossed it to him. He growled as it hit his face. "There's going to be nothing but success today," she told him in a prim voice. Her smile was wide and easy. She felt ebullient and powerful, ready to take on the world. Of course, today was going to be a historical one: it would be the day the Great Elder fixed her father's sealskin.

The thought that it might not work never crossed her mind.

Ceannas shrugged on his shirt and pants with careless movements that set Lyall's blood rushing. The sight of his muscles flexing as he pulled on his clothes was enough to make her want to tear them off of him all over again. But she shook herself, thinking that this was a special day, not one to waste by focusing on budding relationships or new lovers.

Once dressed, Ceannas led her down the long series of hallways, turning here or there seemingly at whim.

"Have you been here before?" she asked as they rounded one more turn that looked identical to the last turn they'd made.

"Once," he tossed over his shoulder. "I was a pup then, but it made an impression on me. I don't know my way around the entire palace, but I know how to get to where I'm needed."

He stopped outside of a set of double doors and turned to face her. He placed his hands on both shoulders, squeezing them to indicate the gravity of the situation. "Now it is vital to keep quiet in here. Don't be shocked by the size of the Great Elder: he's been in this position for at least 2oo years that I know of. Your father once served a season here in this court, if I recall correctly, but that doesn't mean you can assume any special favors.

"Let Trian do the talking. Only speak when spoken to. That's the biggest rule here. The Great Elder sees hundreds of petitioners every day, which means his patience runs thin. And his temper isn't the greatest, so be sure to follow all rules you hear."

"But won't you be with me while we're in there? It sounds like you'll be somewhere else?" The thought filled her with dread. To be alone in the Great Elder's court? Visions of failure rose in her head, of the Great Elder ignoring Trian's petition, or worse, of the Great Elder refusing to help at all.

"I'll be with the other Anchors on the side of the Hall." He pressed his hands down on her shoulders to focus her attention on him. "But you will be fine. There is no reason to worry here. You're in safe hands. Despite being a curmudgeon, the Great Elder is one of the wisest creatures in the sea. There's a reason creatures other than selkies pay homage to him."

Lyall's eyes grew wide. "Wait, what? They do? What kind of creatures?"

But Ceannas was already looking over his shoulder at something. Lyall leaned to peer around him and saw an ordered line of Anchors marching into the Grand Hall by another set of doors. The two selkies in front both held up a fabric banner that gleamed like gold. Most of the Anchors were naked, though some carried hip belts with knives on them. Trodaire was one of them.

"Why are they armed?" she whispered to Ceannas.

"It's a show of force to the other creatures attending today. Though it's a mark of weakness among selkies, it sends a strong message to others."

"How is it a weakness?"

"To selkies, it says your body is not enough of a defense, your teeth are too soft so you need metal ones to take their place. But other creatures don't know that—to them, we are armed well in both the number of Anchors present and those that are armed to the teeth."

Lyall nodded, though she didn't quite agree: it seemed the ones with the knives appeared the most dangerous. She glanced over and realized Ceannas wore no hip belt or weapons.

"What will happen if it comes to blows here?" she asked.

"Nobody dares quarrel under the Great Elder's roof. Here, even enemy factions must behave themselves, or risk the Great Elder's wrath. We put aside all feuds until we are out of his territory."

"What then?"

Ceannas shrugged. "Then we're free to kill each other as much as we want."

Lyall shivered. To hear it laid out so coldly... It was sobering.

Then Ceannas was moving, reaching back to lay a kiss on her forehead. "I've got to go. But remember to follow the rules and everything will be fine."

He turned and strode off to the line of Anchors and took his place beside Trodaire. Confused about what to do, Lyall waited, wringing her hands together, before she saw Trian and his contingent striding into the Hall. She darted forward, merging with the retinue, and hoped she was where she was supposed to be.

The doorway leading to the Grand Hall was rounded, giving the illusion of added height, but once inside, the ceiling vaulted almost a hundred feet into the air, ending with a curving dome for a ceiling. The effect was like walking into a giant, hollowed out egg. Bioluminescent torches lined the space, casting everything in a smooth blue glow. It was like being underwater but on land. She reached out a tentative hand along the wall and found it to be slightly damp, like a sponge. The whole effect seemed designed to recreate the ocean floor, and from Lyall's perspective, it worked.

As her group marched into the Hall, Lyall felt she might break her neck from craning to see everything at once. Groups of people flanked the room, most naked except for the colored armbands they all wore, identifying them as one clan or another. Others were dressed like she was, in ill-fitting clothes, but with their hair pulled back in the same intricate braid work with sea glass and shells threaded through. Other than the large colored banner, Lyall couldn't tell how her clan was set apart from the others.

The line in front of her slowed, and she peered around the bodies in front of her to see why.

In the center of the room, reclining on a large cushion, was a giant walrus. His massive tusks were stained brown near the tops of his mouth but faded into ivory tips at the bottom. They curved almost to the ground, and Lyall wondered why he was in his changed form when everyone else was in their human form. She knew selkies couldn't speak human words in their seal forms.

Maybe he's doing it for effect, she thought, which made sense once she thought about it. The Great Elder was three times the size of a normal walrus, which made him tower over the human-formed selkies in the room. It also gave him an advantage, she guessed, by being able to see over the tops of everyone's head so he could address everybody at once. She glanced around the room, trying to count the number of different clans in attendance. Assuming, that was, that they were all selkies and not some other shape-shifting creature.

"Liath Clann," a deep voice rang out. "So good to see you. Well met."

"Well met," the selkies around Lyall chanted. She frowned. Who were they speaking to? She had seen no person speak aloud in greeting.

Then she turned her head back to the colossal figure in front of her.

The walrus shifted his great bulk to re-situate himself. "I trust your tithes are bountiful?" he said. Lyall stared in shock. His mouth had moved, as had his tusks, but the voice sounded human. How was this possible? She longed to be next to Ceannas so she could ask how this could be. For the time being, she would do well to assume that was part of the magic of being the Great Elder, magic she'd been counting on all along, in fact.

Trian stepped forward, along with a dozen other selkies behind him. Lyall saw they were carrying various woven baskets, which they now removed the lids from to reveal the contents. Lyall saw gems gleaming around the inside edges of the baskets: creamy mother-of-pearl, giant pearls the size of her fist, and other shiny objects that looked like jewelry.

But what does he need jewelry for? she wondered.

Basket bearers brought the offerings forward and laid them at the foot of the Great Elder's dais. He leaned forward to inspect them.

"These look acceptable. I thank you for your gifts and offerings." He leaned back and peered down at Trian. "Is there any issue you wish to bring forth? Any grievance that needs arbitration?"

Trian stepped forward, then turned and scanned the viewers behind him. His gaze settled on Lyall's, and he gestured her forward. But before she could respond, a hand clamped down on her upper arm and began to drag her.

"Hey!" she exclaimed, as she recognized Trodaire beside her, pulling her along. The crowd parted as they approached the front of the line.

They made it to the front of the line, and Trodaire threw her to the ground at the foot of the Great Elder's flippers.

"Who is this?" the Great Elder asked. He cocked his head to inspect them more closely.

Trian gestured to Lyall as she attempted to regain her feet. "A thief, my Lord. The daughter of my brother, who stole his sealskin from me on our journey here."

The Great Elder looked back and forth between Lyall and Trian. "Your own niece?" He inspected Lyall as she stared aghast at Trian. The words that wanted to spill forth felt clamped together, a blockage she couldn't overcome even in her own defense.

"Let's see this sealskin," the Great Elder said. His voice was ripe with curiosity.

Lyall felt movement at her hip and realized someone was fishing through her satchel. She looked on in shock as Trodaire tossed the damaged sealskin to the ground in front of them all.

"The sealskin of my brother, Prince Prion," Trian said in a booming voice that echoed in the cavern. "It was damaged some time ago."

"What do you expect me to do with this?"

Trian paused and made eye contact with Lyall as she looked on with wide-eyed anticipation. His lips curled into a sly grin, then he turned back to the Great Elder.

"Oh, Great One, I don't expect much from you regarding the skin itself—I know the damage is beyond repair. I instead seek justice for a grievance that occurred on our trip here." He turned and pointed a damning finger at Lyall. "That female stole it from me on the way here, and I only just get it back by the grace of the sea. She took the skin intending to destroy it beyond all recognition. I demand you imprison her as a traitor to the royal family."

Lyall stood for a moment in shock, the words all jumbling together and not making sense. Then two selkies snatched up her arms on either side of her and drug her forward towards the Great Elder.

"Is this true?" the Great Elder asked, peering down at her with rheumy eyes.

She gaped at him, then shook her head. Her throat locked up, preventing any words from coming out.

"Speak up for yourself, girl! If this is untrue, now is the time to say so!"

She shook her head, shivering with terror. "N-no, it's not true. I would never do that! My father is Prion. I brought this skin so you can heal it!"

"She lies, Great One. And I have the witness to prove it." He turned and gestured to someone behind her. She turned her head in shock.

Trodaire took a step forward, throwing a superior smirk her way as he passed her. "It's all true, Great Elder. She took it from Prince Trian!"

The Great Elder peered at her as tears fell down her face. "It's not true," she whispered. "It's not true."

Where is Ceannas? she wondered frantically. "I have a witness, too!" she exclaimed. "Ceannas, the Lead Anchor. He can vouch for me!"

The Great Elder looked around the Hall. "Is this true? I demand this Ceannas step forward."

There was a low murmur around the room that died down as soon as it started. Silence weighed heavily over the room. Lyall craned her neck desperately to see him for herself.

After several heartbeats, the Great Elder looked down at her. "Take hold of her. I will arbitrate judgment at another time."

"Do you want her in the cells?" one of her handlers asked.

The Great Elder shook his head. "For now, just hold her to one side while I complete my duties to Liath Clann."

The hands around Lyall's arms tightened and jerked her to one side, out of the way of the rest of Trian's entourage.

"Ceannas!" she screamed as she bucked and thrashed in her captor's hands. "Ceannas!"

But he didn't appear.

"Quiet, girl!" one of her handlers snapped and slapped her hard across the face.

Stung to silence, she stared at him in horror. How could this have gone so wrong so fast? She craned her neck, standing on her tiptoes to see the rest of the Meeting Hall. Where was Ceannas? And would he be back in time to help her before they took her to wherever the cells were?

"Now, about this sealskin," the Great Elder said. His voice dripped with curiosity.

"The sealskin of my brother, Prince Prion," Trian said. "The damage happened some time ago, and I was hoping you could fix it, though I suspect it cannot be done."

The Great Elder let out a soft sigh. "I haven't heard that name in ages! He was a studious learner and a sound strategist during his time in my court. I would do much to help him."

The words penetrated Lyall's stupor, and she gaped in shock. Her father? Apprentice to the Great Elder? He'd never told those stories before.

"Let me see it more closely." The Great Elder leaned forward to sniff at the pelt Trian held up for him. He used one tusk to move the pelt around in Trian's arms.

"This has to be the worst I've ever seen." He sniffed at the sealskin, then sat back with a loud groan of effort. "However, there is nothing I can do for him. This kind of fix requires great magic, of a level that I could not attempt even with my best efforts. This needs the hand of a *buidseach* the likes of which I have never seen before." He bowed his head to Trian. "I'm sorry, but there's nothing I can do."

Lyall noted the smug smile on Trian's face with a detached sense of self. She felt as if she were watching a scene unfold rather than being a part of the scene itself.

"I'm sorry, but there's nothing I can do." The words pounded through her brain, pushing out all other thoughts. Nothing he could do.

It seemed like years had passed by the time the individuals holding her captive pushed her towards the door. As they cleared the Hall doors and began down the hallways toward the prison cells, Lyall walked docilely between them.

She felt drained of energy, still in shock about what had just happened. How could it have gone sideways so quickly? And why would Trian lie? What motive did he have for getting her out of the way? And what would she do now after discovering the damage to the sealskin was irreparable? She had staked everything on the Great Elder being able to help.

It was all too much to concentrate on. There was a low buzzing in her mind that overrode the sounds around her. It drowned out the snickered insults of her handlers as they pulled her down the halls.

They came to a stop in front of a small cave room, carved out from the stone wall itself and with iron bars stretching from the ceiling to the floor. One of her handlers opened the barred door while the other gave her a sharp shove. She fell forward, tripping over the uneven stone of the floor. Behind her, the door clanged shut with a loud clatter.

"Enjoy your stay," one handler snickered. "Don't worry about your decision. It'll come in due time." They laughed together, then walked back the way they came, laughing over the joke as they went.

Tears poured down her cheeks as she stared after them. She hugged her arms around herself, feeling as if she might break into a hundred smaller pieces. How could this have happened? And where was Ceannas?

She walked to the back wall of the cell, pressed her back against it, and slid down until her buttocks touched the floor. She drew her knees close to her chest and wrapped her arms around them. Then she bowed her head and allowed herself to weep at the enormity of her situation.

CHAPTER 19

CEANNAS FUMED AS HE stalked down the hallway. After kissing Lyall goodbye and striding off to take his place in line with the other Anchors, he'd stepped in behind his sire. The second Trodaire had caught sight of him, he'd taken his son aside.

"You know about the tension that's threaded through our clan as of late, yes?"

Ceannas nodded, even as he craned his neck to see where Lyall was. Surely she'd come in by now?

"There's been some division among the Anchors," Trodaire continued, "about who would favor further action against the sirens and who would roll over and accept Prion's decision of peaceful coexistence with them."

Ceannas spared a confused look at his sire. Where was this going?

"We have uncovered one dissenter, and he's awaiting judgment by the Great Elder. We need you to watch over him while he is imprisoned, to make sure no harm comes to him by his hand or anybody else's."

"We?" Ceannas asked, peering at his sire.

"Lord Trian and myself."

"Who is this dissenter?"

"Garach."

Ceannas's eyes raised in surprise. "He had the nerve to come back to the clan?"

"He returned telling rumors of how he helped save Lyall from an attack, only to have you attack him instead."

"But that's not what happened at all!" Several people glanced at the two men as his voice escalated.

Trodaire held out a placating hand. "I know that, and Trian knows that. But we need someone to guard him until the Great Elder can see him."

Ceannas's jaw clenched at the thought of that traitor coming out on top of the situation. But he nodded. He clasped a hand to his heart, noting the disdainful sneer Trodaire returned.

Cheeks burning, he turned and went out through a set of side doors that wasn't as cluttered with bodies in the way. He stalked among the crowd of people lining the hallways, waiting their turns to see the Great Elder. How he hated showing signs of subservience to his sire! It was as if nothing he'd ever done was good enough to warrant the male's approval. Not becoming Lead Anchor, not developing a reputation as a master General during the selkie/siren war, not being a close friend to the royal family. None of it was ever good enough.

He made it to the prison cells a few minutes later. He hated the damp air that lingered this close to the sea. Down here, the walls were spongy and dank from being close enough to the water that the walls absorbed the sea. He walked down the center of the corridor, peering into each cell as he passed.

But all of them appeared empty.

Frowning, he walked to the far end and double-checked himself, stepping up to the bars of each cell and looking inside.

Nobody.

A strange feeling came over him as he turned a confused circle in the middle of the aisle. Why would Trodaire send him down here when there was nobody to watch over? Something was not right about this whole thing. He needed answers, and he knew he would have to find them from Trian. As both a royal and the Migration's leader, he would know what games Trodaire was playing at.

He strode down the hall at a fast clip, taking a shorter route than before, a shortcut he remembered as a pup. When he made it back to the Grand Hall, most of the other clans had filed out.

Had he missed the whole thing? And where was Lyall in all of this? He paused, concerned, and looked around for a familiar face. After a moment, he saw Trian and Trodaire standing with the Great Elder in close discussion.

He stalked to them, nearly vibrating from the effort of holding his anger at bay. As he approached, the Great Elder caught his eye. "Young Anchor, what is it you seek?"

He stopped in his tracks. The Great Elder had just spoken to him, as if he were a person of importance. For a second, he gaped at the Great Elder, who gazed back with a bemused expression.

Trian rounded on him, his face furious. "How dare you approach the Great Elder with such an informal attitude!" He turned back to the Great Elder. "My Lord, my deepest apologies! I will take him to task for his impertinence."

But the Great Elder laughed. "It isn't impertinence that drives him." He peered down at Ceannas. "I can sense your anger from the hallway. What is it you seek?"

"Answers, my Lord," Ceannas managed. He opened his mouth to say more, but his eye caught the torn pelt of Prion's sealskin lying at the base of the jeweled offering baskets. "What of Lord Prion's skin? Was it healed?"

Trodaire clamped a hand on the back of Ceannas's neck and squeezed hard enough to hurt. He laughed between the four of them as if Ceannas had told a joke. "Ah, pups, they get to the heart of the matter, don't they?" He leaned close to Ceannas and growled in his ear, "Now is not the time."

But Ceannas pulled back. "That's the whole reason Lyall came! Why is that not acceptable to ask about?"

Trodaire's hand clenched harder, pinching Ceannas's spine in warning. The message was clear: stop talking, stay quiet, be respectful. But hadn't he been that way his entire life? He shrugged his sire's grip off of him, then rounded on him with a scowl.

"Don't touch me!" He stood tall as he stared his sire down, the two furious gazes matched in intensity. "I demand to know what happened to Lord Prion's sealskin, as well as the female who brought it."

"We have taken care of the traitor," Trian said smoothly. "She will be dealt with accordingly."

"Traitor? What are you talking about?"

He looked between the two males and the Great Elder, who leaned down to peer at him with open curiosity. "Who are you to demand answers for such things?"

"I'm Ceannas, her protector."

"Ah!" sighed the Great Elder. "So you are the one she sought! Unfortunately, she was imprisoned to await my judgment at a later time."

Ceannas's jaw dropped as he gaped at the Great Elder. "She's done nothing wrong!"

"And would you swear to it?" the Great Elder asked.

"Who charged her with this offense? I'll have his head!" Ceannas's rage was a living thing in his chest, a burning flame that longed for violence to rend, to tear, to make right.

Trian narrowed his eyes. "You want to control yourself before you do something you'll regret later."

Ceannas scowled at him. "Who. Was. It?"

Trian glanced between Trodaire and the Great Elder. "Me." He drawled the word out.

For Ceannas, the path was clear. He leveled a finger at Trian. "I challenge you to a Blood Duel on her behalf!" He saw doubt flash in Trian's eyes, and the sight of it solidified his decision.

"This is a very serious commitment, young Anchor," the Great Elder said. "Are you sure you want to take that step? You realize only one is left standing in a Blood Duel?"

But Ceannas only had eyes for Trian. He nodded in agreement.

Trian's gaze narrowed, then shifted to Trodaire with a small nod.

Trodaire stepped forward and bumped Ceannas's shoulder with his chest. The movement made Ceannas break the intent stare with Trian and look at his sire instead.

Trodaire sneered down at him, and Ceannas felt a fleeting moment of remembered childhood fear.

"I volunteer to take Lord Trian's place in the Blood Duel. I fight on his behalf."

Ceannas blinked in surprise. "You?" His voice was half as strong as he wanted it to be.

Trodaire nodded with a slow grin. "You've been on my case all your life," he said softly to Ceannas. "It's time to step up and see who's the stronger selkie."

"You don't have to do this," Ceannas ground out through a hoarse throat.

"Coward!" Trodaire spat. "You've been on your belly your entire life. It's time to stand on your own two feet and be a proper warrior."

Hate flared in Ceannas's stomach as he stared at his sire's derisive expression, even as doubt eased its way into his mind. Had he always been on his belly? Had he ever stood up for himself? Had he been a proper warrior after all, or was he merely playacting at being one?

He shook his head and scowled at his sire. Of course, he had become a great warrior, despite the ruthless course his sire had set him on, with his heavy hands and condemning words. Ceannas had grown past that, despite it even, and deserved to be seen as a male in his own right.

"You've got it." He stared into his father's face, letting all of his hate and anger leech through into his expression. A slow smile oozed across Trodaire's face as he watched the interplay of emotions cross Ceannas's face.

Trodaire turned on his heel and strode to the other side of the Grand Hall, towards a wooden rack filled with weapons. He removed a long, wooden spear, then stepped into the circle of a ring painted on the floor. Ceannas hadn't remembered that ring being there the last time, but it was obviously some kind of fighting arena.

He stalked over until he was inside the large white ring. Trodaire tossed the wooden spear to him from the other side of the circle, and Ceannas caught it in the air. He examined it for a moment, then tossed it aside.

"I don't need any weapons to best you," he said. The hate and anger inside him flared hotter. He didn't have to call on it from deep inside—it was already there, at his fingertips, ready to burst forth at the slightest release.

Trodaire grinned at him with a viper's smile. He pulled two knives from either side of his hip holsters. The blades spun into his hands with the ease of intimate practice.

"Let's dance," he cooed.

Ceannas growled an inhuman sound and leapt forward.

CHAPTER 20

LYALL DIDN'T KNOW HOW long she sat there, but after a while, her buttocks felt flat and cold, as if she were growing into the stone herself, becoming one with the rock. She lumbered to her feet and rubbed her arms to generate some warmth.

For the first time since arriving in the cell, she looked around, taking in the confines she was stuck with. She walked over to the bars of the cell and gripped them tightly. She practiced shaking them back and forth, grimacing as the cold of the metal seeped into her skin. It was like touching ice, and she tucked her hands in her armpits to revive them.

She wandered the edges of the cell, taking it all in from top to bottom. The only way out seemed to be the cell door that was locked with a chain and a clunky metal lock. She tried pulling on it, but only half-heartedly. She knew it was too strong for her to break.

As she walked the perimeter of her cell, she noticed a small puddle, a bowl-sized indentation in the stone that had a puddle of water in it. Upon further inspection, she realized there was a leak above the indentation, which dripped water down into it. She watched for a few moments, counting the timing between drops, losing herself in the waiting since actual thoughts about escape seemed too weighted, too heavy to focus on in the moment.

After a few heartbeats, she knelt down next to it and gazed into the shallow depths. A sheen of oil over the top made a purple and green rainbow of color appear as she looked on. She stared down, letting her gaze go soft, unfocused, into the shifting colors.

As she watched, a new droplet dripped down from the ceiling above. Ripples shimmered from the contact, but behind it, she saw other movement. Curious, she stared harder, letting her gaze intensify to see what was crawling out of the pool.

But she realized it wasn't something coming out of the pool, as she'd thought, but something moving within the water itself. She could make out two figures at first, their forms hazy and indistinct as they moved back and forth in a strange sort of dance.

As she watched, the figures came into focus: Ceannas, with his auburn hair tousled and wild, and Trodaire, his expression hard with rage. The two males circled each other, with Trodaire holding two knives out from his sides and Ceannas keeping rhythm on the opposite side of a white circle painted on the ground.

"Ceannas!" she exclaimed, and she saw the figure in the water jerk in response. It was enough of a distraction that Trodaire leapt forward, slashing with one knife at Ceannas's ribs.

The two danced out of contact with each other, and Lyall saw a fresh red wound slashed across Ceannas's ribs, too high to disembowel and too shallow to be dangerous. It was a slice designed to anger his opponent, not actually hurt him. And Lyall realized Trodaire was just playing with Ceannas. She knew Ceannas had the reputation of being a good warrior—she'd gleaned that much from her father—but she didn't know how good he was when matched by his older and heavier sire.

She glanced wildly around the cell, looking for anything to help her. Nothing stood out to her, and when she looked back at the water image, the two fighters were gone—the water was just water again.

The urge to move, to fight, to act was overwhelming. She stood and paced the length of her cell, her hands buried in her hair to help her think.

She knew what she'd seen was true, though she had no idea how she'd summoned it. There was too much detail for her to have made it up. It was as if the secret magic of the Great Elder's palace was helping her.

But now she needed to help herself.

She walked back to the cell door, touching and grasping around the edges of it to test for any areas of weakness. But the metal was too strong, too immobile. But the lock...

Hefting it in her hands, she lifted the lock to inspect it. There was a single hole for the required key, which she obviously didn't have. And she had no way to get anybody to get her the key.

Or did she…?

"Help!" she shrieked. "I need help! Someone come help me!"

She cried out as loudly as she could manage, but nobody came. After several minutes of trying, feeling like time was slipping away faster than she could afford to wait, she gave up.

She looked at the lock again, growling when its bulk remained indifferent to her actions. She grasped it in both hands and concentrated her attention on the keyhole in the middle of it. Both hands pressed into the metal as if she could imprint herself on it.

After a few moments, she noticed a warmth radiating from her hands into the metal of the lock. Her gaze intensified on the keyhole, and she pictured the clasp of the lock sliding open like a cracked egg. Her fingers sank in the metal, making small indentations as the heat grew to an intolerable level. Smoke escaped from the keyhole as she stared at it, as she willed it to bend to her will.

With a small click, the lock clasp opened.

She dropped the lock, unable to bear its heat any further. Using her shirt to handle the now-heated lock, she removed it, unwound the chain from the cell bars, and opened the door.

Fear gripped her as she took a cautious step out of her prison cell. She expected a yell to go up as someone realized she was free. But there was nothing other than the squeak of the cell door as it swung closed again.

She remembered the vision of Ceannas getting slashed across his ribs. The thought filled her with a sense of dread that made her stomach cramp with fear. She took a moment to orient herself, then raced down the hall in the direction her captors had led her down.

Be safe, be safe, she prayed as she ran. She was only aware of the river of emotion inside her that insisted she run faster, harder, longer. She had to get there before something terrible happened. She just had to.

Her feet flew down the halls, guided by her unconscious gut feeling about which direction to turn when the halls converged. It seemed like she had run for days by the time she spied the arching doors of the Grand Hall ahead of her.

Bursting through the doors with both hands held out in front of her, she exploded into the room.

"Stop!" she screamed at the limit of her endurance. She saw a small crowd gathered around the end of the hall, which all turned to regard her with surprise.

In the middle of the circle, Ceannas straightened from his fighting stance and stared at her with shocked surprise. "Lyall?"

Without missing a beat, Trodaire lunged forward, stabbing Ceannas between the ribs, impaling him on the length of steel in his hand. His blade thrust in to the hilt, and the sound of it seemed to echo throughout the entire room.

Ceannas grunted, then turned a confused expression on Trodaire, who grinned savagely down at him. Trodaire jerked his knife upward, slicing deeper, then withdrew the knife with a savage cry of victory.

Frozen in shock, all Lyall could do was watch as Ceannas sank to his knees and then fell over, the expression of shock still on his face.

CHAPTER 21

LYALL FELT THE WORLD shrink down to the eye of a needle. The only thing she could see was Ceannas's form lying on the cold floor, while his sire stepped forward to intercept her.

"How did you get out?" Trodaire growled.

His words were the catalyst for her movement, and she took three steps forward until she could reach him. Instinctively, she placed her palm against the flat plane of his chest. "Stop," she said, and the word had the gravity of eons behind it.

Trodaire stopped with a puzzled expression.

"Wait for me," she intoned in a soft voice, and he nodded his head, looking dazed as she brushed past him.

She crouched next to Ceannas, tears flooding her cheeks as she stared down at his bloodied body. Silent, because there was no room for sound in her heart or in her mind, she leaned forward, her tears dripping over his skin like rain. He tried to lift his head off the ground but failed.

"Lyall," he gasped in a voice that bubbled blood onto his thin lips.

She made a shushing sound and placed one finger over his mouth, silencing him, too. The other hand moved of its own accord, reaching across him to cover the rib wound, splaying her fingers over the gap in the flesh that made a sucking sound whenever he inhaled.

She closed her eyes and bowed her head, remembering the prison lock, remembering what it felt like to scry in the water pool, remembering Ceannas's shark bite wound coming together. All of those things had required concentration, but it was more like allowing herself to be a vessel for the energy rather than being an active participant.

With each rattling breath of Ceannas's, she breathed the same, so that they were inhaling and exhaling at the same time, in the same way. Imagining herself as a conduit, she poured her desire and her love for Ceannas into the hand laid over his wound.

Dimly she could make out gasps from the crowd surrounding them, but she let that knowledge move past her like water down a river. Instead, she focused on his breathing, inhaling in healing, and a sense of knitting together, exhaling the blood and the danger and the tearing of flesh.

Slowly she built that image in her head, of seamless skin unbroken by a blade. Gradually, her breathing evened out so that she was aware only of her own breaths and not his.

"Lyall?" The voice wavered as it said her name, filled with confusion and uncertainty.

She grabbed onto it like a lifeline and opened her eyes to find Ceannas staring at her with a dazed expression.

The sound of her name on his lips was her undoing, and she leaned forward, letting the tears fall unchecked as she pressed her forehead against his. His hand crept up to tangle in her hair, holding her head close to his as if he never wanted to let her go.

She leaned back and smiled a watery smile that he returned.

Someone cleared their throat, and she leaned back, remembering for the first time that they were not alone. And she had unfinished business to attend to.

Though she felt drained of her energy, she rallied herself and stood, smoothing the front of her shirt to quell the tidal wave of feelings inside her. She felt relief and joy and terror at what might have been. But underneath that was fury and rage and a deep sense that justice needed to be served.

She remembered how Garach had stopped moving when she'd spoken to him in the clearing. And she'd guessed, when she first touched Trodaire's chest, that she could control him with her voice. But now she was certain, and that certainty ran through her like blood.

Trodaire remained where she'd left him, looking dazed. A small frown line appeared in the center of his forehead, but that was the only sign there was anything wrong.

Lyall stepped up to him and placed her hand on his chest again.

"Say your name," she said in a low voice.

"Trodaire." He stared straight ahead, not looking her way. His voice was level, inflectionless.

"And why did you try to kill your son?"

"Because he challenged Trian to a Blood Duel."

"Is that all?"

"And because Trian told me something like that might happen. And if it did, I was to step forward in his place."

"Why?"

"Because Garach failed the first attempt on your life, and Ceannas proved himself too strong a defender. Trian wanted Ceannas out of the way so he could dispose of you."

Lyall felt her own anger rising but pursed her lips against the tirade that threatened to explode forth. "Why did he want me dead?"

"He just wanted to wound his brother more deeply by losing both his skin and his daughter."

"Why did he do that?" A sinking feeling twisted her gut.

"He hates his brother. If Prion died, Trian would be the next in line to be Strategic Anchor Commander. Without that, Trian will inherit nothing."

Ceannas rose and stepped forward, frowning. "But what about the other brother, Andara?"

"Andara is slated to be next on the throne if his father, the King, dies. Prion is Strategic Anchor Commander, and Lyall is his only heir. What is there left for Trian? Nothing unless one of his older brothers dies. And when Trian found out about his niece's intentions, it seemed like the perfect opportunity: he pretends to try to get the sealskin fixed, which everyone knows can't happen, and he gets the glory for the effort and waits until Prion is gone to step into his new role."

"Anchors!" Ceannas barked. "Take him into custody!"

A few Anchors closed in, forming a loose circle around Trodaire, who stood swaying by himself like a man woken from a dream. Ceannas growled and stepped forward with his hands coming up into fists.

But Lyall put a restraining hand on his arm. "We don't need any more violence. I think this will be enough." She looked to the Great Elder, whom she'd forgotten about in the excitement.

He nodded. "I've not seen magic like this before. Young lady, are you Prion's daughter, as you claimed earlier?" At her nod, he sank into a bow so low his forehead touched the ground.

Around her, everyone sank into deep bows, with heads bent or laid low to the ground.

Confused, she looked around at the entire hall laying themselves low before her.

"What's happening?" she whispered to Ceannas.

Grinning, he rose from his bow and leaned close to her so that only she could hear. "I don't know, but I say swim with it. It looks to be in your favor."

She could feel her cheeks warming as she urged the Great Elder to rise. Finally he did, and his eyes sparkled at her as he towered over her.

"My dear, I can say with honesty that I've never seen magic like that done before."

"But can't you heal with your touch?" she asked, surprised.

But the walrus shook his head. "I can heal small wounds. But I cannot bring anyone back from near death. That is a skill only reserved by the strongest of *buidseach*."

"*Buidseach*?" Lyall squeaked. "I've only known one of those in my life, and she's disappeared to wherever the sea would take her. There's no way I am what you say."

Lyall felt a strange buzzing in her head. There was no way she was who the Great Elder said she was. She would have known long before then... wouldn't she?

"How do you know I am this *buidseach*?"

The walrus laughed, a deep noise that made his great bulk jiggle. "That's like asking how I know I need air to breathe—it's an innate sense in my bones, just like I imagine it's a sense in yours, too."

Lyall frowned and looked down at her ill-fitting clothes. Did she sense her difference? She had always wanted to be different, had hoped to be someone special. But that was nothing but a young girl's fantasy, a desire to be otherworldly. Were there markers that she hadn't seen earlier that indicated something special about her?

There was the shark attack, where she'd seen that burst of light. And the earthquake steps she'd taken when she and Ceannas were in the forest. But those were minor. Nothing as significant as scrying in a pool of water in a prison cell or manipulating metal to open a lock.

"Oh gods, is it true?" she breathed.

Ceannas grinned down at her, and she looked up at him in wonder. Then his smile faltered, and he looked down at his feet.

"What's the matter?" she asked. "What's wrong?"

He glanced up at her, then back down to the ground. "This changes everything. You know that, right?"

"It doesn't have to, does it?" Her voice was timid, soft enough that only he could hear her.

"You heard him: you're one of the strongest *buidseach* he's ever known. And I have a vow to my clan. I don't see any overlap."

She put her hand on his shoulder. "I know we can work something out. In the meantime, I think I may need a bodyguard to accompany me safely back home." She offered a gentle smile. "Know of anybody up to the task?"

Ceannas managed an answering grin. "I might know a guy. But he went and got his fool self injured a while back, so you might have to—"

She gasped as an idea exploded in her mind. "Injured," she breathed. "I wonder..."

Pushing past Ceannas, who spluttered at the interruption, she went to where her father's sealskin lay forgotten on the ground. She picked it up, fingering the tears in the skin, the rubbery fat that contrasted with the softness of the fur.

She could fix this. What was dried skin after she'd fixed living skin?

Picking up the skin with both hands, she brought it to her nose and inhaled deeply. Despite the travel, it still smelled of her father, of the ocean and cedarwood, fresh and wild. She closed her eyes and pictured the sealskin whole, without the rough tears and gaping holes. Her hands warmed under the pelt, and she concentrated on pushing the energy from her core outward. In her mind, there was a ball of light in the middle of her, and she shoved it forward so that the light connected to her hands in long, shining lines.

She heard gasps echoing around her, but she shut them out so she could concentrate on the light paths working like thread, sewing together the rips with a thin string of light. *It was just like sewing a dress,* she thought. Only more taxing.

After what felt like a decade of effort, she felt a sense of completion, a full feeling of satisfaction. Her hands tingled with the effort and when she withdrew them from beneath the sealskin, she was surprised to see they were a deep red, as if all the blood in her body had rushed to her hands.

She flexed her fingers, trying to get the tingling sensation to subside. She took inventory of herself and was aware of voices speaking around her. The pelt suddenly seemed too heavy in her hands and she let go of it.

She tried to stand, only to find her legs were too weak to bear her weight. Ceannas was immediately at her side, helping her upright with a bracing hand on her elbow and shoulders.

Why was she so weak? She felt empty, wrung out like a washrag. Leaning heavily on Ceannas, she rose.

"You only just healed a dying man and repaired a sealskin nobody else thought was possible," Ceannas murmured in her ear. "No big deal." She glanced sideways at him. She hadn't meant to ask the question aloud.

"So what's next?" she asked the Great Elder.

"Tomorrow, your clan returns to your island. I will send an emissary with you telling of Trian's exile and betrayal."

"Trian!" Lyall had forgotten him in the excitement. She looked around the Hall for him but he was nowhere to be found.

The Great Elder chuckled. "Do you think there is anything in my palace I don't know about? No person enters or exits my kingdom without my knowledge."

"But where—"

With a jerk of his giant head, the Great Elder indicated the doors of the Hall. "I have my people on him as we speak."

"But how do you know he's not already escaped?" Ceannas asked.

The Great Elder's eyes gleamed as he leaned down, bringing his head closer. "Much like the magic that ties you to your sealskin, I have a similar magic over my kingdom. He cannot leave this place without my permission. It's part of my protective magic."

As they continued the conversation about how the magic worked, Lyall felt a dizziness come over her. The floor shifted beneath her, twisting and turning in such a way that she felt she might be sick.

"I don't think I'm—" she managed, before her legs gave way and she pitched forward.

She had the sense of strong arms holding her, and then there was nothing but cool darkness that she gladly fell into.

CHAPTER 22

He didn't know what to do.

After he carried Lyall back to her room to rest, attendants of the Great Elder, three diminutive ladies in flowing cotton gowns, shepherded him from the room.

Instinct told him he needed to wait until she was conscious, to tell her of his love and make sure she was all right. But the rational part of his brain told him that waiting outside her door did no good. Besides, he preferred to keep busy when faced with uncertainty.

So he took a walk, wandering his way through the palace with no real desire or intent. He knew he wouldn't be needed until tomorrow morning, when Liath Clann was scheduled to depart.

As the Lead Anchor, he was the next in line after Trian to usher the clan home. But at the moment, all he wanted was to be by Lyall's side, to be the first thing she saw when she opened her eyes.

He found himself in front of a door, not having walked there on purpose, but once he realized where he was, he knew it was the right location. He knocked three times, then waited.

"Enter," called a muffled voice beyond the door.

Squaring his shoulders, Ceannas opened the door and stepped over the threshold.

Inside was a man, dark-haired and obese. The bulk of him reclined on a plushy bed-pod adorned with decorative pillows and gold threaded sheets. His hair was a shining waterfall of darkness, draped over his nudity like a sheet. The man's eyes were kind as he regarded Ceannas with a small smile.

"Young Anchor, well met. What brings you to visit me? Not that I mind, of course, but I would figure you to have remained by her side for the rest of the visit."

"Great... Great Elder?" Ceannas frowned in surprise. He'd only ever met the Great Elder in his walrus form, presiding in the Grand Hall over the court of attendees that required his attention. This human form, so soft and vulnerable-seeming, was disarming.

"I can come back later, if you'd prefer...?"

"Nonsense!" The Great Elder waved him to come closer. "You obviously have something on your mind, or you wouldn't have sought me out. What are you thinking?"

Ceannas looked down at his hands, which were clasped in joined fists. "I need to know how to be with her."

The Great Elder watched with limpid brown eyes that seemed to radiate a welcoming warmth.

"I took a vow," Ceannas continued after a moment of silence. "And she did, too, in a way. And I can't see a way for us to resolve them."

"Well, you know how to resolve them," the Great Elder corrected. "Both of you remain true to your words and accomplish your respective goals." Ceannas let go a sigh he hadn't realized he'd been holding. "But," the Great Elder continued, "you're wondering how one can mesh the two so that you both get what you want. What *do* you want?"

Ceannas thought for a moment, glancing around the room. He took in the sandalwood dresser with its gleaming glass mirror, the receiving chairs that made a reception area at the far end of the room. Gold and purple and silver threads composed most of the colors used to decorate.

"I want her to be happy." Ceannas's voice was soft.

"And what would make her happy?"

"To save her family and know where she belongs."

The Great Elder made a humming sigh of acceptance. "I see. And do you think she's found where she belongs?"

Ceannas shook his head. "At first, I thought so. She could turn into a selkie, after she worried she couldn't. Then she healed her father's sealskin, which was her goal the entire time. But now that she's a *buidseach*, I worry she will feel distanced from the clan, just as she found a home with us."

The Great Elder nodded. "'*Us?*'" His voice held a gentle reproach.

Ceannas met his eyes with an anguished expression. "Me."

"But you're an Anchor. Those don't have room for close relationships."

Ceannas sagged and nodded. "I don't know what to do."

The Great Elder cupped his chin with one hand, thinking. After a long silence, he jerked as if he'd just thought of something important. "Ceannas, do you know my name?"

Ceannas's eyebrows lifted as he looked at the other male in surprise. "No, my lord. Nobody has ever told it to me."

"It's Seanóir. Does that change how you look at me, now that you know my true name?"

With a skeptical look, Ceannas asked, "Why would it?"

"Because it's not how you met me. You met me in my ocean-self, as most visitors to this palace do. But here you now know a different part of me, in my human form."

"But you're still the same creature. You just have a different version of yourself being shown."

Seanóir's eyes gleamed at him. "You're right. And why do you think I approach most of my interactions as the Great Elder and not as Seanóir?"

"I don't know."

"I have a certain reputation to uphold. The Great Elder is a myth, much like the *buidseach*. It's not a person, per se, but more of a persona. Creatures that come to the Great Elder expect a certain presence, a sense of grandeur and magic that they can believe in. The Great Elder before me died with no one but myself knowing about it. I accepted his crown seamlessly, so that nobody knew another walrus had taken his place.

"Your lady is much the same, a myth come to life. Though she may not understand the depths of the power she holds, she can be anything or anyone she wishes. But she is also a daughter and a princess. Like myself, she has different personas she must put forth based on others' expectations of her. Do you see now?"

But Ceannas didn't see. He shook his head. "What are you saying, Great... Seanóir?"

Seanóir sighed and ran his fingers down the length of his long hair. "I'm saying that we all serve multiple masters, depending on what persona we have to put forth. She is no different from me, and no different from you. You just have to take ownership of which persona you put forth. In this, you will find your answer."

Ceannas blinked at him. Multiple personas? Myths becoming legends? The latter was easier to comprehend than the former, he realized. He'd seen it with his own eyes. But how could he serve his clan while remaining true to his heart?

"Thank you, Seanóir, for trusting me with this information. I have much to think about."

"The least of which is how you'll accompany your clan safely back home, I imagine?" Seanóir said with a smile.

Ceannas nodded and returned a rueful smile. "I feel like it will be an easier journey than it was coming here."

Seanóir nodded gravely. "Speaking of which, I heard someone say you were injured on the way here. Something about a shark attack? Do you need me to heal a wound before you go?"

With a smile, Ceannas shook his head. "When she healed me... saved me inches from death... she healed that small wound, as well, not just the knife wound. I feel better than ever!"

"She truly is a miracle in the flesh," Seanóir said. "Keep her quite safe, Ceannas. And you will find what you seek."

Ceannas bowed and put a fist to his heart. "Well met, Seanóir."

"Well met, Ceannas."

He turned and left, wondering at the puzzle of words the Great Elder had imparted to him. If Seanóir's words were true, he had to figure out what persona he must put forth to solve his problem.

He had to admit that he had successfully been a warrior and a lover. Could he not be the same to the clan? Much like Lyall would have to be a *buidseach* and a lover and a princess? It was worth a try. He would appeal to his king and queen and hope they saw eye to eye on this topic.

In the meantime, he would pray to whatever gods might listen that it turn out in his favor.

He rushed down the hallways, convinced of his purpose. If tonight was the only night he had left with her, he would take it a thousand times over. And she would wake knowing that she was the most incredible creature he'd ever met.

HE ARRIVED AT HER door just as the female attendants were leaving.

"Is she awake?" he asked. The first two attendants ignored him, but he caught the arm of the last one as she slipped through the door. "Please, I need to know."

She glared up at him and jerked her arm from his grasp. "She is awake. But she's been dealt a great emotional blow. Make sure that she rests so she can make the sojourn to your home tomorrow."

He nodded as relief flooded through him. He pushed the door open, squinting in the darkness. A single bioluminescent lamp was on a wall sconce in the corner. Moving as quietly as possible, he crept over to her prone figure on the bed.

"Lyall?" His voice was a hoarse whisper.

She stirred on the bed, lifting herself up to a sitting position. "I'm here. Where were you?"

"Your nurses sent me away while they tended to you. So I went and met... well, I saw the Great Elder."

"And? What did he have to say?"

Ceannas cocked his head. "He said a lot of things that made little sense to me, to be honest. But there was one conclusion I came to."

Lyall raised her eyebrows in question. In response, he stepped over and sat down on the opposite side of the bed from her. "He told me we are all different things to different people. You are a *buidseach*, a daughter, a princess... You're always those things simultaneously, at every part of the day. But just like there are different times to be one persona instead of another, you are still only ever just Lyall."

When he stopped and waited for her response, she gave a confused smile and shook her head. "I don't understand."

"I didn't either, at first." Ceannas smiled ruefully. "But on the way over to see you, I put it together: I am a warrior and a lover. I can be those things when I need to be. So there's no need to worry about how an Anchor can be together with a *buidseach*. We will each be what we need to be in order to stay together."

"Are you saying that you're giving up your Anchor's Vow?" she asked in shock.

He shook his head. "I am bound to my clan. But I'm also bound to you, however unwilling I was to admit it at first. I can't bear the thought of being without you, not touching or smelling or tasting you. I know you have other responsibilities, but I need you to know that I am wholly yours, in this life and the next, regardless of what happens."

Lyall's mouth fell open in surprise. "I feel the same! I can't imagine being apart from you. I love everything about you: your strength and compassion and dedication. But how can we be together within our clan? The only other alternative seems to be to run away, and I won't leave my family."

Ceannas took her hand. "I'd no sooner ask you to leave your family anymore than you'd ask me to give up my vow. I'm saying there's got to be a way to make it work. Maybe it's time for the Anchor's Vow to change, to allow for mates and close relationships."

She regarded him soberly. "How are you going to push for change that large? You're only one male."

Ceannas leaned forward so their foreheads touched. "I may only be one male. But you are a member of the royal family and a *buidseach*, one who is above the law. I'm sure we can figure something out if we don't give up hope."

Lyall frowned as she thought. As she remained quiet, Ceannas prayed she'd come to the same conclusion he had. Finally, a slow grin spread across her face.

"I am above the law, aren't I?"

He nodded with an answering smile.

"Do you know what the first thing I want to do is?" At his curious expression, she grinned wider. "Bed you until I pass out again."

He leaned away from her. "They gave me strict instructions not to let you exert yourself."

"Damn your instructions! I am above the law." She leaned forward to kiss him on the lips. "At least, that's what my bodyguard told me."

He rolled over so that he could cradle her in his arms. "Bodyguard, huh?" he growled into her neck as she giggled. "Who in their right mind would put me in charge of a headstrong, willful *buidseach* like you?"

As an answer, she tilted her head and kissed him, letting all of her pent-up emotions flood the effort so that they were both gasping when she pulled back.

They matched gazes for a moment, then each began shucking out of their clothing as quickly as they could. Ceannas got through first and walked around to the other side of the bed.

Lyall was struggling to get the shirt over her head, and he held her arms, still raised above her head, so that the upper half of her face was still covered.

"Hey!" she exclaimed.

But he silenced her with another kiss as his hands trailed down her body, starting at her breasts and moving down over her ribs. She made a wordless murmur of appreciation when he cupped one breast and ran his thumb over the nipple.

"May I be free, my lord?" she teased.

In response, he leaned forward and nipped her lower lip. "Not yet," he said with a smile. "I want to play a game."

"A game?"

"It's called Talk and Touch." He grinned at her mischievously. "You are Talk, which means you tell me what you want me to do, explaining it in graphic detail. And I am Touch. I touch you exactly how you describe, doing nothing other than what you say."

"So you do what I tell you to do and nothing else?"

"Correct."

"I want you to take this shirt off so I can see you," she demanded.

"Ah-ah," he chuckled with a mischievous grin. "You have to stay blindfolded."

"That's not fair!" she exclaimed.

He leaned forward and licked the pulse that beat frantically in her neck. In response, she shivered and smiled.

"It may not be fair. But it's how the game is played." He felt the desire building in his loins, and he longed to touch every part of her. But he held back, delighting in the delayed gratification that he knew would come in due time.

"So what do you want to do?" she asked in a tentative voice.

"I want to devour you," he murmured.

"I want to let you," she countered.

"But you have to tell me what to do first."

She licked her lips. "I want you to lick your way down my body."

He grinned, loving her acceptance of the game.

Placing a hand on her sternum, he leaned her back so that she lay flat on the bed. He situated himself between her legs, feeling the pressure of his manhood press against her delicate juncture.

"In me, Ceannas," she panted, looking up at him.

"In due time, my lady. First things first."

Maintaining eye contact, he kissed his way down her body. He pressed a kiss to her bellybutton, then her lower stomach, then each hip, and then lower.

He paused with his mouth against her intimate lips. "What now?" His voice was husky with need.

"Lick me."

With a broad swipe of his tongue, he licked at her, savoring the musky taste of her desire on his lips. He lapped at her, then suckled at the tiny nub of pleasure that had her crying out his name.

"Ceannas, more! Inside me! I want you inside me!"

Without ceasing his attention on her, he slid two fingers inside her, thrusting in time with his tongue's caresses.

"Yes!" she cried, arcing off the bed in delight. "Oh, baby, I'm so close!"

He pulled his face back, long enough to take in the sight of her so near release because of his touch. "Do you want to come now?"

She shifted her hips, considering. "You're right," she panted. "I want you at the same time."

"Then tell me what you want."

"I want you in me."

"Gladly!" He drew himself up her body, holding his upper body up on his elbows, then slid his manhood deep inside her.

She gasped at the pleasure and the pressure of it. "This, exactly!" she sighed.

Being in her was like coming home. He tried to keep it slow for her, but she bucked her hips to increase the rhythm. "Faster, Ceannas! I want all of you!"

He didn't need to be told twice. Pumping into her, he pushed all his pent-up desire for her into each thrust. He gazed down at her, then pulled the shirt blindfold off so that he could see her face.

"I want to see you," he growled.

Her expression was one of surprise, as if she couldn't believe such pleasure was possible.

He felt the tide rising in him and guessed, from her delighted gasps, that she was close as well. He leaned down to where her legs wrapped around his waist. In a smooth movement, he hooked one of her legs over his elbow to increase the depth of his thrusts.

"Ceannas!" she cried as the wave of pleasure crashed over her.

It broke in him at the same time, and he felt her body clenching his manhood as he climaxed with her. There was the sense of two heartbeats beating frantically like birds in a cage, then the sensation of two lungs gasping for breath together. He leaned back to look at her as a languid sense of satisfaction washed over him, covering him like a blanket. It felt like a glowing ember in his stomach, but also like a golden thread stretching out, anchored some place outside of himself.

He frowned down at her. "Do you feel that?"

She grinned. "Feel what?"

He sent a feeling of confusion along the thread, and she shivered.

"What was that?" He felt an answering wave of confusion echo back through the thread.

"Can you feel... well, anything different?"

She frowned, thinking. "I kind of feel like there's another presence nearby. Like I have this connection to something outside of myself."

Ceannas grinned and sent a wave of desire down the connection.

"No more!" she groaned, rolling away from him. "I'm exhausted!"

He laughed. So the rumors were true: True Mates could sense each other's emotions. But it didn't seem to include actual thoughts, just emotions. He sent a wave of love down the connection and felt an echoing flare of affection in response.

He lay on his side and nestled her into the curve of his body. "So this is what it's like to be mated."

Lyall propped her upper body on one arm so she could look at him in the face. "Are you okay with that?" Her voice was soft and hesitant.

But he just smiled and sent a wave of intense love through the bond. "If I'd have known it would be like this, I'd have accepted it the day I met you on that beach."

She grinned at him. "I'm not so sure I would have." He pushed a wave of shock through the bond, which made her giggle. "You *were* a little intimidating," she laughed.

He flashed an indignant look. "*Were?* I'll not have you infringing on my reputation with that nonsense."

With a smile, she reached over and kissed him on the nose. "Just think of how it will affect your reputation to have a *buidseach* as a True Mate."

Ceannas's eyes rose to his hairline. "You're right!" Then he sobered. "But we're not done yet. The rules regarding an Anchor breaking his or her vows trends towards exile at best, death at worst. I will have to be charismatic to change the minds of our king and queen." He smirked down at her. "But I've been planning my attack. I know what I will say to them. And once they hear our story, I don't see how they could demand we stay apart."

Lyall shook her head with a beautific smile. "We'll cross that current when we have to. But for now, we stay where we are and appreciate what we have." She sent wave after wave of affection to him through the bond, and he let himself relax into the feelings.

She was right. They would handle that issue tomorrow. For now, he was content to cuddle his True Mate and savor the afterglow of their joining. He tucked her into the crook of his arm so that their bodies touched from shoulder to toe and let himself fall asleep.

CHAPTER 23

THE ENTIRE CLAN MET at dawn at the small exiting pool they'd once used to enter the Great Elder's kingdom. The Great Elder, in his walrus form, had been waiting for them, and cast a blessing over them for safe travel and a speedy return.

Lyall, draped in her grey sealskin, had her father's skin in the satchel hung around her neck. She struggled not to fidget as everyone made the final farewells. Before they left, the Great Elder called her forward and placed one large flipper on her shoulder.

"Be safe in your life and your magic, and know that you always have a home here, should you ever choose it."

She bowed, both hands clutching the cross-bodied strap between her breasts. She shivered in her nudity, despite the warmth of her sealskin across her shoulders. "Thank you for everything," she said through chattering teeth. Beside her, Ceannas brushed the back of his hand against hers in a covert caress.

The Great Elder turned to Ceannas. "Have you figured out the solution to your dilemma?"

Ceannas shook his head. "We are True Mates, my lord, but our clan doesn't look favorably on Anchors who abdicate their duties, even for love. I will have to get permission from my king and queen on how to handle it."

"Nonsense!" the Great Elder boomed in an incredulous voice. Everyone standing around the exiting pool cringed back. He looked back and forth between the two of them. "Surely you aren't suggesting a clan's royal family has more power than the Great Elder?"

"Not at all, Great Elder!" Ceannas said, with a hand clasped to his fist as he bowed low in front of the giant walrus. "I merely meant to convey that I would need their permission—"

"You need no such permission," the Great Elder said. "You have broken the Anchor's Vow with your acceptance of the True Mate bond. That alone is punishable by exile."

Lyall exchanged shocked looks with Ceannas, who appeared pale.

"Great Elder—," he ground out, but the walrus spoke over him.

"Lyall." The Great Elder turned to regard her. "You are a *buidseach*, one of the most powerful ones I've ever met. Would you rather go your path alone, or would you rather a protector on hand to keep you safe?"

Lyall looked back and forth between the Great Elder and Ceannas. She was so shocked that she didn't know what to say. Was the Great Elder suggesting that Ceannas could be a protector? Did this mean they had the freedom to be True Mates and still uphold their own vows?

Ceannas nudged her hard, digging his elbow into her side, which jolted her back to reality. She bowed at the waist. "Great Elder, I would be more than glad to have a protector by my side."

"Then I decree it: you may choose one Anchor from Liath Clann to serve as a guardian, a Sworn Protector who will remain with you for as long as you'll have him or her."

Straightening, she looked in shock at Ceannas, who could barely contain his mirth.

"I choose you, Ceannas," she murmured. "If you want the position?"

She pushed affection and adoration down the bond between them. When the feelings registered with him, they flared hotly at his acceptance.

Ceannas bowed low with his fist over his heart. "My lady, I would have it no other way." She leaned over and touched his shoulder, and he rose. He sent a returning wave of desire over her, and she blushed.

"This, then, is your punishment, Ceannas," intoned the Great Elder. "To abide with her as her protector for as long as you are capable. Your life goes before hers, and you can only step out of her service upon your death." The Great Elder re-situated his bulk and cleared his throat, taking on a less formal tone. "You can inform your king and queen of the developments that occurred during this Migration. I dare say you'll have a great deal of things to broach with them."

"Thank you, Great Elder," Ceannas said.

"Well met, young Anchor. Return your clan safely to your home, then your Sworn Protector duties will begin. I wish you both the most success."

Ceannas and Lyall glanced at each other, sharing suppressed grins.

Then, one by one, with the Anchors leading the way, the entirety of Liath Clann's entourage dove into the water. Some, like her, waited until they were in the frigid water to change, while others, like Ceannas, changed mid-dive so that their seal forms hit the water first.

I should've done that, Lyall thought as the icy cold of the ocean shocked the breath from her body. She gasped, then tugged her fastened sealskin closer to her body and curled into the change.

An elephant seal escorted them out of the coral tunnel and into the open ocean. Lyall couldn't tell if it was the same individual who'd led them to the palace in the first place, but she found she didn't care.

So many transformations had happened over the last day that she still felt awestruck, unable to process the depth of her emotions. She swam strongly, keeping an eye out for Ceannas's lean form a few yards ahead of her. His presence was comforting, even just being within eyesight of her.

She felt a calm assurance as she glided through the water, a confidence that hadn't been there before. What was the limit to her powers? she wondered. And what other things was she capable of? She saw a pair of pups swimming near her and timed her breathing breaks to theirs, so she rose to the surface and took air in tandem with them. It was a solid practice, and she never felt she was near her limit.

Perhaps it was the knowledge that she was a *buidseach.* Or perhaps it was a sign of growth that she could manage herself and protect herself when the need arose.

But the one thing that she avoided thinking about, the only thing that dampened her radiant feelings, was what to do when they arrived back at Selbane. She was a different creature than had started out so long ago. And she didn't know what place there would be for her, or for Ceannas, for that matter.

Would she be on her own, like Harper, the only other *buidseach* she'd ever known? Had that been a choice on Harper's part, or had her clan exiled her? These were all questions she would have to ask of King Righ and Queen Mairi when they returned.

Ahead of her, she saw Ceannas split away from the head of the group as another Anchor took his place. He let the clan swim by him until he caught up to her. He swam close enough to bump her shoulder with his. In response, she barked at him, and he twirled in a tight spiral. She sent a wave of affection down the bond, and he sent back a wave of mischievousness that made her smile.

She may not know what the future held for her, but she was confident that she wouldn't have to do it alone. The Great Elder said that she was a *buidseach*, the likes of which the selkie world had never before seen. She had a True Mate that was also her Sworn Protector.

No, she would never be alone again.

EPILOGUE

L YALL WAS SURPRISED TO find a group already waiting to welcome them home upon their return to the bay on the western side of Selbane. Ceannas must have sent a pair of Anchors ahead of the group to herald their arrival.

She hung back as the rest of the clan surged forward to reunite with loved ones. Slowly, the seal forms gave way to human forms as the bulk of the clan hugged and kissed their welcome.

Lyall swam to the side of the shallow end, staying on the outskirts of the group as she scanned the crowd for her parents. When she didn't see them, she began to fret. What if her father was too sick to come? What if he had died while she was gone? The thought filled her with dread, so that she felt on the verge of tears as the crowd filtered out of the water to shore.

She changed, the last of the clan to do so, and edged her way to the shore, covering her nudity with the sopping mass of her sealskin.

Then she spied them, standing on the opposite edge of the crowd, scanning the emerging selkies with frantic expressions. Her father leaned heavily on his cane, stooped nearly in half, while his mother stood on her tiptoes to look over the heads of the exiting bodies.

Lyall and her mother made eye contact, and her mother let out a whoop of joy. Lyall slogged through the water that came up to her thighs as she made her way over to her parents.

Before she could exit the water, her mother was wading in, heedless of her dress becoming soaked as she clutched Lyall's shoulders into a firm embrace. For a moment, her mother clung to her, her own shoulders shaking. When she pulled back to inspect Lyall's face, she saw her mother was sobbing in joy.

Her mother cupped her face in her hands. "You made it back! We were so worried when you disappeared!" She sucked in a ragged breath as she noticed Lyall's grey sealskin. "And you've changed!"

Lyall ruefully rolled her eyes. "You have no idea," she murmured. But her mother was already turning to her father, who huddled on the edge of the beach where the pebbles began and the water ended.

"Hugh! Look at this!" Her mother held up the wet sealskin. "How amazing! We're so proud of you!"

Lyall grinned at her mother, then sobered as she looked at her father. Would he kill her for running away *before* she could give him the fixed sealskin? Or would he wait and kill her later? His expression was blank, with just his blue eyes shining like shards of ice in his face, so she couldn't figure his mood.

She stepped forward, fiddling in her satchel for the folded sealskin. Stopping a few feet away from him, she pulled out the wet mass. Without saying anything, she held it out to him with an earnest expression.

For a long moment, he merely stared at her with his hard expression. Then he looked at the sealskin she offered.

"What is this?" His voice was the softest of whispers and as gravely as the beach itself, and it broke her heart to hear it.

"Your sealskin." It was difficult to hold the heavy pelt out, but she didn't dare lower her arms. "It's fixed."

"That's impossible," he ground out, with the beginnings of a scowl forming on his face.

"It's not! I took it to the Great Elder to see if he could fix it and—"

"And we healed it," a voice broke in from behind her. She closed her eyes briefly, savoring the sound of her mate's voice, feeling through the bond the security and support he was sending.

"What is the meaning of this?" her father said. "Why do you play games, Lyall?"

"I play no games, Father. Ceannas speaks the truth. The sealskin is healed."

Prion stretched out a hand and caressed the proffered pelt. Lyall felt the jolt of electricity that heralded the changing of the magic to its rightful owner. By the shock on her father's face, she knew he felt the same.

Dropping his cane, he lumbered forward, tripping over the shifting pebbles on the beach, and only preventing a fall by Ceannas leaping forward to catch him by the arm.

"Easy, my lord," Ceannas murmured, but Prion wasn't paying him any attention. He pulled the wet sealskin to his chest, running his fingers over it with the expression of a dreamer who had just awakened.

"It's true," Prion whispered. "It's really true."

He dropped the sealskin and began to rip his clothes off. Leannán stepped forward to assist him, and Lyall looked away to give her father some privacy. When she risked a glance back, she saw her father standing stooped-over, trying to pick up his sealskin from the beach.

A coughing fit wracked him, and he bent over further as he hacked his lungs to pieces. This time, when he pulled his hand away from his mouth, Lyall saw the bright crimson stain of blood on his fist.

We got back just in time, she thought as she shoved aside the guilty feelings that threatened to overwhelm her. If only she'd swum faster. If only she'd learned her powers sooner. If only...

Her mother picked up the sealskin and draped it over her father's stooped body like a cape. Lyall watched as her father tried to fasten the small hooks with his shaking fingers, only to growl in exasperation as they slipped through his hands. Her mother fastened the rest of them down his front until he stood encased in his sealskin.

He looked down at himself in wonder, then with shining eyes at his wife. "I never thought I'd see the day," he said in a low, shocked voice.

"Do it, Prion," Leannán urged. "Do it for all of us."

He nodded and plodded into the water. Her mother stepped to one side to clench Lyall's hands. On her other side, Ceannas's strong presence pressed his warmth into her arm.

They watched as Prion curled forward into the water as if falling. Lyall tensed, ready to dart forward, but Ceannas laid an arm around her shoulders.

"Wait for it," he murmured.

Next to her, Lyall's mother gripped her hand tight enough to hurt, but she barely registered the pressure.

"Come on, father," she chanted to herself. "You can do this."

Suddenly, a head broke the surface of the water a few yards out. A grey seal with shocking blue eyes barked at them, then disappeared under the water again.

Her mother gasped, and Lyall realized tears were rolling down her own face as she watched the grey seal caper about in the water, performing spiraling dives and twists out of the water as if filled with unconstrained joy.

Lyall's mother pulled her into a fierce hug with one arm and squeezed. Lyall glanced at her and saw happiness and longing on her face and remembered that her mother had given up her ability to shift as well, back when she mated with her father. So Lyall had given *two* members of her family the ability to change again.

A surge of pride reached her from the True Mate bond, and she leaned against Ceannas while she surveyed her father cavorting through the water like a pup. She had done this. Her father and mother now found peace because of her. And though he hadn't changed back into his human form yet, she had a sneaking suspicion he wouldn't be sick anymore, as they had hoped.

She put her arm around Ceannas, and he hugged her to his side. This was where she belonged, here and nowhere else. *Buidseach* or not, she knew that this was what coming home was like. And it was everything she could ever want.

AFTERWORD

Thanks so much for reading *Saving the Selkie's Heart*! I knew two books ago that Lyall and Ceannas deserved their moment in the sun, and here it is. I'm so glad you've followed along in the lives of these inhabitants of Selbane—just wait, there's more to come! I really hope you enjoyed reading this book, and if you want to start a discussion about it, feel free to email me at ellarose@ellarosebooks.com. Also, don't forget to leave a review on Amazon or Goodreads!

If you'd like to read more about this world, you should DEFINITELY sign up for my newsletter (http://www.EllaRoseBooks.com/newsletter) to get a free novella, *Losing the Selkie's Skin* (Prion and Leannán's story), and to stay up-to-date on all new and upcoming releases. I've got a few short stories set in The Selkie Seas world, and you can find out more about them on my website, www.EllaRoseBooks.com/Books.

Of all the social media channels, I'm most active on Facebook (http://www.facebook.com/EllaRoseBooks) and TikTok (@EllaRoseWrites), though I'm also on Goodreads (@EllaRoseWrites), Instagram (@EllaRoseWrites), and

Pinterest (@EllaRoseWriter). My website is www.EllaRoseBooks.com. I look forward to seeing you around teh interwebz!

Acknowledgments

And the band plays on my friends!

This book would not have been possible without Cathy Yardley and her Rock Your Writing instruction (http://www.RockYourWriting.com)—you are worth your weight in cheese, my friend, and I can't wait to work on the next adventure with you!

Further thanks to my editor, Tiffany Tyer (http://reedsy.com/Tiffany-Tyer), whose encouragement and hard work made this book what it is. Any gaffs that you find, dear reader, is fully on me and not her.

And finally, to my friends and family who never gave up on me, even when I wanted to give up on myself. Know that I'm raising a toast in your honor now. And let us never be too old for fairy tales!

ABOUT THE AUTHOR

Ella Rose is a paranormal romance author who loves kink, ink, and cake, and hopes you do too. She is a bi-sexual author writing through a Bi-Polar Disorder lens and thinks representation and mental health matter. She is the author of the Selkie Seas series, which includes *Losing the Selkie's Skin*, a Selkie Seas prequel novella (http://books2read.com/losingtheselkiesskin), and *Stealing the Selkie's Heart*, Book 1 (http://www.books2read.com/stealingtheselkiesheart). Her latest selkie short stories appear in Dark Rose Press's *Worlds Apart* and Dragon Soul Press's *Beyond Atlantis*

anthologies. She is a member of Romance Writers of America and the Paranormal Romance Guild.

You can follow her on:

- Facebook (http://www.facebook.com/EllaRoseBooks)

- TikTok (@ellarosewrites)

- Goodreads (@EllaRoseWrites)

- Instagram (@EllaRoseWrites)

- Pinterest (@EllaRoseWriter)

And find out more about her at www.EllaRoseBooks.com. To stay up-to-date on all things Selkie Seas, sign up for her newsletter (www.EllaRoseBooks.com/newsletter).